#FASHIONVICTIM

#FASHIONVICTIM
A NOVEL

Amina Akhtar

CROOKED
LANE

NEW YORK

Copyright © 2018 by Amina Akhtar

Published in the United States by Crooked Lane Books, an imprint of The Quick Brown Fox & Company LLC.

Crooked Lane Books and its logo are trademarks of The Quick Brown Fox & Company LLC.

Cover design by Melanie Sun
Book design by Jennifer Canzone

Printed in the United States.

Crooked Lane Books
34 West 27th St., 10th Floor
New York, NY 10001

ISBN 978-1-64385-061-0

#FASHIONVICTIM

Dedicated to my parents and DRN. The best support combo anyone could ask for.

Elmer's glue sticks changed their formula. They used to smell better, more toxic. More likely to get you high. I bet a bunch of fifth graders used to sniff and lick the shit out of them, and their mommies complained, so the company had to dial it down. They were barely usable now, but I still liked them; they were good for mood boards. Some people like to use pins for mood boards, but where was the dedication in that? The commitment? If you want to have a fucking mood, own it. Put some elbow grease into it.

I cut carefully along the photo, making sure to get her hair in. Her perfect fucking hair. I wanted hair like that. Long, cascading, blonde. My hair wasn't like that—it was just below my shoulders and dark brown. Too thick, too wavy. She had extensions in this shot. I know because I've sneaked into the same parties as her just to catch a glimpse. Her eye makeup sparkled; her lips were ultraglossy. She wore Gucci boots and supertight jeggings and carried a comically large bag by Céline. She wore her hair at different lengths during the week, courtesy of extensions. Later, I copied that look to a T. It was amazing what those bags could carry.

My mood board was filled with shots of Sarah out partying, going to fashion shows, beaming at the camera. She was an associate editor at *La Vie*, and she was perfect. Her family

1

was rich, she was gorgeous, and her closet would make you cry. She was the opposite of me. I didn't have photo spreads in magazines. I didn't have summer houses and beach cottages. I had barred windows as a kid and a paper cup full of pills. Now I had a small apartment, but it wasn't as nice as Sarah's. (There were photos online.)

I wanted to hang out with her, wear her perfume, do nails with her. I wanted to have an old-fashioned slumber party at her giant apartment (in Tribeca). I wanted to go out to bars with her and let guys buy us drinks. I wanted her to text me nonsensical abbreviations and emojis and take selfies with me and make fun of everyone else. I wanted to work with her, and I would. (I had a meeting with *La Vie*'s HR department next week.) I'd stared at photos of Sarah for years. We practically grew up together. Sarah at her fancy socialite galas, me in my sad rooms at school. We were *connected*, thanks to all her photos, which appeared in every society and Manhattan mag you could find. I wanted to be Sarah's one and only true friend. I wanted to be loved by her so much that I could taste it. I hated myself for it just a bit. I was aspiring. I picked up a glitter pen and wrote *Sarah Taft* at the top of my board.

We were going to be BFFs. That meant forever.

1

Three blonde PR girls with iPads stood behind a velvet rope, slowly checking people in. I waited for one to glance up.

"Hi, I'm here—"

"Name?"

"Anya—"

"Oh, hold on! Lauren, we totes need a selfie. We're twinsies!" She called to a younger, even blonder girl, also wearing a headset. I sighed. The girls converged for a group shot, ignoring the line of impatient partygoers. I cleared my throat.

"One second, babe." One of them called to me, holding up a finger.

I wanted to bite that finger off. Finally, after ten or so flashes, the girls turned back. I forced a smile.

"Sorry! Had to post to Insta! Okay, what's your name again?"

I ground out each letter. She popped her gum while typing into her iPad.

I could hear Celia Avery's voice in my head: *A La Vie woman doesn't wait in line.* Shit. If she caught me standing around like a fucking plebeian, she'd fire my ass. We weren't even covering this event, but Celia needed a favor: she wanted to borrow (and keep) a dress. And any excuse to do her a favor was a good one. The PR firm throwing this bash repped designer Alexander King. The official story was that Celia wanted the dress for a shoot, but reality check: she wanted a freebie.

Blondie was still typing. I rolled my eyes.

"Do you need me to spell it again?"

"No, no. Which outlet are you with?"

"*La Vie,*" I said through gritted teeth. Her eyes widened. I should have stabbed the dumb PR girl through her stupid little eyes right then. Shish-kebabed her for the line to nibble on while they waited.

"I don't see your name on the list . . . It's, like, not on here?" Everything was said like a question.

I could have told her my name was Beyoncé and she wouldn't have known the difference. The grumblings behind me were getting louder.

"Check again." I started to hear a buzzing sound. It was like a drill going off in the background. I wondered if there was construction inside, an installation piece maybe.

"Do you hear that?" I asked. Check-in girl looked up from her iPad and stared at me blankly.

"Hear what? The music?" She popped her gum.

"Never mind."

She started typing again. "Oh! There you are. Your name was right in front of me! Ha! I'm, like, blind. I'm Lauren, by the way. We emailed earlier." She beamed. I wanted to pat her on the head, but she was wearing three wool scarves despite the heat, and beads of sweat were starting to roll down her face.

"Hey! Great to finally meet. Grab me inside and let's have a drink." I winced as I heard myself say the words. God, I hated myself sometimes. I knew that later, when she offered to do lunch, I'd take her up on it. Because that was my job and I was soulless.

"For sure!"

Fucking idiot. This was my life.

This was my second event of the evening. The first one had been for a Fitbit accessory—an accessory for the accessory that tells you you're not walking enough. You wanted to show off that you were actively trying to get in shape but then you had to hide your Fitbit inside chunky gold jewelry. What would they think of next? But I'd wear it. Maybe if I lost ten more pounds, Celia would bump me up from associate editor. Eyes on the prize—and the pounds.

This party was for a new scarf, which explained Lauren's sweatfest. Not a world-saving scarf or child-hunger-ending scarf or even an animal-friendly, organic alpaca scarf. (They wait for the animals to drop dead before culling the wool. How *thoughtful*.) Just a plain gray scarf. The PR girls were all draped in them; Lauren really was wearing three. It was July in New York and eighty-nine degrees outside.

It was also time for a drink. I don't get drunk. Losing control is tacky. You know what happens when you lose control? You get sloppy. But if I didn't drink, I'd have to use my phone incessantly—or worse, talk to people. Sarah always drank like a fish at these things, but she didn't care about the impression she made. Why should she? She was untouchable.

"Anya! There you are!" Another Lauren stood in front of me. I had lost track of who was who anymore, but PR girls always seemed to be named Lauren. They all looked alike; they wore David Yurman jewelry, their highlights were chunky, and their manis were French. Laurens hailed from Long Island, obviously.

"Lauren!" I hated myself for my fake enthusiasm.

"You remember me!"

I didn't.

"O-M-G, how much did you love that event last week for the light-up mirrors? Don't you love using those?"

"Yeah, I use mine all the time. Is this your event too?"

"Yes! The scarf is *amazing*, right? You can wear it, like, five different ways! Who knew you could do all that with just a scarf? It's, like, changed my life."

This Lauren was wearing four. You could see sweat pooling around her armpits, turning her pale-blue blouse a deep indigo. I tried to look away. There was a weird spicy scent in the air.

"You don't say. But aren't you a bit hot?"

"No! I feel great. Besides, I'm detoxing, so sweat is so great for me right now. I only eat kale and garlic, so this is really helping."

So that's what I was smelling.

"You can never have enough scarves," she added, scanning the room for someone else to talk to. "Oh! There's Annie from *Mince* magazine. Go get a drink! Try on a scarf!"

Twenty minutes later, I was weighed down with knits. Every time a Lauren came by, they managed to drape another one on me. Perhaps this was a rite of passage, a test of some sort? If you could survive the night wearing five heavy woolen scarves, you're officially a woman or something. Smiling, I downed my third glass of champagne. At least the booze was top shelf for once. The idea of taking in empty calories nearly sent me into a panic, until I rationalized how much I was sweating out. It seemed an even trade.

"O-M-G, we have to Instagram you! You look so great!" Lauren again. The first one. Or the second. No, wait, definitely the first. Her shirt was pink, and the armpits had turned a deep mauve.

"Oh, I'd rather not—"

"Don't be silly. Smile!" *Click!* "You look so chic." She snapped the photo while I was talking. My mouth had been open. That was the opposite of chic.

"I feel like I'm being swaddled." Too many layers can make you look heavy. Heavy was bad.

"It's the new look. I heard Alexander King is totally wearing his knits this way. Oh, shoot, be right back. Gotta tinkle."

"But can I see the photo? I think my eyes were shut."

"No, you look great. I'm posting it. I'll tag you!"

She walked away before I could grab her. I could have made a scene and pulled her by her pretty hair, but I didn't want to create a ruckus. Imagine the social media shitfest that would ensue.

Instead I checked my Instagram. There it was: one eye closed, lip semisnarling. How many chins did I have? My neck had disappeared into the wool. Worst of all, she hadn't used a filter. I looked like something that had washed up on the beaches of Montauk. Tomorrow I'd be ridiculed in our editorial meeting, lectured about putting my best foot forward. Because *A La Vie woman must always present herself in her best light.* As if Celia and Sarah didn't have bad angles.

They didn't. Those perfect bitches.

The buzzing had started up again. It was a saw. I knew it was. Was there another room where an artist was cutting something up? Or maybe they were doing ice sculptures. That would explain all the scarves. Where the fuck was the VIP room, anyway? Why was I stuck here? Determined to make my night better, I walked up to another Lauren and tapped her on the shoulder.

"Hi."

"Hey!" She flashed a toothsome smile. Veneers, all of them. I guess she could handle a lot of pain.

"Where's the VIP room?"

"I'm sorry?"

"The VIP room, with the artists?" I said slowly, raising my eyebrows. Was her programming in need of a reboot?

"Um, there isn't one," she replied, looking around.

"Then what's with the buzzing?" I asked, annoyed. First that shitty photo, then no access? What kind of party was this?

"What buzzing? I'm not sure—"

"Listen, Lauren. *La Vie* doesn't put up with this kind of bullshit. Okay?"

"Anya! There you are!" I turned to see the pink-shirt Lauren beaming at me. "Everything okay?"

"No, it's not okay. This . . . intern of yours won't tell me where the VIP room is!"

"Okay, calm down, there's no VIP room. Not at tonight's event, sweetie." They always called you by lovey nicknames, like they cared. Sweetie. Honey. Sugar tits. Darling. Lauren-bots were the absolute worst. "Let's get you a drink though, okay, hon?"

I allowed her to lead me to the bar. I hated this party. I hated this PR girl. She was treating me like a child. Sarah would never be treated like this. And why was that buzzing noise still going?

"Why don't you have a drink while I go tinkle. And then I'll get you a gift bag, okay, sweetie?" I heard her say.

I nodded stiffly and closed my eyes, trying to block out the barrage of sounds.

I opened my eyes and watched Lauren—at this point, I wasn't sure if it was the first or second one, but really, it didn't matter. The bot models were interchangeable. She left the main party room and slipped out a door. She was going to the VIP area where the big story was. *Liar.*

How could they not think I was VIP enough to go? Hello, I worked at *La Vie*, for Christ's sake. They'd never pull this shit with Sarah. I downed my champagne and followed the bot.

Lauren walked down an empty hallway and through a door. Where was security? Where were the ropes? I pushed on the door, but it was locked. I waited—someone would have to come out soon enough. It seemed like hours went by when the door finally opened.

"Anya! Hey!" the bot said. "Did you need to go too?"

"Obviously, you know I did!" I pushed her back through the door and shut it behind us, locking it.

"Uh, what's going on? Are you okay?"

"Yeah, we need to talk, is all." I surveyed the room. It wasn't much of a VIP area at all. Toilet, sink, mirror—they made the major peeps hang in the bathroom? I mean, if they wanted their Kate Moss coke moment, fine, but who even did that anymore?

"Oh, about what? The scarves? Don't you love them?" She smiled nervously.

"Totes, Lauren. They're so chic." I was on fashion autopilot. I could spout any gibberish now and it'd make sense to a bot. "I'm so into them. Maybe I can do a pull?"

She nodded enthusiastically, like a bobblehead. I don't know when I decided to smash her head into the mirror, but all of a sudden I did, and glass went everywhere. She stopped bobbing and looked at me, horrified.

"O-M-G, Anya, W-T-F?"

She didn't even say the words. She said the acronyms. Even in this moment, she couldn't say *Oh my God*. I really fucking hated bots. When she opened her mouth to shriek, I had to power her down. Somehow, I knew there was an off switch behind the left eye. Hit it just right and *bam*, the bot turns off. Lauren fell over, and I checked to see if she had fully powered down. Yep, no breathing.

I wiped down the sink, resisting the urge to kick her before I left. Her blood was seeping out of her eye. I've always enjoyed the color of blood, but oddly, I can't watch bloody shows on TV. Weird, right?

* * *

"Anya? Anya? Hello?"

I opened my eyes and looked at Lauren. "Oh, hey."

"Were you sleeping?"

"Ha, no, just zoning out." It wasn't real. I didn't just stab her through the eyeball. Just a daydream. Cool, totally normal.

"Did you want another drink?"

"Oh, sure." I smiled, watching her run off to the bar.

"Oh, hey, listen," she said, handing me a glass of Veuve a moment later. "Before I forget, I have a dress for Celia. Mulberry emailed a request in. I'll send it over tomorrow." Mulberry was Celia's latest assistant.

"That'd be great!" I said. A six-inch shard jutted out of her left eye. Did anyone else see that? "Celia will be thrilled."

"Well, we're just happy *La Vie* loves Alexander King as much as we do." She beamed, and her eyes crinkled, making the shard move. Was this real? I needed to ask Dr. M to up my meds.

"Okay, well, I think it's time to call it a night. Thanks for everything!"

"You'll write about the scarves?" Lauren looked concerned.

"Uh, sure . . . gotta go. Email me."

She leaned in for a cheek kiss, but I ran. I didn't want to touch the shard. This wasn't real.

None of this was real.

2

The ten AM editorial meeting at *La Vie* took place in the smaller of the two conference rooms on the seventh floor of Blanchett Publishing's giant glass tower building in Midtown. We were surrounded by curved metal and shiny surfaces. The walls were Frank Gehry inspired, and the chairs looked straight out of *Beetlejuice*. We had this meeting every Wednesday for FFD, or fashion, features, and digital—all the things I covered. It would be twenty minutes of pure hell.

"Nice photo of you last night." Sarah Elizabeth Taft laughed, flipping her gorgeously perfect hair. "You know Halloween isn't for a few months though, right?" She had been checking out my Instagram feed. My heart began to race.

"Ugh, I know. They posted it without giving me approval."

"You really need to take a course in how to get your photo taken. I mean, it's just tragic." She wrinkled her nose.

"What's tragic?" Celia walked in wearing leather shorts. For someone in her early forties, she managed to make them look good. Her secret? Planks. Celia was the master of the five-minute plank.

"Another bad photo of Anya," Sarah said, gesturing to me.

"Another one? You just can't represent us if you look like an ugly whale!" Celia glared, waiting for me to acknowledge that my hideous deformation of not looking like Gisele

Bündchen would be the ruin of *La Vie*. I nodded, attempting to put on a sorrowful face. I hated today. I hated Sarah Taft.

"We can't all be perfect, Sarah." I aimed for venomous, but it came out sounding slightly forlorn. I hated how much I loved her. She was wearing a floral dress by Preen with cowboy boots. Her look screamed "fresh off the prairie." I wanted to churn butter right then and there.

If Blake Lively and Blake Lively had a baby, it'd be Sarah Elizabeth Taft. Tall, willowy blonde, and rich, Sarah was born to be a fashion editor. She was wearing Chanel by the time she was two—there were photo spreads in magazines. Shots of toddler Sarah playing with her mom's Birkin were so damn chic. (My mother only ever splurged on Coach.) Her parents were heirs of heirs, owning some coffee bean factory or plantation or something. No one really knew anymore, except that at some point there were slaves and it was all rather scandalous. She had the kind of life magazines claim is possible if you only aspire a bit more. Make the effort, spend the money.

Sarah possessed a magical gift: she could make anyone, anything hot. She simply had to wear it, Instagram it, or glance in its direction. If you were her friend, you were in the front row. I'd seen it unfold before. She'd graced Lisa Blitz and Jack Archer with her attention, back when they were loser nobodies. And a few months later, they were fashion fucking royalty. Total upgrade. Just by snapping photos with Sarah, Lisa got funding for the site she was launching. Jack booked stylist gig after gig and then landed at a men's mag. Sarah was the source of all things fashionable. Everything I wanted.

On the flip side, if Sarah hated something, it was never seen again. Piles of bags were tossed out because she decreed they were lame. You never wanted her to wrinkle her nose at your product, at you. It meant it was ugly. That you were ugly. If she welcomed me into her life, I could be everything. I could be amazing.

I could be her.

When I first started at *La Vie* two years ago, I did as Dr. M instructed and told Sarah how much I admired her, that she inspired me. She was my reason for getting into fashion. It was my first day, and I was young and really dumb. I wasn't a true fashion girl yet. Dr. M was thrilled that I'd been so open and honest with my feelings. That moron. For the next two years, Sarah brought it up every chance she could, rubbing salt in my wounds.

"I want salad for lunch. Let's go. You should have one too. You're, like, so puffy." She did the nose wrinkle. "Since I *inspire* you, you'll skip the burger."

I wanted to die each and every time. Sarah couldn't be won with earnestness. I should have known that. But when I stopped responding to those taunts, she picked something else to lord over me.

"Anya, are you still doing your little *blog*?" She'd erupt into giggles over the word.

Blogs were lame, she'd decided. I had killed my blog once I got hired at *La Vie*. It was a means to an end. With the right amount of faked articles, bought traffic, and paid followers, you too can be the hot new shit. Photos of me at the same events as Sarah (sneaking in when the door bots weren't looking) and write-ups of fabulous runway shows I never attended filled the site. I overheard conversations and reported them as if they had been spoken to me. None of it was real. Fake it 'til you make it. (My résumé listed magazine jobs I'd never held. No one remembered. Staff turnover is brutal in the media world.) There was no set list of credentials to get hired at fashion mags. No requirements beyond passing the edit test and dressing well—and having a good (faux) reference or two. I was just another young editor no one paid attention to. And it was all worth it because now I was here, an editor at *La Vie*.

"Okay, well, let's get to it. What's on the agenda?" Celia said, clapping her hands. As the HBIC (head bitch in charge), Celia always led the FFD meetings. Mulberry sat in the corner scribbling notes, next to our intern, Cassie. Cassie stared at her phone throughout the meeting.

"We need to do our Fashion Week preview," Dalia Joshi, our accessories editor, offered. She was the only person on staff who was nice to me and also one of the only minorities in editorial. She was Indian. (There was another brown woman on staff in the sales department, but we never mingled with sales. Ever.) Dalia should have been the beauty editor; her skin was perfect and glowing. She also posted really amazing how-to beauty videos on her own time. (I watched them studiously; my winged eyeliner had never looked so good *and* I learned how to contour.) But Celia wouldn't ever think of having a brown woman run *La Vie*'s most lucrative department.

"What if she has to do TV? No, that will never work. We're not an *ethnic* magazine."

Insert facepalm emoji here.

The accessories department was professional purgatory. There was nowhere to move on to from there. At best, Dalia would get hired away by a brand. If she were lucky.

"Right. So new designers, who's doing that?" Celia asked. I raised my hand. She shot me a look but acquiesced. She was still mad about the photo. But I wasn't ugly like the Elephant Man; bad angles happen to good people. "Great, I want Alexander King in there."

"Sure thing." I smiled. Always smile. Dr. M taught me that. Smiling makes people like you.

"Sarah, can you do a shoot on the models to watch? Nothing too crazy; it's just for the website."

"Of course, Celia."

I knew what this meant. Sarah would pick the models, and I would write it for her. That's how it worked with us. She used to want me to eyeball her pieces for her, tweak a few things. Soon that shifted to me writing everything based off Sarah's notes. I was the better writer, so of course I did it. I was helping her. I enjoyed it, as a matter of fact. Writing

Sarah's stories brought us closer together. Sarah had to talk to me about her thoughts sometimes. We were almost friends. We were united.

"What else?"

"We should totally do something on crash dieting for Fashion Week," Evie Rose Smith, the beauty editor, chimed in. "You know, how to lose twenty pounds in a month. That sort of thing."

"Is that even possible?" Celia asked.

Evie shrugged her bony shoulders. "Probably not, but it will be funny to find out." She snickered.

I felt everyone's eyes on me as the room grew quiet.

"Let me guess . . . this one's for me?" Smile.

"Well you *are* trying to lose weight," Sarah said in her most charitable voice. "I mean, you'll never fit into a size two if you don't do something drastic."

"Very true." Celia nodded, scrutinizing my chest and arms. "Great. Work with Evie on this. Keep a log of everything you eat. And daily weigh-ins. Oh, and remember: A *La Vie* girl does not cheat on her diet. That's it. Thanks everyone. Anya, Sarah, stop by my office." She walked out of the room with Sarah and Mulberry on her heels.

I trudged after them, dreading whatever torture Celia had cooked up for us next. Sarah was already sitting in Celia's office, smiling coyly, when I arrived. Mulberry smiled at me sympathetically as I walked in. (I hated that. I didn't need pity from an assistant. Who did she think she was?) Celia sat behind her black leather desk. She'd had her office redone six months ago, wanting more "dramatic texture." Her chair was upholstered in chinchilla fur; the ones across from her were covered in sequins. Clearly she didn't want us to ever feel comfortable sitting in her office. Celia's Louboutins were lying on the floor. The smell of feet tickled my nostrils.

"Ah, Anya, good, you're here. Shut the door." She rested her chin on her index fingers. This was her serious face. "Now, as you know, you've both been here for a while—"

"Some of us longer than others," Sarah cut in. She wasn't wrong. She'd been at *La Vie* for years, starting as an intern, then assistant, then assistant editor, and finally, associate editor. Years that she had on me. I'd come in with the same title as her but was paid fifteen thousand less. But it was worth it. I worked next to Sarah Taft.

"And you're associate editors. Well, I'm going to promote one of you to style editor. The other one will report to your former colleague."

"Um, who are you promoting?"

"Good question, Sarah. Promotion will be based on traffic. The person who does the most to boost our traffic on the website wins. You each have until Fashion Week to prove you have what it takes."

"But what does that have to do with—?"

"No buts, Sarah. You're dismissed." Celia had already picked up her phone and was yelling orders to Mulberry.

Sarah was my competition? This was bad. Celia loved Sarah. Sarah was perfect. Sarah was gorgeous. Sarah was my reason for even being here. Sarah had been here longer than me—but I didn't want to be her inferior. That would be social suicide. If I worked for her, I'd be stuck fetching her coffee, not having drinks with her. But if I were her boss, everything Sarah would be invited to, I would too. (It was, like, masthead law of nature or something—the higher you were on it, the more people wanted to see you and be near you. Invites would simply pour in. Like magic.) Our seat assignments at shows would be nearly identical. Right now, I usually sat behind Sarah. No one knew who I was. But next to her, our bags touching, whispering my runway thoughts to her, I'd be just like Sarah. No, better than. Because I was self-made. She'd have to accept me as her friend. And being Sarah's friend would make me untouchable.

"Wow, can you believe that?" Sarah asked when we were back at our desks. A low wall stood between us, separating our cubicles. I hated it. I could only see the top of her head unless I popped up like a meerkat (which I did twenty times a day). Her side was covered with love notes from designers. Mine had to-do lists and editorial calendars.

"Crazy," I agreed.

"I mean, traffic? That's, like, so not our job!"

I shot her a look, staying quiet. Maybe this wouldn't be that hard after all. I had more than six weeks to best my bestie, and my work outshone hers every day. Sure, I wrote her work, but I didn't make it as good as mine. I'm not stupid.

"Besides, it's so not fair to you," Sarah continued, her voice dripping with pity.

"What does that mean?" I asked.

"Everyone knows that promotions are based on your social standing, no matter what Celia says. And you have none. You're a total nobody. Seriously, no one knows who you are. Which is just so sad because you're, like, really great." She tilted her head, nodding as she said this.

She thought I was great! My heart skipped a beat. But she was right about the nobody part. No one knew me, or anything about me. I would have to show her and Celia that I deserved the new title. And any money that went with it. Living on less than fifty thousand a year was impossible when you had to be fashionable. The shoes alone cost me more than my rent. Thank God my trust fund was still full. I had to win this. *Be brave, you can do it.* Mantras were useful. I would win, I'd show her.

"What's the matter, Sarah? Scared of some competition?" Bravado, my only weapon.

"Um, okay, whatever!" She laughed. "I'd be totally happy if you won the promotion." She widened her eyes as she said it. That meant something, right? I felt strange. Like a balloon puffing up.

"Aw, thank you. And I'd be happy if you won too."

"Good, because I will."

Before I could hiss out my reply, I heard Celia screaming at some poor soul that she was going to ruin them.

"Goddammit!" Celia threw her door open and stalked up and down the hallway (still barefoot), yelling at anyone who was stupid enough to make eye contact. Celia wasn't a crazy boss, exactly, but when something didn't go her way, it was best to stay out of sight. She stopped at our cubicles and took a few deep breaths.

"Do you girls know anyone at White & White PR?" We both nodded.

"Of course we do," Sarah said enthusiastically. "What do you need?"

"I need my fucking Alexander King dress! So call your friends over there and get it!"

Sarah paled at Celia's tone. When I became her boss, we'd get manis and pedis together and expense it.

Celia turned to me.

"Lauren said she'd send it over this morning," I practically squeaked. "Doesn't Mulberry have the info?"

"Mulberry can't find the emails," Celia ground out before stomping back to her office.

"We'll take care of it, Celia." I glanced at Sarah as she picked up the phone. When she hung up, she sighed heavily. "Nothing?"

"*Nada.* They have no idea where Lauren what's-her-name is, and she has the dress. How fucking inconsiderate. I mean, I bet she's over at *Mince* right now handing it to their fashion department. That's our dress to debut!" *Mince* had stolen three dresses from us in the last four months. They were designer exclusives, launching to the world on our pages. The versions on the runway were often not what ended up in stores. So it was necessary for us to get the best looks first. We were *known* for it. And *Mince* was kicking our ass.

Ugh. *Be a team player, Anya. You can do this.* Insert whatever other stupid corporate euphemism here to make what I had to do easier. I called Lauren's cell phone.

"Hey Lauren! It's Anya." My voice was so chipper, it made my head hurt.

"Anya! What's up, babe?"

I cringed. "Nothing much. Listen, I think there was a dress that was supposed to come here for Celia."

"Oh, shit, the Alexander King didn't arrive? O-M-G, my assistant forgot to send it! So sorry babe!"

My shoulders tensed. "Celia's not happy."

"Oh, fuck. Okay, tell her I'll bring it there myself in the next hour."

"Cool, thanks." I hung up.

"Sarah!" Celia yelled from her office.

"Shit," Sarah muttered. She ran to Celia. I could hear her saying she had no idea where the dress was and maybe she should find a new one. Time for my move.

"Actually, guys, Lauren said she's bringing it within the hour," I said from the door. "There was some mix-up with delivery, and she's really sorry about it."

Celia shot me one of her steely stares and nodded. "Good job, Anya. That's how you get a promotion."

"But you said it was going to be based on traffic!" Sarah cried.

"It'll be based on what I want it to be, okay? You're dismissed."

"You could have told me you found the dress," Sarah said while walking back to our desks.

"You didn't ask." I smiled.

Smiling makes people like you.

* * *

Thirty-eight minutes later, Lauren ran in, sweating and out of breath. I checked her eye for any signs of stabbing or blood but found none.

"Hey, Anya! I—I have the dress," she wheezed.

I nodded and picked up the phone to call Mulberry. Celia's assistants never lasted long, but there was a bonus if you got through an entire year. We called it the shit payout. Mulberry had been there for ten months, which was a record at *La Vie*. She was blonde—they were always blonde—and the daughter of a former model and hedge fund guy. People think models and rock stars usually get together, but the real matches are the bankers and the catwalkers. Money talks. It's also how Mulberry landed this job.

"You can have a seat right here." I led Lauren to the extra chair at my desk (for minimeetings). Mulberry came running over, wearing a pair of vintage Marc Jacobs backward heels. You know, the kind that looks like the heels were hacked off with a machete. They came out in spring 2008—totally vintage. But right as she got to Lauren, her ankle buckled, and down Mulberry went, like a wounded giraffe. I heard cackling next to me.

"God, she can't even walk in heels." Sarah laughed.

Mulberry wasn't getting up. She rolled around moaning, acting as if her ankle had broken. It hadn't. Nothing snapped; I have an ear for these things.

"Get up," I ordered. "Take those ridiculous shoes off and get back to your desk."

"But they're my faves," she whispered, crying.

She was crying over shoes. I wanted to slap her. I wanted to take those shoes and smash her head in. She had pitied me, that idiot. I wanted to watch her bleed, to wipe that look from memory. Instead, I took a deep, coping breath.

"Honey, you can't cry over something like this. This is fashion. Celia will fire you. Now get the fuck up and do your goddamned job." I turned on my heel (Valentino rockstuds) and walked back to Lauren. "So sorry about that. She's new," I lied. "Let's go in to see Celia."

I led her to Celia's office. The buzzing noise was back. Were they doing construction in the building? Could this day get any worse?

Celia was happy. No, Celia was fucking thrilled: her Botoxed lips almost smiled. The dress had arrived; I had saved the day. Points for me. The promotion would be mine.

But when I turned back to my desk, I caught a shimmer out of the corner of my eye.

The shard was sticking out of Lauren's eye again. Six inches of mirrored glass hanging out of one of her baby blues for all the world to see. Just what was she playing at? How had she hidden it before?

"Anya? Is there anything else?" Celia asked.

"What? Oh, um, no." I hurried back to my desk.

"I don't even know why you helped her," Sarah's voice came over the cubicle wall along with more buzzing.

"What?" Was she making the noise? Was there a vibrator over there? You think I'm joking, but you'd be surprised at the shit publicists send us. But when I looked over the cubicle wall, nothing.

"Why'd you help Mulberry? She's obvi a loser." Sarah really despised the girl. It was a socialite thing; they were sworn frenemies. But Mulberry was no Sarah. Sarah was perfect.

"Because she's practically a child, and someone had to clear her out of the way."

"Whatevs."

Maybe she was right. I could have left Mulberry there to die in the hallway in front of my desk. Everyone stepping over her, ignoring her until she finally rotted away. The weak didn't survive here. The weak didn't belong. Mulberry wasn't one of us. She had to go. I needed to be more like Sarah if I wanted to survive, if I wanted upward mobility.

"Maybe you're right. But I felt—"

"What, bad for her? Come on, Anya, you're not doing her any favors. She's going to get fired anyways."

I nodded.

"What's with you? Why are you covering your ears?"

"What? You don't hear that?"

"Uh, hear what? Stop being so freaky. God, Anya, it's amazing we let you work here. You're such a weirdo."

I dropped my hands and smiled. Flashed teeth. Everything was fine. I was fine. Nothing to see here. "You're so right about Mulberry. What a fucking weakling." I sat down.

"Duh," she replied, the telltale sound of her filing her nails coming through over the buzzing. I was not a freak. I was not a freak. I belonged here. I was one of them. Mulberry was weak. I had to show that I belonged.

3

Sarah popped up over the cubicle wall when I arrived the next morning. "Oh my God, did you hear?"

"No, what? Did someone wear last season's Alexander King?" She didn't laugh at my joke.

"God, no, this is serious. They found Mulberry."

"About time. Where was she?" Celia's assistant had vanished the afternoon before. From embarrassment, probably. I popped a piece of bagel in my mouth, a move that Sarah's eyes followed. I stopped chewing and casually spit the offending carbs into a napkin.

"How can you put that in your body? Don't you know what gluten does to you? It attacks your system. It's like poison."

"That's not how it works—"

"That's exactly how it works. Dr. Shinasky told us, and she never lies."

"Dr. Shinasky isn't even a real doctor." She wasn't. She worked at Sarah's gym.

"Wow, I'm just trying to save you. Besides, do you really need carbs?" She eyed my waist. Shit. She was right. I had the new diet to start. There was a diet meeting on my calendar today.

"Right, you're right. Anyways, Mulberry?"

"She was in some computer closet. Can you believe it?"

"Doing what? She doesn't know anything about computers." My heart was pounding in my ears. *Act normal, Anya.*

"No, she's, like, dead! They found her with those stupid shoes bashed into her head. The police are coming, and the dead-body people are here!" She meant the medical examiners.

I paused. *One. Two. Three.* "Shit, is this actually happening?"

"Yes! The police want to talk to us, Anya."

"Oh." I hated talking to the police. They asked too many questions. And if you didn't answer correctly (or even if you did), they took you away. And then you had to live with crazies and criminals until you aged out. They never believed that shit just happened. Friends caught on fire. People died all the time. It's not a big deal.

"Are you worried?" Sarah asked.

"I'm just upset about Mulberry," I replied breezily. "I mean, how brutal. Also, like, did someone do that to her? Or did she fall and hit her head? No, that wouldn't be possible, even for her. Someone . . . here maybe? So . . . what does that mean?"

"Oh, shit. O-M-G." Nothing could get her to actually say "Oh my God," not even the thought of a killer on the loose. "You're right. Holy shit. We should do something. You don't think the police will, like, search our bags, right? I mean, not without a warrant?"

"Uh, I don't think so. Why, got some extracurricular items in there?" I grinned to show I was cool, just like her. Drugs didn't bother me.

"No! I mean, maybe. Whatever." Sarah paced around our cubicles.

"I doubt they'll search anything. Just relax."

"Wow, W-T-F Thursday, man." And then she took a selfie, captioning it just that. She didn't offer to take a photo with me.

"I'm going to see if I can take a selfie with the body. Maybe the shoe's still in her head!" Sarah bounded off. I shrugged, getting up to follow. After all, if Sarah did it, then it was fine. No, it was *chic*.

* * *

The computer closet was a narrow cupboard in a small hallway next to the supply room. It was filled with old keyboards and monitors, along with some outdated and ugly *La Vie* merch. The only people who went near it were the IT guys. Today, the tiny hallway was packed with people. Uniformed police officers; some guy with a camera and a bright flash snapping photos; *La Vie* girls forming a semicircle, fake tears rolling down their faces. I saw Sarah and pushed my way next to her at the front of the gawking line.

"Holy shit," I managed to say.

There she was, sitting in yesterday's YSL leather mini and Balmain tee with one shoe on, one bare foot hanging out, crammed into a space barely wide enough to hold her. The other shoe was in her head. Not on it, but actually in her face. Smashed in so hard, her nose was gone. I suppose the weird heel mechanism helped it stay lodged where it was, but still—wow.

I had tried to make it look accidental. With a girl as clumsy as Mulberry, you could get away with a lot, but it still didn't look right. No, it was pretty obvious someone had done this to her. *Stupid Anya. Always rushing to get things done. Take time, slow down*, I chastised myself. But I hadn't been able to get the look she'd given me out of my head. *She* felt bad for *me*. For me! Ha, that was a riot. The more I thought about it, the more enraged I became. It was like one of those crimes of passion deals. I had to very *passionately* show her that her pity wasn't welcome.

So while everyone was at lunch yesterday, I went to Mulberry with some computer closet questions. She cheerfully led me to the small space. Dr. M always says to seize opportunities. And hello? She hadn't even screamed. But she did ruin my dress. Blood was such a bitch to get out of silk. Still, she'd gone without a fight. Typical Mulberry. She was weak, just like Sarah said.

I'd done it, I killed her, but it didn't feel like I had. You know that feeling? Like when you unplug your flatiron but then aren't sure you did? I remembered killing Mulberry and changing my clothes. But it all felt so far away from this moment with Sarah so close to my side.

Sometimes it felt like I was sleepwalking through life, and what I did (or didn't do) was a vague blur I couldn't put my finger on. But that's normal, right? Maybe my meds were messing with me. Anyway, Mulberry was dead. She'd never pity me again. That's all that mattered.

"Death by accessories," Sarah muttered. Was she going to tweet that?

"Killer shoes," I whispered back. She giggled.

"Fashion victim," she practically cackled, snapping a photo before the officers shooed us away.

"Ladies, we need to speak to anyone who worked with Mulberry and saw her yesterday," one police guy said. He was wearing a suit, so he must have been a detective. Detectives always wear suits. At least, that's how it worked on *Law & Order SVU*. This guy was no Elliot Stabler, but damn if he wasn't hot. He looked like a Calvin Klein model. No, beefier. Like one of the Chanel models. (Karl totally liked some muscle on his guys.) I could stare at him all day.

"Sarah and Anya probably saw her," I heard someone pipe up. It was a girl in credits. You know in magazines when there are those impossible-to-read captions listing the clothing pictured and where to buy them? Those are credits. It was some unlucky girl's job to do them for each issue. This girl was dressed in the identical outfit Sarah wore the day before.

"Fuck," Sarah said under her breath. "Yep, we're here!" Bright, perfect teeth flashing. You could practically see the sparkle bouncing off her pearly whites.

"Great, let's go somewhere to talk," Hot Detective said.

"The small conference room is available," I offered. He looked me in the eyes. This was one of those detective tricks, those moments where they test your mettle. Younger Anya may have fallen for some of them, but I was smarter now. I was not taking the fall for Mulberry. God he was really hot. It was shallow and lame, but a pretty face can do almost anything. Look at Sarah. She practically got away with murder all the time.

I blushed and stammered. He had really intense green eyes. "I-I mean, we can go there."

"Easy, Anya, don't melt into a puddle." Sarah laughed. I could kill her.

I smiled and led them both to the room.

"Can I get you a drink or something, Detective . . . ?"

"Hopper. And no, I'm fine. So you're—"

"Sarah Taft," Sarah interjected. She was easy in these situations. So calm. I needed to be more like her. Bounce the hair, smile, beam. She never got rattled.

"That would make you Anya."

"Anya St. Clair." I practically mumbled it.

"Anya's our social reject." Sarah laughed again. "So, Detective, what can we tell you?"

"When did you last see Mulberry von Gratz?"

"Well, yesterday when she tripped and fell and Anya dragged her away."

Was she trying to make me look guilty? WTF, Sarah? This was not how BFFs behave. I wanted to smash her face into the glass conference table to shut her up. Teach her a lesson. Now I had to tell everyone what really happened. Detective Hopper's green eyes turned to me. Did you know that only 2 percent of the world has green eyes? This man was a fucking rarity staring at me.

"You dragged her away?" he asked.

I sighed. "No. Mulberry was wearing those vintage Marc Jacobs shoes and couldn't walk in them. She tripped and went flying in the hall near our desks—and just lay there.

For, like, ever. And you just can't do that here. If you trip, get up. If Celia saw her like that, she'd be fired." My explanation had to make sense, right?

"Oh, *so* fired," Sarah chimed in.

"So I made her get up. I told her to stop crying and get back to her desk." Later I bashed those ugly shoes into her face. Nobody pities me. "I think she went to the bathroom or something to pull herself together."

"Did you see her after that?" I shook my head. "And where did you go after?"

"I came back to bring Lauren White, the publicist, into Celia's office. That's what Mulberry was supposed to do before she fell."

"And can anyone verify that?"

"Oh, I can. I was there," Sarah said, smiling.

Okay, I wouldn't smash her face in. Maybe I'd just give her a bad haircut. And then keep her hair for a wig. I imagined myself with Sarah's perfectly highlighted locks. I looked amazing—in my head.

"So did anyone see Mulberry after she went to the bathroom?"

"I wasn't really paying attention, to be honest. I don't think I saw her later, at least I don't remember seeing her. Maybe she was too embarrassed by how she acted and knew she was going to be fired so she hid in the ladies' room? Celia hates it when assistants act out."

"God, she so does." Sarah couldn't resist.

"Did Celia find out about the scene in the hall?" A lock of his dark-brown hair—it was nearly black, but, really, no way could it be black-black. Was he that perfect?—fell in his face. I wanted to touch it. Smell it. Make tiny dolls with it. Shit, what if he and Sarah had perfectly cheekboned babies together? The hair on their kids alone would be world changing.

"Maybe?" I shrugged. "Lauren could have told her about it in their meeting."

"Did anyone have it in for Mulberry?"

"That idiot?" Sarah snorted. I elbowed her in her ribs. "Sorry, it's just that she wasn't very bright, and it's not like she was going to work here for long. None of Celia's assistants do. They all leave. No one's ever lasted a full year."

"Why's that?"

"Well, Celia's kind of tough to work for. She usually just fires you, and if she doesn't, you quit," I said. "But Mulberry was hanging in there, sort of."

"Has anyone ever told you that you look like a model?" Sarah said suddenly, pouring on the charm.

"Uh, no, but thanks, Ms. Taft."

* * *

The talk around the proverbial water cooler (a.k.a. the green juice delivery bag) was that no one could believe what had happened. Surely there had to be security camera footage of it. ("Wait, no, they only film the hallway with the fashion closet," Dalia reminded us.) And was Sarah going to post that photo she snapped?

"Oh, God no! I was just curious. That'd be so gauche."

"But how hot was that cop? What did he want with you guys?" Evie asked.

"So many questions, right, Anya?"

I nodded. "Ugh, that was so annoying. I can't believe you asked him if he was a model!"

"No, I said he looked like one. Whatevs, he did."

Dalia laughed, Evie filed her nails. An uncomfortable silence grew. We all scrolled through our phones.

"Hey, Sarah, I thought you weren't posting that photo?" I asked.

"I'm not, why?"

"Because it's up. And come on, the hashtag?" #FashionVictim. It was funny when she said it, but on Instagram? Tacky.

"I didn't post it! Take it down! Someone help me!"

"W-T-F?" I gasped. "It's been reposted and faved like a thousand times. You're in such deep shit." This was better than smashing her head into a table.

"Seriously, that is messed up, Sarah," Evie clucked. "What if her family sees that?"

"God, for real," Dalia added.

"I didn't post it!" Sarah yelled. "Fuck this, I'm getting a mani."

The day passed in eerie silence after she left, which was more than welcome. Everyone spoke in hushed tones, avoiding the Murder Hallway and police tape. That's what we were calling it now. Celia spoke with the police from her home on East Sixty-Second Street. Apparently it was all "too much" for her, and she was taking the rest of the week off.

Everyone assumed the murderer was someone from the messenger service.

"They, like, hate us!" Evie moaned to us when Sarah came back. (Her nails were pink and silver.) The only reason people thought that was because most of the guys weren't white. The unspoken—and spoken—racism of magazine land, where the masthead was all pretty white girls and the support staff was everyone else.

"Jesus, you're so white, it hurts," I said.

"Thanks!" She was *that* white. Her skin was the color of curdled cottage cheese. But Dr. M always said to pick your battles, and this one wasn't going to be won.

"Whatever, I just don't think anyone from the messenger center did it. It has to be someone who knew Mulberry." I watched Sarah's face. I wanted to impress her. She looked concerned.

"What do the police think?" Evie asked.

The police. They'd asked us all the questions, but they never offered us up any info. I needed to change that. I needed to know what they knew.

"Let's go get froyo from downstairs!" Dalia suggested cheerfully.

"Um, that's all sugar and chemicals. We're organic now," Sarah chastised.

I nodded. "Green juice?"

"O-M-G, totes."

* * *

If it bleeds while wearing designer shoes, it goddamned leads. The news of Mulberry von Gratz's demise didn't take long to spread. It wasn't that people were particularly devastated by her death; it was just such a juicy story. A beautiful, rich kid dead? Murdered while working at a fashion magazine? *"Fashion Victim!"* was splashed all over the *New York Post* the next day, along with a story about how awful the death was, how beloved Mulberry was, and all that bullshit—including a mention of the cold fashion bitch who Instagrammed the body.

Social media got in on the effort, and #PrayforMulberry was trending in New York, Ibiza, and Biarritz (where she'd gone to school). I almost choked on my coffee when I saw that one. *A bit too late to pray for her, guys.* #FashionVictim was also trending. Twitter was full of vicious bitches. No such thing as too soon in this business.

And all this because Mulberry wanted to pity me. She wanted to show she was better than me. Pity means people look down on you. Well, I showed her. That weakling. She was so damn useless. She couldn't fetch anything. And that's what assistants did. They fetched. Coffee. Shoes. Xanax. Whatever we needed. She could have gone on to be anything: a stylist, a consultant, a trophy wife. But she gave up in that hallway.

Sarah was right. Mulberry was a weakling. Sarah was always right. I'd done this for her. She had to love me now. I flashed to our police interview. Sarah telling the detective details about me. Her hair was shining even under the fluorescent lighting. (Maybe I *should* get a wig.) Sarah had to love me. BFF meant loyalty. She would have to learn that. I'd have to teach her. Help her.

Too bad about Mulberry's shoes. They were cute, in a conceptual way. And now, no one could ever wear them without thinking *killer shoes*. Maybe I did the world a favor?

4

Mulberry's funeral was held a few days later. It had the same solemn air as before a major fashion show. Hushed chatter, lots of pinched faces. Mulberry hadn't received this much ink for anything while she lived—unless the mother-daughter spreads from when she was a toddler counted.

Everyone dressed in their best event attire. Fashion event, not normal event. I even wore Alexander McQueen, this season. (Sarah laughed at me. "You don't have to be so damned goth!") The entire event went off without a hitch, except for the police presence. They stood out in the crowd, their suits rumpled, the pant legs too long. (Why don't men use tailors anymore? Even a cheap suit looks chic when fixed up.) The lone exception was Detective Hopper.

I felt his eyes on me throughout the service. *Shit. Anya. He knows.* I was bracing myself to be led away in cuffs, a scene in front of the entire industry. (Seriously, everyone showed up to Mulberry's funeral. She really would have thanked me.) When Detective Hopper made his way over to me, I started to hold my wrists out. He shot me a puzzled look.

"Oh, just my bracelets—they're bothering me," I said in rush. He nodded. My face felt hot. "Do you have any leads?"

"We're still investigating. Nothing I can comment on right now. But we may need to speak with you again." I nodded. He wanted to speak to me. Was that good or bad? He smiled, and I left, quickly.

The "Twenty-Six Best Funeral Looks" article came out the next day. Celia was included, posing in that ghastly ruffled Alexander King dress. The unholy trinity—Sarah, Jack Archer, and Lisa Blitz—were all given proper placement. Sarah had worn a sedate and boring Tory Burch dress in the hopes of looking appropriately sad after her social media snafu. Everyone had the decency to look somber in the photos, but they still did their best street-style poses: ankles crossed, head angled downward, chin titled, hand on hip.

* * *

Dr. M wasn't thrilled with the developments at work. No surprise there; dead bodies weirded him out. And the whole police thing rattled him. He worried so much about me.

"Anya, are you anxious?"

Our relationship was the best I'd ever had. Dr. M was in his midfifties and wore round glasses. His hair had turned grayer over the last five years. (We'd been together for at least thirteen, since my teen years.) Things had gotten rocky between us some years back. He was mad at me for not progressing quickly enough, but you can't rush good mental health. He threatened to cut me off, fob me onto some new shrink in training or something. I felt like killing him when he said that, but we worked it out. Now he said he'd never leave me again.

"Um, maybe. But mostly because someone was murdered near me. But otherwise, I'm okay." I smiled to show him I was fine.

"But the police?"

"O-M-G!" I said it just like Sarah: oh-em-gee. "You should see the detective. He's so pretty. He and Sarah would make excellent babies together."

He shot me another worried look. "Do you think perhaps you're putting Sarah on too high a pedestal? That she may not be as perfect as you think she is?"

"Uh, no. You'll see when you meet her. I mean, she and I have so much in common. We could be sisters."

He cleared his throat. "Maybe you need some distance from Sarah."

I glared at him. "No. The more Sarah likes me, the higher my profile will be. Dr. M, that's how Fashionlandia works." We had had this argument before. He felt I was putting too much effort into getting Sarah to love me. I think he was just jealous I had someone else in my life.

"Doesn't that mean you're using her?"

"What? No. No! We're *helping* each other. I help her manage her workload. And in turn, she'll help me climb the ladder."

"Are you still writing her stories for her? You said you'd stop." He was disappointed in me.

I shrugged. "She *needs* me. Anyways, you did always say I should aim high." He did. He said it to me constantly. *Anya, do better. Stop lashing out at people.* I was merely doing what he told me to. I was aspiring; I had goals. And Sarah Taft was the key to achieving them all.

"But you're putting conditions on your friendship," he pressed. "If she doesn't help you, then what?"

I rolled my eyes. "Just being friends with her elevates me. Don't you see?" He had to get it. I had come in as a nobody. As some girl who liked what she saw in magazines. I was lower than nothing. And now I had the chance of being the BFF of Fashionlandia's top star. Short of chilling with the Hadids, this was the pinnacle.

"I'm just concerned. Shouldn't you focus on your work and being happy?"

I sighed. "This is my *work*. What's the point of doing a good job if no one notices?"

"I notice."

"You don't count. You're paid to like me. Or not hate me."

"What happens if Sarah doesn't want to be friends? You two are competing against each other. What if it drives a wedge between you?" Dr. M was such a worrywart. I'd simply have to win the promotion. Invites and accolades would pour in. Sarah would embrace me as her equal. And if that didn't happen, if somehow I lost, I'd have to fix it. Fix her. But that wouldn't happen. This was my destiny.

He shot me a pointed look.

"I know what you're going to say. It's Meredith all over again." Why did he have to always bring her up? Meredith was gone. Dead. I would never have to see her again, but Dr. M was obsessed with her. With my relationship to her. She was just some psycho I was friends with when I was a kid. We grew apart; that happens to all besties eventually. And then she died. It was her own fault.

Dr. M blinked.

"It's not the same!" I insisted. "Meredith was totally different."

He sat back.

"Whatever, you weren't even around then."

The same. Hmph. Meredith's name began with an *m*. Like Mulberry. And Mariana, the old me. Anya was the new me. The fashionable me. Safe from Google searches and prying people. I grew out of *m* names. Except for Dr. M. I was way into *s* names and words now. *S* for superb. Stunning. Sartorial. Sarah. I even had an *s* in my last name. It truly was kismet. With an *s*.

* * *

"Have you lost any weight? Are you even trying?" Celia was facedown on the ground in her office, hovering a foot above the carpet. "It's been, what, a week? You should be down ten pounds by now."

"That's not even healthy."

"Fuck healthy. You need to be thin. Look at you."

She swiveled her head up from her plank, which she'd now been holding for two minutes. Her furrowed brow was an alarming shade of red.

"You're never going to be a real fashion editor if you don't look like one. And editors at *La Vie* are not chubby. This is not the way to win a promotion, Anya."

"I thought the promotion was traffic related."

"Do not argue with me. Until you can hold a plank for five minutes and fit into a size two, this experiment is a failure. Do you understand?"

"Yes, Celia."

"Good. Now get down here and plank."

"I—what?"

"You heard me, plank!"

The buzzing drill in my head was back. Was I dying?

"But I'm not warmed up." I had to get out of here.

"Excuses, excuses! You will never get anywhere with that attitude. On your knees. Now!"

I wasn't going to win this battle. I kicked my heels off (Manolos, obviously) and sank down to my knees. Was the promotion really worth it? I imagined reporting to Sarah every day, having to do menial tasks for her. Pouring her drinks while she chilled with Marc Jacobs or taking her shoes to be reheeled. It would be a nightmare. I'd never catch up to her.

"Okay, now get in position and . . . go!" Celia commanded.

I hoisted myself into a plank, or as planky as I could go in skintight jeans. I cursed under my breath. Celia hadn't budged from hers even once.

"Keep going! You can do it!"

I was going to kill this bitch.

"Everyone starts somewhere. Keep it up!"

I was going to make her suffer.

"Just ten more seconds!"

I was going to rip her heart out and eat it on top of a giant plate of pasta.

"And done! Great job! Now go have your protein shake—you earned it, finally."

"Thanks, Celia. That was fantastic." I flashed as many teeth as possible, the buzzing in my ears growing louder. Bronwen, her new Mulberry, smiled as I walked by.

I hustled back to my desk and stood, popping barbiturates to dull my headache. Dr. M said my headache pills were fucking with my memory and I shouldn't take them anymore. But they worked better than the pathetic over-the-counter shit.

"It's your own fault, you know," Sarah said, shoving avocado slices into her mouth.

"What? I can't hear you over the noise." I motioned to my ears.

"It's your own fault!" she shouted.

"Oh."

"You just need some willpower. Size two is the maximum you should be. She wanted you at a zero. But I told her it wasn't possible. I mean, you have such big-girl bones." She said the last part pityingly.

I wanted to punch her. I wanted to rip her blown-out-to-perfection blonde hair until she was bloody and bald. I wanted her to say I was stunning and gorgeous, her ideal vision of a best friend. *Be cool, Anya. Let it all wash over you. Nothing bothers you.* I looked at her and laughed loudly . . . for ten seconds. She furrowed her brow. I wanted to stab my head with scissors until the pain ended and the world went quiet.

"But you look good, Anya. I mean . . ."

Smile and the world smiles with you.

She shifted focus to her phone. A group chat with the unholy trinity, no doubt. Jack and Lisa, always around. Sarah snickered as she typed. Was she talking about me? Were they all laughing? I needed to see the texts. Thank God I'd installed parental monitoring software on her phone. I sat down at my desk and pretended to work while I pulled up the app.

Sarah: *Wait what are we doing later? I wanna go outttttt.* (Kissy face emoji)

Jack: *There's that party tonight.*

Lisa: *But it's in Brooklyn.* (Sad face)

Sarah: *Ew! Gross. OMG, you guyyyyys, Celia made the whale do planks. Planks! Can you die?* (Crying laughing emoji)

Lisa: *OMG, you should have filmed it. Record that shit so we can all laugh.*

Jack: *I'll bring popcorn.*

I was not a whale. I was barely a size six. Fine, a six to eight. I wanted to scream, to pick up my computer and smash it on my desk. But that wasn't an adult reaction. I was supposed to breathe when I felt like burning everything down. Because Dr. M said breathing would make that impulse go away. (Spoiler alert: it didn't.) He had this big thing about walking and breathing. That somehow, with each step you took and every breath you exhaled, your troubles would melt away. He used to make me go on superlong walks with him. So annoying.

But the trinity was mocking me. I would never be accepted by them. And with them around, by Sarah. They made her act so petty. Couldn't she see I was above that? Above them?

Remember, Anya, you're a winner. Dr. M said mantras were helpful in getting my mind on track. Eyes on the prize, all that bullshit. I took a sip of my protein shake—thirteen grams of protein, zero carbs, eight calories, and absolutely no flavor.

"Oh, aren't those amaze? I love them!" Sarah gushed, leaning over the partition. "I drink them all the time."

I tried to smile without gagging.

"If you drink two of those a day and water, you'll lose all the weight. Trust me," Sarah said wisely.

"Oh, you're so smart, Sarah!" Cassie, our intern, chimed in. She had been hired to help us out while she got school credit and was always hovering around. She probably heard and saw a lot. Had she seen me in the cupboard with Mulberry? No, couldn't have. She'd have told someone by now. She was getting close to Celia's new assistant, Bronwen. They were bonding over their administrative duties. Bronwen was blonde and wore flowers in her hair. Cassie was brunette and followed Sarah around like a puppy. She had painted her nails just like Sarah's: pink and silver. I hated Cassie. I hated Jack. I hated Lisa. I needed some motivational poster that told me to turn my hate into love, my frown upside down. Maybe a kitten hanging by its paws. Or Cassie hanging by her neck.

Sarah was wearing the new Prada mules (in blue), and they looked stunning on her. I needed to buy a pair, ASAP.

* * *

I spent the weekend working on mantras, breathing, and learning to control my thoughts. Okay, fine, I watched *Law & Order* and had Chinese food delivered. But on Monday, I was ready for the week. I sat at my desk, breathing deeply. A Diptyque candle in the John Galliano scent burned next to my computer. Dr. M felt it was important to center myself first thing. Because before you knew it, one wrong thing led to another, and your day was ruined.

Besides vegging, I'd updated my mood boards over the weekend. One for me and a new one for Sarah. Finding photos of her was ridiculously easy. When you're rich and famous, or society famous, everyone writes about you. Weird blogs and fancy magazines were obsessed with the Tafts. Where they holidayed, summered, shopped. (There was, I learned, a distinct difference between holidaying and summering. The latter was done in the Hamptons only.) There were profiles upon profiles of Sarah. Of her life at fancy boarding schools. Of her wardrobe. I'd read them all so much that I had memorized the details. Younger Anya loved to see every photo of Sarah. I held them up to my chest and wished again and again that we could trade places. That I'd wake up in her body, in her family home, with her parents. With her wardrobe.

Sarah and I are a lot alike actually. We're both only children. Our parents were absent. Hers were off yachting while she was stuck with the nanny. Mine died in a horrible car accident, leaving me with an ugly scar on my arm and my inheritance (in a trust. Jerks). We were both abandoned, sent away to school. Sure, Sarah's was more upscale and elite, but Dr. M said I had as good an education as was possible, all things considered. You know, those schools for kids like me are never that great.

You've probably never been to one of those schools—for damaged and difficult kids. For wayward girls. Call them whatever you want, but they're basically prisons for tots. I spent nine years in one before leaving at eighteen. Nine long years of following rules and being medicated. *Yes, ma'am. No, sir. I sure am sorry for everything.* All because the police believed I had done something to Meredith. I hadn't acted traumatized enough for their liking. I had a dead bestie and dead parents. I was walking trauma! The police are the worst.

I wasn't alone-alone back then. This isn't a fucking pity party. Don't go all Mulberry on me. I had roommates. New girls throughout the year, each year. I never learned their names. What was the point? They were in and out. I was there to stay.

But I had my magazines. Photo spreads that promised me a better life, a life like Sarah's. Sarah had been photographed from the day she was born. Sarah with her folks, Sarah as a toddler. Sarah walking down the runway as a teen at socialite fashion show. That's the age I first saw her. We were both fifteen. Her perfect face stared out at me. She would smile then. Now she poses. The magazines that featured her promised me that life. So long as I bought the clothes and wore the right makeup. I, too, could be on a sunny beach surrounded by hot models. The people shown weren't stuck in a school full of freaks, in a bedroom barely large enough for two twin beds, with the windows covered in bars. The magazine people were happy, gorgeous. No shitty friends or clueless parents. No drugs, no doctors.

I used to rip up each issue and cover my walls with the pages using scotch tape and chewing gum. Happy families like the Tafts could be mine, the magazines promised. I could be pretty and rich and loved by everyone. But even better than that, I could be envied. And I wanted that more than anything else. I wanted someone to make mood boards of *me*.

Sarah was destined to be my friend, even back then. And you just can't argue with destiny. I applied at *La Vie* two years ago just to be near her. And look at me now! We were almost BFFs. *So* close.

"There you are!"

I looked up to see Greg Davies standing over my desk, his wrinkled Adidas tracksuit looking out of place in the chic office. He was our publisher and Celia's boss (and therefore my boss).

"Did you see this?" He waved a paper in front of me. Greg used to be a model, or so he said. Catalog, at best. He was only five foot nine, and as much as he tried to hide his accent, his Staten Island roots betrayed him. His black hair was always slicked back, and I could see chest hair poking out from under his track jacket. The only jewelry he wore was a diamond pinky ring and a gold Rolex.

"No, what is that?"

"It's a comment! Engagement!"

"Let me see." I took the sheet, which turned out to be a printout of one of my stories—"Ten Date-Night Dresses Straight from the Runway." Designers had given recommendations on what to wear on a first date. It had done quite well. But at the bottom, Greg had circled—in red sharpie—a nasty comment from a troll. The comment said, simply, *U r stoopid*.

I sighed.

"Look at this one!"

He shoved another paper in my face. It was my "Ten Ways to Survive a Social Faux Pas" piece, and my regular internet troll, fasi0n-419, was giving it his or her all: *This story iz a faux pas. WTF?* and *This iz so stoopid*. If sighing burned any calories, I was so ahead of the game today.

"These comments kind of suck." I grimaced.

"They do. So let's tweak our content for the readers. They're who we do this for. They drive traffic. Make them happy *or else.*"

"Or else what?"

"Or else I'll find a writer who can make them happy. That goes for you too, Sarah." He moved toward her desk. Sarah stood to stare at him. "I want *more* comments. Happy comments. For both of you. Understand?" He pointed at us both with one hand, using his thumb and pinky. We nodded before he walked away.

"Was that all he wanted?" Sarah was annoyed.

"Yeah. Ugh, I hate the commenters."

"I didn't know we had any. But really, why is anyone even talking about your stories? Mine are so much better." She sniffed as she said it even though her stories were my stories. "I mean, who even reads you?"

"Sarah, are you . . . jealous right now?"

She gasped, then narrowed her eyes and pursed her lips. "Of what? You? Puh-lease." She flipped her hair for emphasis. "There's nothing about you worth being jealous over." She smiled coldly.

"I dunno. I don't see Greg running here to see you."

Her face darkened even more. "You know what? Fuck you, Anya."

5

I cycled my legs, left, right, left, right, pumping them as sweat dripped down my face and chin, pooling onto my chest. The music was loud. Too loud. The instructor was a peppy little wisp with no body fat. She smiled as she yelled at us, "Cycle harder, be a warrior!"

I hated Soul Cycle. Every second on my bike made me want to murder the bitch next to me. (That would be Celia.) If the bikes weren't bolted to the ground, I'd throw mine on top of her. This had been her doing. She pounced on me first thing Monday morning, as I sat down at my desk with hot coffee.

"There you are!" Celia grabbed my arm. "Let's go do Soul Cycle. I signed us up for the nine thirty class. Did you bring shoes?" She half dragged me to the elevators. My coffee was abandoned. Sarah waved.

"Come on, keep pushing! Do this for yourself! You're worth the sweat! The pain! Cycle through it!" I hated the cheerful instructors telling me to feel the rhythm. It was forty-five minutes of pure hell. I closed my eyes, cycling as hard as I could. I could be thin and happy if I did this more often. I could get my rage out on the bike. I could be like Sarah.

I got chills thinking of her, and not in a good way. I dreamt about her last night. Again. Her hair billowing behind her like at a photo shoot. She's laughing, her perfect teeth glinting.

"Be a legend! You can do this!" the instructor roared at us.

The dream was a bad one. Sarah was mad at me. She told me she likes Cassie, that she and Cassie are going to hang out now. Cassie was joining the trinity. Can you believe that? Hanging out with an intern? *Quel* nightmare. It was just a dream though. And dreams have no power. Sarah would never betray me like that.

"Everyone, cheer for yourself! Give yourself the applause and approval to live your life!" The instructor was soaked through, her skin glistening. I bet *she* never binged on cheesecake. "You did it! I am so proud of you!"

I was going to drown her in a bucket of her own sweat.

"This keeps me sane." Celia giggled, climbing off her bike. I wanted to devise a torture device that made Celia ride until she died. Or better yet, start my own class: Psycho Cycle. It'd be the ideal workout for today's woman: half the class has to get away from crazed killers (spoiler alert: they die), and the rest of us come out looking like Kaia Gerber. Million-dollar idea.

Celia was so mellow after the workout, she touched my arms and shoulders as if we were friends.

"You know, I don't want to tip the scales, but you're ahead in my little competition." She winked at me.

My heart stopped. I was winning. I was going to be Sarah's boss, and then Sarah would have to hang out with me whenever I wanted. I was going to be a real *La Vie* woman. Everything was going the way I wanted.

Sarah was at her desk when I came back. My leg muscles were vibrating. I was certain they had turned to Jell-O during my workout. She laughed when she saw me.

"Kill me" was all I could say.

Sarah looked gorgeous, as always. Her lips were so glossy, it was mesmerizing. Her secret? She applied five coats of gloss (by Fenty), waiting ten seconds between each coat. Watching her make fish faces while she did it brought me such singular joy. (Matte lips were out.)

The day got even better after I discovered the name of my number-one fan (thanks to the IT guys. They were *so* helpful. I almost felt bad I ruined their computer closet). Diana Williams—username: fasi0n-419—was the troll commenter getting Greg so excited about "engagement." I didn't know what I was going to do with her—hug her for making Sarah jealous or lash out at her for leaving such shitty comments. Greg's "or else" hung in my mind. I was going to have to keep an eye on Diana.

* * *

I was remarkably cheerful the next morning as I settled into my desk. Maybe there's something to that whole endorphins thing after all. My cheekbones were practically jagged. Soul Cycle and not eating *were* making me thinner, but was that any way to live? Chalky shakes and kale until I peed green for the rest of my life?

I felt pretty damn good, until I noticed printouts left by Greg. Diana's comments on my recent stories were once again circled in red sharpie. She'd made her displeasure known by commenting *This is lame* and *U don no fasion* again and again. She left each comment nine times, just to get her point across. My morning protein shake began to rise in my throat.

"Celia's looking for you," Sarah said curtly. She didn't say hi or stand up to deliver the message. Didn't she want to see how good my cheekbones looked? Maybe she had gotten comments too. I hurried to Celia's office.

"Oh, good, you're here. I think what your diet needs is the right motivation. So hop to it."

I looked at her blankly until I realized, with horror, that she was gesturing to a scale. "You want to weigh me?"

"Yes, every morning. I told you we'd have weigh-ins. This should inspire you not to cheat." Gone was girlfriend Celia. In front of me was boss bitch Celia. But we had bonded the day before. We'd sweat together. She'd touched my shoulder.

"Are you kidding me?"

"No, I'm serious. Now get on."

My day had officially gone to hell. I hated Wednesdays. They were the worst days.

"Now, Anya. We don't have all day."

I stepped on the scale and watched as Celia recorded my weight in a notebook. Fashion people never let you forget that you don't belong.

"And you're five foot four?"

I nodded.

"I think ten pounds won't be enough. You're almost one hundred thirty pounds. You need to be one hundred and ten. By Friday, you have to be down five pounds. Understand?"

That left me two days. I cleared my throat. "Um, Celia, yesterday you said I was in the lead for—"

"That was yesterday. What have you done to please me *today*? Nothing. The only way I could promote you is if you lose the weight. A *La Vie* woman is not obese."

Celia pinched my stomach through my caftan (it was a *chic* caftan). She held the fabric, skin, and fat in her fingers, eyeing it clinically. "All of this has to go. Oh, and I was thinking, we really should do a post on planking. I mean, isn't it the best thing ever?"

Her mouth hung open, waiting for a reply. I was still shocked by the fat pinching. My mind went into a rage-induced blankness. I had to reply.

"Well, haven't we already done that story?" We had. Several times over.

"Yeah, but this time we'll do a new one!"

"Okay . . . 'Fifteen Ways to Make Planking Work for You'? Something like that?"

She wrinkled her nose to show she was thinking. It was her way of avoiding frowning.

"Or 'Ten Ways to Add More Planks to Your Day.'"

"That's it! That's perfect! You may be chubby, but you're a genius!" And with that, I was dismissed. Chubby. I was chubby. The buzzing was at deafening levels. I want to say I didn't cry. My eyes welled, but I did manage to hold it in, at least until I got to the bathroom.

I had to call Dr. M for an emergency phone session before I did anything rash.

* * *

"But I feel so violated," I whined. The ladies' room was thankfully empty. My voice echoed off the tiles.

"Mariana, you know how to stand up for yourself. I don't know why you're playing the victim now."

"Anya. I wish you'd call me Anya. Like, Mariana is dead." There was an edge to my voice.

"Sorry, dear. Force of habit. You don't have to do anything you don't want to. Just stand up for yourself. Remember, *Anya*, nobody likes a victim."

"I know. And there's Lisa. She and Sarah called me a whale." I sounded like a child tattling. Dr. M sighed.

"You know how to handle this. How to handle yourself. Be a doer, not a whiner."

Way harsh, Dr. M, but also spot on. I was a doer. And I'd have to do something about Lisa sooner rather than later.

After my conversation with Dr. M, I made myself go back to my desk. I held my head up and smiled at everyone who walked by. I was fine. I was breezy. See? I was smiling.

"I'm going to grab lunch. You want something?" Sarah popped up and peered at me with curiosity.

Had she heard me with Dr. M? I didn't have anywhere private to talk except the restroom. I thought no one else came in. I waved her away, staring at my computer. I had to do something about Celia. I was not a victim. Maybe I'd wait until my promotion. Then she'd learn to not overstep boundaries. (That was another Dr. M-ism; boundaries were some kind of mental-health boogeyman or something.)

I raided the art department and began cutting out health photos from our archives for my diet mood board. Maybe I'd get a *La Vie* body by osmosis. The mood board would help, at least until I figured out what to do about my boundary-crossing boss.

At my schools, they fed you nothing but carbs. Starch on starch on starch. I didn't know if it was a weird health thing—like, with enough carbs, we'd all crash eventually—or if they were just cheap, but I learned to inhale my potatoes with macaroni salad. I learned to love them. But now I was at *La Vie*, and carbs were on the don't list. I had to change. I had to be better. I scrawled *Size Two* in a sharpie at the top of my board.

I started another board on Detective Hopper. It was filled with *Law & Order* images and Gucci men's runway pics. He hadn't checked in with me in almost two weeks, not since the funeral. Should I call him? No. My need for attention was going to ruin me. I had to play it cool. I drew a heart on his board. See? Nothing but love and positive vibes.

* * *

My improved cheekbones and I took a tour of a few events after work. I had no idea who or what they were for. It didn't matter. Every night there were countless parties to attend. I usually did drive-bys, popping in, kissing a few cheeks, downing a drink, gift bag in hand. Tonight I wanted to show off my thinner face, have someone tell me how good I looked. I needed that. I got out of my Uber near the Highline Hotel. It used to be a monastery and still had the forbidding look of a religious building. It was a favorite location for clothing presentations and parties.

Male models held trays of red and white wine, welcoming everyone with a smile. I grabbed a red, took a sip, and grimaced. People who cheap out on wine selection shouldn't go into party planning.

The usual panic started to rise up. Every event, every time I walked in, I had that moment of *Fuck. What am I doing here?* I glanced around for a familiar face. Any familiar face. Walking into a room full of the rich and fabulous can make anyone doubt herself.

I spotted Lisa's frizzy hair escaping out from under a vintage hat. (There was an attached veil. Can you even?) It was her look, her way of setting herself apart. She only wore vintage, paired with bold-red lipstick. Her dress was forest green. Greens, beiges, pale pinks, and corals always reminded me of institutional walls, the strange palette all schools and lock-ups shared. Sarah and Jack were standing next to her. Jack had on a mishmash of colors that should have clashed but didn't. I had to go over there. I had to say hi, despite just seeing Sarah at work. Why hadn't she told me she was coming to this?

"Hey, guys." I raised my eyebrows in lieu of a wave.

"Hey, Anya. Cute dress," Lisa said. I had changed into a black, sleeveless dress by Opening Ceremony. I couldn't tell if Lisa was being facetious or if she liked it. Her perpetual smirk kept me guessing. Dr. M's voice whispered in my head, *Be a doer.*

"Hey," Sarah added.

"I love the accessories this designer is doing." Lisa turned to me. "Don't you?"

I shrugged. "I guess. Not my thing." I had no idea who she was talking about. The designer I was wearing? Or the one who was throwing the party?

She laughed. "No shit; we can tell." What did that even mean? "I heard you're Celia's new pet project. How's the weight loss going?"

"Great, down a lot. So close to my goal weight," I lied. But I had cheekbones.

"Your face looks almost gaunt," Jack said approvingly. He even smiled at me.

"You still shouldn't be drinking wine. What with all the calories. Such a shame—you'd be so pretty if you lost the weight." Lisa's mocking voice echoed in my ears until all I could hear was her and my heart beating like a drum.

My head felt like it was going to explode, and my face burned. *Deep breaths, find a mantra. Do something! (Kill her.*

No, don't. Not yet.) I wanted to scream that she was a frizzy-haired bitch.

I cleared my throat. This was it. I was going to take her down. "Aw, thanks, Lisa, so sweet of you!" Okay, it wasn't the most cutthroat thing I could have said. Not even close. I smiled politely at her, which seemed to enrage her.

"Is your dress fake too?" she hissed.

"Lisa, I love that you make do with used clothing. That's so . . . cute."

I glanced at Sarah. She was grinning. She enjoyed this.

"Whatever. Don't think I don't know about you. Because I do. And soon I'll know more." Lisa spat the words out.

The ominous threat hung in the air between us. What did Lisa know? No one knew me, who I used to be. I wanted to grab her by the throat and force her to tell me.

I shrugged. "Whatever you say!" Bright smile, wave, exit. *Exit now.* I'd like to say I didn't spend the rest of the evening focusing on Lisa and her threats. But that'd be a lie. And Dr. M said telling lies only hurt you. But he didn't have to survive in Fashionlandia.

I stopped to buy myself a new present on the way home. A blonde wig, long and wavy. Like Sarah's hair. Like Meredith's. They were both blondes, but Mer had that supersoft kid hair. The wig cost a fortune; the good ones always do. I tried it on when I got home. It made me look like Sarah's sister. I was perfect. This was exactly what I needed.

That and Lisa's head on a fucking platter.

* * *

I wore black jeans (denim and leather was always a winning combo), a black silk tank, and an asymmetrical blazer. All from Barneys, my happy place.

I was determined to be happy and positive. To not let the party from the other night get to me. Fuck Lisa and her taunts. I was better than her. But my mood soured right as I got to my desk. Left on my chair were more printouts of my stories with comments. Diana's comments. Greg had written in red sharpie, *Do better. Or else.*

"Dammit," I muttered.

"What?" Sarah asked.

"More shitty comments. Are you getting them too?"

"Not really. I guess my stories are just better than yours."

I closed my eyes. My head was already pounding. How could this be happening? This Diana person was targeting me. Did I know her? Did we go to school together? I had to talk some sense into her. She was seriously messing up my work life.

Which was weird because Diana had no life of her own. I'd stood outside her apartment yesterday after work. I skipped all my parties; this was more important. I saw Diana come home, go upstairs. She dressed in boring outfits from the Loft. She wore no makeup, and aside from a pedicure—which I unfortunately had to see thanks to her heinous flip-flops—it was clear she wasn't trying. She was not a *La Vie* woman. So why was she trying so hard to get my attention? Diana needed to get—or lose—a life. Maybe I could talk to her, woman to woman. Or break her fingers off—*snap, snap, snap*—so she couldn't comment ever again.

"Why is Greg so obsessed, anyway? Doesn't he know you shouldn't read the comments?" Sarah didn't answer me. She was busy clack-clacking on her phone.

Fucking Diana. What was her problem, anyway? Why my stories and not the ones I wrote for Sarah? Trolls were the worst. They picked on one person and tried to break them. I'd seen other editors deal with them. Evie had one that always called her ugly. (Okay, it was me, LOL.) But Diana just hated me.

I stewed. All damn day. Every word I wrote, I wondered what Diana would think. Not Sarah, but Diana. This commenter was winning, and Greg would fire me if I didn't do something. Or at least not promote me. That "or else" echoed in my head. Followed by Dr. M's advice: "Be a doer."

"Anya! Did you weigh in today?" Celia bellowed. TGIF.

Dammit. Also, my Fitbit broke. The fashion gods were clearly against me. Sarah looked like a beam of sunshine was following her around. Life was not fair.

When I got home, I started to finalize my Diana plan. Then I ordered a new Fitbit. Essentials. The rest of my evening was spent searching through Sarah's emails. She always used the same password: Blondie1. I liked to read through them every few days. She hadn't mentioned me, like, at all. What was wrong with her? Maybe she was trying to be stealthy. There was something endearing and exciting about being her secret friend. Also, she was definitely porking Greg. I had to save her from her bad choices. This is what BFFs did. We were the dream team, even if Celia wanted to pit us against each other. I saved a few emails, including one to Evie about how much she hated Mulberry.

I ordered Prada mules in yellow. They were just like Sarah's.

* * *

My Manolos were completely soaked through with blood. Goddammit. They were ruined. I don't know what I was thinking wearing stilettos tonight. But I ran straight here from work and didn't change. Not even Martha-freaking-Stewart could DIY these babies back to wearable condition. Whatever, at least my new Pradas were at home. Gotta love Net-a-Porter's insanely quick turnaround. A black shopping bag containing a designer shoe box can make any Monday better, even today.

Still, I wondered if I could write them off on my taxes.

Diana's apartment in Chinatown was disgusting. From the outside it looked normal. But once I got inside, I was horrified. The woman had never heard the words *cleaning lady*. There were moldy food cartons everywhere. Pizza boxes (with left-over crusts) piled up on her floor, takeout-containers-turned-biohazards in the kitchen. And God, the soured milk stench, the source of all things putrid.

And here I was contemplating taking my fucking shoes off. Fact: at least fifteen different diseases can spread from skin-to-skin contact. But I was going to have to swallow my pride and fashion sense and put on my flats. The indignity of it all. I tried imagining Sarah's face when she saw this place and burst out laughing. As if.

I kicked my right foot, shaking some of the excess blood off. A towel would have been helpful, if Diana had any. I put the saw on the ground and limped over to the bathroom.

"Manolos may be the most comfortable shoes, Diana, but when they're wet, they're brutal to wear," I lectured while climbing over the debris of clothes, shoes, boxes, cable wires, coat hangers, and crumbs of who knew what, trying to not gag the entire way. Vomit equaled DNA. Sometimes it was only my paranoia that held me together.

There were ripped yellow towels on the floor of the living room. They looked like Diana had bought them at least five years ago, and that was probably the last time she washed them too. Gross. *Eye on the prize, Anya. Focus.*

I squeezed each shoe in a towel, soaking up as much blood as I could. I'd have to destroy them. What a pity. Such craftsmanship. The arch was pure art, the way it cradled your foot. It drew the eye up a woman's leg, just so. It took talent to create shoes like these. Well worth the $595 I had spent on them. I put the wet shoes back on and wiped down where I had stepped. No prints.

I lifted Diana's head by her hair—which was a rather pretty shade of brown with naturally red lowlights. I knew they were natural because (according to her credit card statements) she only went to get a trim at MasterCuts every two months. Did everyone have perfect hair but me? I cut her mane off. Waste not, want not.

I had watched her all weekend before deciding to just pull the trigger. Get it over with, Monday be damned. After she'd let me in, I'd Tasered her, and now she was a bit worse for wear. Was she getting it? Was this all going over her head? God, why was she just staring at me like that, glassy eyed?

"If. You. Hadn't. Been. A. Goddamned. Annoying. Troll. We. Wouldn't. Be. Here," I said, emphasizing each word with the buzzing of my electric saw.

Diana had nothing to say to me.

The human and pig anatomies are shockingly similar. Which is why I've taken three different pig butchering courses at the Bedford Cheese Shop, honing my skills on the blade. It's trendy to want to butcher meat, especially if you're a girl. Fabulous course, by the way. Highly recommend it. So after severing Diana's arteries first—both the carotid and femoral—and bleeding her into large bowls, I fired up my saw again.

When I was finished, I had to do some major cleanup. This night was amateur hour. Still, rule of thumb when trying to move a body: don't leave a mess everywhere. The last thing an overworked cleaning lady needs is a wall of splatter. Hey, I care, okay?

* * *

When I got home, I ordered a new pair of Manolos from Barneys. I know, I just got the Pradas. But I deserved a treat after all my hard work. Instead of blue, I went with red. It was more apropos. Yes, definitely red. Diana had inspired me.

Steps taken: 32,045. Calories burned: 2,184. Celia would be so fucking happy with me.

Countdown to Fashion Week: twenty-one days.

6

The weeks leading up to Fashion Week always pass in a drunken blur. Summer cocktails, rosé on a rooftop, invites to Montauk (as long as you promoted the brand hosting you)—I did it all. It was required, and frankly, I needed to toast myself. Diana's comments had turned positive. It wasn't a sudden 360, but she was loving my work—and hating Sarah's. Greg now flashed thumbs-ups at me in the hallway.

Diana started commenting, *This is good.* Then she wrote, *Your so smart!* But what really made me like the dead troll was when she wrote on Sarah's stories: *You r so lame.* I laughed for five minutes straight in the ladies' room over that.

"I just don't get our readers!" Sarah wailed. I was at her desk, patting her back reassuringly. Greg had left printouts on her desk. Did he lecture her about engagement while they were fucking? I made cooing noises at her. That's what you were supposed to do, right?

"Ouch! Anya, not so hard." She swatted my hands away.

"Sorry," I mumbled. My face grew hot.

"Ugh, this better not fuck up my promotion," she added.

There was no way Sarah would win. But just in case, I'd already started doing a shitty job writing Sarah's stories, making them all but impossible to read. She hadn't even noticed. (Sarah had stopped reading what I wrote for her a while back. She trusted me, she said.)

But I'd make it up to her. We were going to the same event tonight. She didn't know that. It was my surprise for her.

My phone rang.

"Anya St. Clair," I said, using my best phone voice. Authoritative and slightly husky.

"Ms. St. Clair, it's Detective Hopper." Silence. I opened my mouth a couple times. This was it. He was going to tell me I was being arrested. For Mulberry. And Diana. Wait, they didn't call ahead of time to make an arrest reservation.

"Detective, how are you?" I smiled as I said it. You can hear when people smile.

"I'm afraid we need more information on Mulberry von Gratz. Do you have time to talk?"

"Of course. What do you need?"

"Well, we know about her life outside of work, but no one has said who her office friends were. You know, work pals." Oh, I knew.

"Huh that's a good question. The assistants kind of keep to themselves. Like, they're too busy to socialize, you know? Perhaps she commiserated with other assistants? I can ask around for you."

"You mean you don't know? Why is it that no one at *La Vie* seems to know who she was friends with?"

"No one? Oh, you asked Celia about it, didn't you?" I laughed. "Sorry, it's just that she wouldn't know. She barely knows the names of her assistants. It's very hierarchical here, you know?" He did. He got me. Him and his green eyes.

"So you can get me what I need?"

"I can try. I'll call you back. I have your number." His card was on my bulletin board. It had been one month since Mulberry's death, and the police had seemingly questioned everyone. They'd come up with nothing.

"What was that about?" Sarah stood, leaning on the flimsy wall between us.

I shrugged. "The police want to know who Mulberry's work friends were."

"Ha, she didn't have any." Sarah giggled.

"Maybe Cassie would know?"

"Maybe." She paused. "Why'd they call you and not me? Rude."

I nodded. Why did he call me? Did he just want to talk to me? I felt my face get warm.

"O-M-G, you're blushing! Ha! You so like that cop."

"I do not." I rolled my eyes. I didn't. We were working together on Mulberry's case, that was all. "I'm gonna go ask the other assistants if they know who Mulberry hung with." I didn't want to do that. But I also didn't want to sit under Sarah's interrogatory gaze any longer than I had to.

Before I left for the day, I left a voice mail for the detective. I practiced what I meant to say in the bathroom. I wanted to be light and easy. I had nothing to hide. I was helping, even!

"Hi, Detective. It's Anya St. Clair. I asked around, and most of the assistants didn't really hang out with Mulberry. They said they spoke with her in passing, but no one, like, hung out with her. Hope this helps!" I put my face in my hands after I hung up. Ugh, I sounded like a loser.

* * *

The event tonight was at the Gramercy Hotel rooftop bar. Sarah was already there when I arrived, holding court with Lisa and Jack. Jack wore yellow pants with a T-shirt, somehow looking both ultracasual and chic. Lisa was in some awful vintage number. Sarah wore gingham head to toe. Around them, girls were dressed in their very best prairie looks. Just like Sarah, a few weeks back. I rolled my eyes. I was in my summer black.

"Hey, guys." I aimed for bored, nonchalant even.

"Hey, Anya," Jack drawled. He wore sunglasses and was scoping out the waiters.

"Oh, surprise, Wednesday Addams is here," Lisa said. Sarah giggled. "Um, all these seats are taken," she added, motioning to the empty chairs next to them. (No one dared sit unless invited.)

"Aw, by your imaginary friends? How cute, Lisa!" I plopped down. I hated her. Maybe I could make her night miserable enough that she'd back off. She turned to Sarah, sneaking a glance at me.

"Did I tell you about that story we ran recently? It was all about hiring a private detective to . . ." She paused and glanced at me. "*Investigate* things. People. Dig up dirt. He's so interesting." She took a big sip of her champagne. I mentally willed her to choke on it and die.

"Oh, cool," Sarah said. She was bored; you could hear it in her voice. The conversation wasn't about her. A real friend would know to always keep Sarah engaged.

"Oooh, we should totally hire him for something!" Jack piped in. "I mean, maybe he could find out who killed that girl. What was her name again?"

"Mulberry." I was the only one who said it.

"That's not a bad idea," Lisa said. "But I may want him to investigate something else. *Someone* else." She grinned at me. "What do you think, *Anya*?" The way she said my name told me everything. Lisa knew. She knew I wasn't real.

I shrugged. Never let them see you freak the fuck out. That's when they win. "It's your money, Lisa." I didn't care. I didn't. She wouldn't get under my skin. She glared at me. Her taunts weren't working.

"O-M-G, guys, you know how I used to work at Fashionista? Well, isn't it weird how at the same time I was there, Anya was supposed to be working there?" She laughed, loudly and harshly. "And my friend at *New York* has never heard of her. Bizarre when it's all on her résumé."

She had just escalated this to all-out war. I closed my eyes briefly. I could take my glass of champagne and shove it in her mouth. Force Lisa to chew on glass. The imaginary sound of chomping paired with the image of blood pouring from her mouth sent a thrill up my back. That would teach her to talk shit about me.

"Lisa, I was a contributor. So I wouldn't be in the office or on the masthead even. Hello?" I shook my head, smiling. I pantomimed *This bitch is crazy.* "Anyways, I have all the clips if you want to see them." I was bluffing. I had written stories, but they'd never run anywhere. But Lisa didn't need to know that. Story links got lost all the time with redesigns.

Sarah looked puzzled. Lisa leaned in to whisper something to her. I was going to be sick.

"Guys, I don't mean to throw water on this, but I know people who've worked with Anya," Jack chimed in. "Like, sorry, but the girl's legit." He winked at me. What did that mean? I winked back. Sarah nodded along.

"Ugh, whatever. Can you just go sit somewhere else in your funeral garb? So over this." Lisa dismissed me. Fine, she practically shoved me off the rooftop with her words. Sarah looked slightly confused, but then she shrugged. I had to know if she believed Lisa. Fashion didn't care if you faked it; they just didn't want you to get caught. It was too messy.

What if Sarah—and by extension, everyone—fell for Lisa's antics? I'd be ruined. I had to do something. But short of shutting Lisa up permanently, I didn't know what I could do.

"Guys, I think Greg is cheating," I heard Sarah say as I left. Just when things were getting good!

The night hadn't been a total loss. Jack Archer had defended me. I had no idea why, but it seemed I needed to reevaluate my relationship with him.

* * *

It was the week before Labor Day weekend when everything came crashing down. Fashion Week started in six days. My gray silk blouse was soaked through by the time I got to work (even though I took a car). My entire body was sweating. Sarah, of course, looked perfect. Slightly dewy, but no unsightly dark spots. I stupidly imagined this would be the worst part of my day, being gross and sweaty. (I had to change into a *La Vie* T-shirt courtesy of marketing. How embarrassing.)

I was summoned to Celia's office and part of me hoped it was about the promotion. She said she'd decide by Fashion Week. But the rest of me wondered if she had come up with some new draconian way to make me svelte. What if she planned on sending me to a fat camp for the weekend?

"Anya! Finally." She was sitting behind her desk, her Louboutins on the floor next to her. Celia never wore them when in her office unless she was meeting with someone important. The shoes looked good, but they were hell on your feet. Not like Manolos. "So I want you to know that you've made some great improvements over the last month or so."

I nodded. Was this it? Would she tell me I had won? Would Sarah now report to me and do everything I ordered her to? The mere thought made me dizzy. My stomach did flip-flops. I prepared myself to be gracious. A perfect winner.

"But I don't think you're ready to be promoted."

Did everyone in the world gasp in unison?

Celia's mouth moved, and it made the sounds. I know I heard them. But none of this was real. It couldn't be. I was supposed to win the promotion. The buzzing noise was back.

"But my traffic is up. I have the reports! I got good comments, even!" I could hear the whine in my voice, and I hated myself for it.

"Dear, I know. And you worked your butt off. Figuratively, at least. But Sarah embodies the *La Vie* woman so effortlessly. It's almost unfair to pit her against anyone." She made that scrunched-up face that said, *You're sad, oh well.* "Sarah will be the style editor. You will now report to her. And to me still. Especially in regard to your diet."

She continued to speak, but I didn't hear her. This was like that nightmare you have where you're standing in front of a classroom and you're naked, and everyone is dead and bleeding. This wasn't real.

61

"This isn't real," I repeated out loud.

"It is. It's done. I want you ladies to handle how things will work, but keep in mind, Sarah is very concerned about your behavior. All this acting out that you do. I get it, you're different. You're artistic, even—or you think you are. But you simply must start behaving like a proper *La Vie* woman. Do you understand what I'm saying?"

I stared at her. I'd have replied, but I had no idea what to say.

"You can't be such a goddamned loose cannon, Anya!" she snapped at my silence.

I nodded and forced myself to smile. What did she mean? I'd have to ask Dr. M about it.

"Thank you, Celia. I will be sure to improve."

She nodded. "Good, good. And keep up the level of work you're doing. You're so close to being a *La Vie* woman." She was being charitable.

"May I ask—you mentioned weeks ago that I was the front-runner for the job. What can I improve on?" There, I was trying to be better. That had to count, right? If you're going to have to eat shit, at least find out why.

Celia rolled her eyes. "At that moment, you were. But Greg felt Sarah should get the job. And he made some compelling arguments. Now, the matter is closed. You can go." She shooed me. I had killed Diana for Greg, to make him happy. And it was all for nothing. Sarah was dating him. I should have seen it coming.

"Thanks for even considering me, Celia," I said stiffly. "I'll speak with Sarah about . . . everything."

I was certain I walked through the door, but suddenly everything went black. The next thing I recalled, I was sitting at my desk. My hands were bleeding from my fingernails digging into my palms. I had lost to Sarah Elizabeth Taft. I'd report to her. I'd never be her equal in the eyes of fashion. I'd trail behind her, fetching coffee like I was Mulberry. I'd sit at least a row behind her at shows. I wouldn't get invited to the best events. I had failed to aspire. I was nothing but Sarah's minion now.

"How's my favorite employee?" Sarah sang out, her voice carrying over several rows of cubicles. She had announced it to everyone. I was a loser.

I glanced at her, nodded, and pretended to look at my computer monitor. My blood dripped onto the keyboard. I needed to clean myself up.

"Where are you going?" Sarah demanded as I stood up. I held up my hands. She actually shrieked. "What the hell happened? Ew, go clean it up. You're such a biohazard, Anya!"

I walked down the Murder Hallway, nodding at Mulberry, who watched me from her closet. She hadn't left the office yet. Why was she still here? Celia would have to call security.

Alone in the bathroom, I washed my hands, wincing as the cold water hit my nail marks. I had gone deep. I wanted to break things, compelled to destroy more than myself. I took off my shoe and smashed it against the mirror. The stiletto snapped in two. I took a deep breath and screamed as loudly as I could. I screamed until my throat hurt. I needed to talk to Dr. M. Stat. I bandaged my hands and dialed his number.

"Anya, is it really a big deal that you didn't get the promotion? Come on, be honest."

"Yes! What the hell do you mean, not a big deal?" Hadn't he been paying attention?

"You'll still be doing the same work. And maybe you can learn from Sarah. Is a heavier workload really what you want? Let her carry the weight."

"But now she'll never respect me. No one will respect me. I'm gonna be a nobody for years!" I was wailing. I was making a scene. Thank God I was alone.

"Then maybe she wasn't meant to be your bestie, as you say." He chuckled then, as if he'd made a good joke.

"I'm going to pretend you didn't say that."

"You need to be calm and rational. Think of this as an opportunity to grow."

"Whatever. I'll talk to you later." Maybe it was time for a new shrink. Dr. M just wasn't getting me anymore.

Back at the cubicles, Cassie was sitting on a stool near Sarah's desk, holding a notepad.

"Okay, so this is what we need to do. I want you to order some crystals. Oh, and some sage spray. The vibes in this office are horrendous, especially after Mulberry." The intern studiously wrote down everything Sarah said. "Call my guy in Arizona." Sarah always had a guy. "Oh, good, you're back."

Her eyes shifted to my hands and then the shoe I held. She shrugged. My drama wasn't her business.

"Listen, I know it's gonna be an adjustment to take orders from me, but I promise nothing will really change. We'll still be Sarah and Anya. You'll see. This is going to be great."

I nodded, fishing out a pair of spare heels from desk drawer. Every respectable fashion girl had extra pairs at her desk. I had six. Something for every kind of emergency. Flats, boots, block heels, stilettos, evening shoes, and even sneakers.

Sarah cleared her throat. She wanted more of a response. I smiled, or tried to. It was more a baring of teeth. I wanted to ask her if she liked me still. No, if she loved me. If she believed Lisa. But I didn't.

"Where do we begin?" I asked.

Sarah smiled triumphantly.

"I knew you'd get on board. Okay, let's go over our Fashion Week plan." She chatted on about designers and models.

I was only half listening. I could fix this, right? I could somehow find a way to make this work. *Think, Anya, think.*

"Anya? Hello? Are you even listening? That is so something we need to work on. Like, you're off in your own little world all the time. And stop muttering to yourself. It's full-on creepy. That's why you didn't get promoted, you know. All your weird little habits and tics."

Sarah was right. I was not a *La Vie* woman. But I would be, even if I had to murder everyone to make it happen.

"The bloggers will be dressed to kill." I switched to a safer topic. *Talk about anything else but me and my history.*

"I know. I hate them. They, like, come out of nowhere."

"Like roaches."

"O-M-G, yes!" She snickered.

Roaches. That would be *our* joke. We'd say it again and again and then double over from laughing. Jokes were essential. I liked having them with BFFs. Meredith and I had one. We would always point out a boy and say, "That's who you're gonna marry." And then laugh until we cried. She always picked the ugliest ones for me. She was such a bitch.

"You know," Sarah added, "if you work to make *me* happy, we'll *all* be happy."

* * *

Sarah went to lunch with Cassie. She did it to spite me. It was my nightmare coming true. But it just made her look bad. What was she even thinking, hanging out with an intern? I had to help her. For her own reputation's sake.

"Sarah, have you noticed Cassie's wardrobe? It's, like, the *best*," I said when she got back. "I think she might be the best-dressed person at the mag. Now that Mulberry's gone. Don't you agree?"

"The best? Anya, you need your eyes checked. I bet you she's wearing something from a *sample sale*." She spit the last two words out. Only poor people went to those. Unless it was the Manolo one, of course. Sarah crossed her arms as she eyed Cassie at her desk. "I mean, what *is* that outfit?"

"Looks like Stella McCartney, current season. I just saw that dress in Barneys. So not sample."

"Where did she get the money to buy that?"

"Maybe she has a trust fund? You're not the only one with a rich daddy, you know."

"You're one to talk. Where'd you get that Rick Owens jacket you've been wearing?"

She had noticed my clothes. I had only worn it twice so far. You can't rewear something that major too often.

"Sample sale," I lied.

"Liar. It's not on sale yet."

I stuck my tongue out at her.

"Why is Cassie dressing like—"

"Like she works here? Because she should. What's the issue, Sarah?" I raised my eyebrow at her.

"I just don't like her. She's bugging me. Always hanging around. Can we exchange her for another intern?"

Success.

"Just make her deal with Celia for a week. That'll scare her off." We both laughed. Best friends forever and ever. We were both standing up to talk. We were together.

"Have you lost any weight?" Sarah scrunched her face. It was her sympathetic look. Or as close as Sarah would get to sympathy.

"Ugh, like a pound? But I'm not eating anything. It's not healthy. Celia won't be happy until I have an eating disorder. Why is she so obsessed?" We were talking like friends. Like buddies. This was heaven.

"It's the Botox thing. You know . . ."

"Uh, no?"

"Her Botox doc retired, and she swears he was magic, and she won't go see anyone else. So now she's working out like a maniac so her husband won't leave her. Also, I think she kind of hates Mulberry two-point-oh," Sarah explained.

"Bronwen, you mean?"

"Yeah, what's up with those crowns she wears? So weird." Celia's new assistant (who she still called Mulberry) always had flowers or plants in her hair.

"I don't know. It's kind of cute."

"Ugh, you have the worst taste, I swear." But she laughed.

I had to keep the conversation going. She was into this, into me.

"So Celia's just going to get as skinny as possible?"

"It's the *La Vie* way!" She grinned.

Sarah was right. The joke was that if you were above a certain size, you might get hired here, but you'd be forced to lose the weight (see: me). On the surface, the magazine was very prohealth. *Lose weight the smart way, be healthy*—all that jazz. But in reality, there were scales in the bathroom. At lunch meetings, some editors didn't allow their assistants to eat the catered food that was provided. Celia liked to come off as someone who ate and drank whatever she wanted, but if you put a burger in front of her, she'd probably punch you for thinking she ate.

But now I had an idea of what to do with Celia. I didn't ask about Lisa. I didn't want to ruin the moment. Our moment.

That night after work, I made a Celia mood board. Then I logged into Diana's account and went on a commenting spree. She loved all my pieces, hated Sarah's. It was petty, but it would (hopefully) get Greg off my back since he didn't think I was promotion material. Whatever, I'd show him.

Dr. M checked in to see if I'd calmed down (I hadn't).

"Worry only about the things you can change. Everything else is out of your control."

He was right. I had to take control. "Thanks. You're so right."

7

"Where are we with the up-and-coming designers, Anya?" Celia asked loudly the next morning. She affected a faux Continental accent for good measure—it was the fashion voice. Women of a certain age in the industry all had it. Somehow, going to Paris four times a year meant they'd "studied" abroad. "Fashion Week is looming."

"The story's done. I sent it to you last week for approval."

"Well, why didn't you remind me?" She sniffed. I shrugged. There was no sense in arguing. "And, Sarah, update me on the models-to-watch piece."

"Well, we did the shoot, but—"

"But?"

"But it turns out that four of the models aren't being cast this Fashion Week, so we can't really say they're models to watch."

"Then why did we use them?"

"Because you liked them?"

I closed my eyes as she said it, savoring the brief moment of joy as Sarah fucked up. It was the wrong answer. Celia's eyes sent death rays. We all waited for Sarah's head to explode. If she died, I'd be next in line for her job. But reality check: she was alive and my boss.

I cleared my throat. "Can we just call up a couple smaller designers—perhaps the ones in my story—and ask if they can use the girls we shot so we don't have to redo the entire spread?"

Celia looked at me appraisingly. *You made the wrong choice, Celia.*

"Good idea. Get on that. And how's the diet coming?"

Dammit, even a good idea couldn't spare me this indignity.

"It's coming. I'm down eight pounds."

Celia just nodded.

"If you think I'm going to help you call the designers, think again," Sarah hissed at me as we walked to our desks. I wanted to slap her on the forehead. Hard. But she was my boss now. I had to get in line. Besides, I was the one who had to rewrite the story.

"We can have Cassie call them, and I'll rework the story for you." See? I was helping her.

"Whatever." That was as much of an acknowledgment as I was going to get. I'd take it. "Anya, are those the new Pradas?" She pointed at my shoes. I nodded. They went perfectly with my leather pencil skirt and Marni top. "O-M-G, did you copy me? They're totally the same as mine!"

No, hers were blue.

"Sarah, your style is just so amazing, I couldn't help myself!" I heard the words pour out of my mouth. I was worse than Cassie. I was kissing Sarah's taut and toned ass.

"It is, I know. But you can't just copy people. Ugh, Lisa was so right about you."

Red. I was seeing red. Literally. Was this some kind of brain disease?

"I'm sorry. I should have asked you first."

"At least you got them in a different color. Just check with me next time, okay?"

I nodded. If I made Sarah happy, we'd all be happy.

Our next meeting with Celia didn't go much better. It was a run-through, where she approved clothes and accessories for an upcoming shoot. She liked all of us to show up, to provide input she would then ignore.

"What the hell kind of shoe is this?" Celia held up a jeweled sling-back and waved it in Dalia's face. "Seriously, what the fuck is this shit? Are we doing a tacky trend? This isn't fucking India or wherever you're from."

No one breathed. No one made a sound. Had she really said that out loud? I glanced at Dalia. She looked like she was going to strangle Celia. But she couldn't say anything, not without getting fired. HR didn't care about Celia's antics. As far as management was concerned, she was a genius, and that meant she could say and do whatever she wanted. Even with brown and black models and actresses gracing our covers, our bosses were firmly stuck in decades past.

The silence was killing me. You could hear someone's jaw grinding, though not sure whose. I had to speak. I had to do something. My palms were sweating.

"Um, I like that shoe." I tried to smile. I heard Bronwen gasp from across the room.

"No! No! No!" Celia screeched, before throwing the shoe. Later, Celia would claim she was merely *tossing* the offending footwear into the declined pile, but we all saw her aim for Dalia's head, like a hunter lining up a kill shot. Dalia ducked, and the shoe hit Evie in the face. She had to walk around with a mark on her forehead for the rest of the day. (She'd get a "sorry-I-hit-you" present from Celia later.)

I'd like to say that run-throughs aren't usually such violent affairs. But they were at *La Vie*. It all depended on Celia's mood. Tornadoes of shoes flew around us, earrings went airborne, belts were snapped so fiercely, we flinched. And yet Sarah placed Cassie front and center. It was cruel; she would get hit by flying accessories.

"Cassie, you really need to sit here and take notes. We need to make sure we know what's in and out of the story so we know what to write about." If she'd added a cackle to the end, it wouldn't have been out of place. She still hadn't forgiven the intern for being so well-dressed. I smiled.

"All I ask is that when we do a story on disco in St. Petersburg, you have the right accessories, Dalia. How hard is that?" Celia demanded, glaring at each of us in turn. "It's disco, it's Lenin, it's glamorous Russia. It just works. But apparently, not for you. This intern"—she gestured at Cassie—"could do a better job. Perhaps we should give her the story assignment?"

It really could have been worse. The story wasn't yet killed; Dalia had a day to redo the entire concept. It wasn't her fault. The idea was pretty idiotic. Celia had been weirdly in love with Russia for the last few weeks. She'd recently watched *Dr. Zhivago* and was obsessed. Maybe she had a new Russian lover?

* * *

The next couple days were a blur of Fashion Week preparation. Which really meant calling in clothes to "borrow" (and never return) for Celia, Sarah, Evie, Dalia, and myself.

Cassie, meanwhile, was in charge of RSVPing for all our events. We couldn't exactly be expected to do it ourselves. We each had about forty-five runway shows and presentations, along with dinners and parties every night. But it was a learning experience for her; Cassie got to learn what it was like to be invited to things. (Bronwen was handling Celia's invites. They were always called invites, not invitations. Verbs as nouns and nouns as verbs were the fashion way.)

"I thought you were getting your hair done?" Sarah stared at my head as I walked past her desk to get to mine.

"I did?" Didn't she see the waves and layers? How bouncy my blown-out hair was?

"But it's still the same color. Like, ew, Anya." She wrinkled her nose. That meant she hated it.

"We agreed I was just getting a cut." I was not proud of this moment. She had decreed that I needed a new do, and off I went to John Barrett at Bergdorf. It was even layered the way she'd suggested. And she had been right, really—my hair was in need of some TLC. I wanted it to be Instagram worthy. I wanted her to love it.

"Ugh, brown is *so* boring."

"Sarah, you didn't mention dyeing my hair," I said through my teeth. My heart was racing again. I needed a Xanax. I had done what Sarah asked me to do. Why wasn't she praising me?

"Whatever. You need to do something edgy with it. You're just so . . . dull."

"Okay, sure. I'll keep that in mind next time." My voice was too bright, too loud. She was helping me. Like a friend does.

"I mean, I bet Celia would love it if you went for the silver-gray look. Or lavender."

"That's not really me."

"That's the point! You're boring!"

I watched her wrap her long blonde hair into a topknot. I imagined using her locks to strangle the life out of her. Nothing was good enough for her. I knew that already, but now, as her underling, the point was made even clearer. Sarah had expectations no one could meet, mainly because they shifted hour to hour. She loved me, but she hated how I looked. She wanted me to take style pointers from her, but she never wanted me to copy her again. I rarely knew where I stood, and that made me anxious. Where the hell was my Xanax?

I was desperate for a Sarah win. But the more I craved it, the more annoyed I got. At Sarah, not myself. She would never be satisfied. I glanced at my Instagrammed selfie from the salon. My hair looked good, dammit. What would it take for Sarah Taft to tell me I was perfect?

Dr. M was not going to approve. He would give me an F for the week. He was the only shrink I'd ever met who graded his patients. The categories were physical health, social, dating, personal care, and overall well-being. You had to get at least a B in everything to make him happy and not up your meds. (I had to lie to pass.) He would so fail me on social. The mere thought of that made me panic. I needed to scream.

Then my ears pricked up as I heard Cassie's phone convo.

"Don't you know who I am? Yes, well, I work with Sarah Taft and Anya St. Clair, so I expect a good seat. It doesn't matter if they're already going, I need one too!"

I glanced at Sarah, who frowned in reply.

"Great, and can you send a car too—"

I grabbed the phone out of her hand and hung it up. "In what universe do you think it's appropriate to demand access like that?"

"Well, I mean, I work here, so—"

"No, you *intern* here. You fetch our coffee and our packages and transcribe our interviews, and if you're lucky—and pull your head out of your fucking ass—you just may learn a few things while you're here. But you most certainly do not work here!" I shouted the last part. The cubicles near us went eerily quiet. I knew I was taking my issues with Sarah out on Cassie. But it was helping, sort of.

"But you and Sarah demand things all the time."

It's true, we did. Sarah shrugged at this.

"You are not me and Sarah. We have worked a long time in this industry. The PR companies know us. We only make demands when appropriate." Lies. We demanded shit all the time. "They don't know or care who the fuck you are! And right now, you're about to be the intern who got shit-canned!"

"Anya's right, Cassie." Sarah nodded. "You really can't do that. I mean, you're not even important." Watching Cassie's face fall at that moment should have moved me. She was a kindred spirit, someone who just wanted acceptance. She wanted Sarah's love. Just like me. But the idea of being like my intern filled me with disgust. She was so fucking needy. I despised her more than ever.

"How many designers did you call and demand seats from?" My head was starting to pound. And with each throb, the sound of buzzing grew louder. I pinched the bridge of my nose to make it stop.

"Eleven," Cassie whispered.

Sarah snorted. "Call them back," she ordered. "Anya will supervise."

I nodded. This wasn't one of those things where she was showing how much she trusted me. Sarah simply didn't want to deal with it.

"And email them for good measure. CCing me. Let's hope Celia doesn't find out."

Cassie wiped her eyes.

"Just dial. I don't have all day to fix your mistakes." I glared.

Sarah grinned at me. She was enjoying this. I had made her happy.

* * *

While I nibbled at my Celia-approved lunch (kale salad with lemon juice and nothing else), I thought about what to do about Cassie.

"Give her a chance. She just goofed," Sarah said. Had they made up behind my back?

"Um, since when do you like her? You've wanted to get rid of her for days." I stood up to watch her while we talked. Eye contact says someone is important to you, that you see them. Sarah didn't even glance up.

"I know, but she's really good with my dry cleaning."

"She's an intern, not your maid."

"Well, yeah, she's cheaper than my maid."

"She's always going to Greg's office. I wonder what that means," I said as innocently as I could. Sarah glared at me.

"Is she? We need to fire her." She seethed as she opened one of dozens of packages on her desk.

"Oh, look at this!" Sarah held up her newest gift: a necklace with charms and beads hanging off a rather unusual matted material.

"What's it made out of?" I asked. I knew what it was. I was the one who made it for her. I swallowed a giggle.

"The card says it's the first bionatural organic cilia-woven jewelry line. What does that mean?"

"Oh, ew. It means it's hair!" I laughed.

"No, like dog hair?"

"Maybe. Or bunny hair, like angora?"

"Oh, totes. It's kinda cute, right? Just what I need for Fashion Week! I'll have to show it to Dalia."

And that's how Sarah started wearing Diana's hair around her neck. Di's hair was too pretty to toss, and I wanted to give Sarah just the *right* present, something with meaning. Diana would have loved going to Fashion Week—and now she could! I wanted to tell Sarah it was from me. That I made it myself, just for her. But Sarah wouldn't like that. She'd probably never wear it if she knew.

Detective Hopper left me a message. He wanted to get coffee. Was that a date? I pushed it back until after Fashion Week. Priorities, people.

I checked Sarah's text messages while she went to get her nails done. Lisa and Jack. Always Lisa and Jack. When would I be invited to the group chat?

Lisa: *Is there any way we could do NYFW without your freaky coworker?*

Jack: *OMG, you are so obsessed with her! LOL*

Sarah: *LOL, I wish. She does so much work tho.*

Jack: *You know what they say: you're either a workhorse or a show pony.*

Sarah: *She's such a workhorse.*

Lisa: *She even has the build for it.* (crying face emoji) *But really, you guys know she's a fraud, right? Like, I'm getting proof.*

Jack: *Babe, you need to let this go. You're starting to sound crazy.*

Lisa: *Ugh, whatever. You'll see.*

* * *

Labor Day weekend should have been one of rest. I had more than forty fashion shows to hit the following week, and all while wearing high heels. I needed to chill. But I couldn't. Not with Lisa Blitz whispering about me at every turn. She was planning something big, I knew it. She was going to out me at shows. In front of everyone. I could picture her now, sitting front row with Sarah. Pointing at me. Laughing. Having me removed by security. Just envisioning it made me throw up.

Every minute I was awake, I thought about Lisa, and really, I should have been focusing on Sarah and what my next steps were. (Dammit, Lisa!) I imagined every single thing she'd say about me. Had she hired the investigator? Were there files on me? Would she run a giant exposé? I had to fix this, deal with it before everything blew up in my face. I'd be a laughingstock if I didn't. Just a punch line to people like Sarah.

"No!" I screamed, throwing my Prada mules at my mood boards. "That won't happen!"

My neighbor downstairs pounded on his ceiling.

Get it together, Anya. Fix this.

Unlike Sarah, Lisa was spending the holiday weekend in the city. She had claimed (to Sarah) it was to avoid the hoi polloi who flocked to the Hamptons. But the truth was that Lisa didn't have a beach house. Sarah laughed about it at work.

"It's so sad. She has, like, no money. She totally makes it work, but she's been crashing at everyone else's beach house all summer. Mine's full this weekend." Her parents were coming in to see her and lounge by the pool. Lisa was on her own. All alone. I didn't ask why I wasn't invited. I would be, soon.

"Is Greg joining you?"

She whirled her head around. "No, why, what have you heard? Do you know what he's up to this weekend?"

I held my hands up in retreat. "No, I just was curious. Calm down." Sarah pouted. Trouble in paradise. But more important, I had a chance to deal with Lisa Blitz.

When an opportunity knocks, grab it by the fucking throat. Or something.

Saturday came. I was up early. No sleeping in. No resting before the sartorial storm hit. I stood across from Lisa's apartment on Eldridge Street on the Lower East Side. She was home, I was certain of it. I hadn't seen her leave, and I'd been there for hours.

I buzzed her apartment; she let me in. I think she thought I was Sarah. I wore my blonde wig. I felt fabulous. Best purchase ever.

"Baaaaabe! Why haven't you left yet?" she said loudly, throwing open her door. Then her face froze. She took in my wig, my clothes, my face. And then she laughed. "Oh my God, you are such a stalker!" She doubled over laughing. My hands flew to my wig. No, I was perfect.

I smiled and pushed her back into her apartment, closing the door behind me. "Lisa, let's chat." She rolled her eyes. "Listen, I'm not sure where you're getting your weird info about me, but it's not cool to spread lies."

"Wait, you came here, dressed as Sarah, because I know about you? You are so pathetic!" Her face twisted as she taunted me. She was so ugly when she did that. If she had just been nice, even once, I would have tried to resolve this peacefully.

I shrugged to show I didn't care. (God, did I care.)

"Wait 'til I tell Jack and Sarah. O-M-G, they won't even believe it! That wig!" She laughed, holding her phone to text.

"Wait! I have a peace offering. Let's have a glass and then move on." I held up a bottle of Veuve. She pursed her lips but acquiesced. Lisa couldn't resist free champagne, even in the morning. "Fab, I'll pour." I love opening champagne bottles. You squeeze, you don't pop. All that foam everywhere is such a waste. I was in her tiny kitchen area, my back to her. I made a show of washing out the dust from the glasses but really, I needed to block her from seeing what I was doing. I dropped some fentanyl into her flute, poured the champagne, and turned back to hand it to her. "Cheers!" I had to know how much info she'd shared with Sarah. Not just her snide comments, but proof. I had no doubt that she had some. She knew too much.

"You know, we're a lot alike. Self-made in a land full of Sarahs."

She rolled her eyes at me as I said it. We should have been on the same side. Why didn't Lisa see that?

"Except I'm not a fraud like you. 'Anya St. Clair' doesn't even exist before a few years ago. What, did you pick the name out of a hat? Just make up something that sounded good? Who are you?" She narrowed her eyes, watching me. "What are you hiding? I'm going to find out sooner or later. You may as well tell me. My private eye is working the case. You're going to be totally exposed." She threw her head back and laughed. "It's going to be so good! Anya the faker! You'll never work in fashion again!" She snorted, wiping tears from her eyes.

I kept an idiotic smile on my face. "Jeez, Lisa, you really are obsessed with me! I guess I just wasn't important enough to get Google hits. I can tell you all about me, but it's really boring." The sneer on her face fueled me. This bitch was enemy number one. "Look, if it makes you happy, pay some man to look into me. Hell, I'll even sit down with him," I lied. "But I'd really like us to get along. We're not that different, you know." Her eyes narrowed. "I say let's have a truce and toast to a good Fashion Week." *Or to dropping this line of questioning.* But she wouldn't. She'd never let it go.

"Whatever. Let's get this over with." She threw back her champagne, swallowing it in one gulp. "Okay, get out."

"Oh, come on. Let's finish the bottle. It'll go flat." And I poured more. But her eyes were already glassy. She'd be out soon.

Lisa was a lightweight. I got no info out of her. My fault; I pour with a heavy hand. At least I styled her after the drugs kicked in. Dead Lisa wore three veils—one on her face, one over her crotch, and the third stuffed in her mouth. Her Chanel pearls were strung so tightly, they almost broke. Her accessories wall alone was reason enough to kill her. So much to choose from, so little time. But this was *self-defense.*

Lisa was out to ruin me. She wanted to take my job from me, my livelihood. My friends. My social standing. Everything I'd worked so damn hard to achieve would be gone in a flash. I'd have to leave New York, go live in a yurt somewhere. All because of stupid Lisa Blitz. People like that don't deserve to live. Dr. M would be so proud of me for taking action. For doing.

I searched through her computer files, emails, and direct messages until I found what I was looking for. Emails from three different editors I supposedly worked for saying they'd never heard of me. Those bastards. And some calls and texts from her "guy." My to-do list was growing every second. Faking your way into this world isn't easy; it's not *less* work. You have to constantly push to stay afloat. Be aware of attacks. Fucking Lisa and everybody like her didn't get that I was *self-made*. She should have looked up to me. I was doing what she couldn't.

The mystery guy she'd hired to dig up dirt on me had texted her a few times. *The situation is resolved*, I wrote. And then Venmoed a few hundred bucks to him from Lisa's account. I screengrabbed some texts on Lisa's phone before turning it off for good. I didn't know what to do with it when I was done, so I decided to hide it in the cabinets at work. There was so much junk in them, so much of Sarah's stuff, that no one would even notice.

I took one last look at the body, snapped a photo, and left. The rest of the weekend I spent watching Netflix and *Law & Order*. I was trying to feel calm, relaxed. One major thing on my to-do list was officially done at least. Line crossed through and all. Now to take on the rest.

8

I t was finally here: Fashion Week. And I was down thirteen whole pounds and one and a half sizes. In the week leading up to my final weigh-in, I lived off of kale, water, and kale juice. I'd like to say I exercised a lot, but truthfully, after dealing with Lisa, I slept. Or rather, I kept passing out. (What was Labor Day for if not resting?) But the result was a five-pound drop in my weight in that last week, however temporary. Enough at least to do the story. I was pretty damn proud of myself, as was Dr. M. (Though he wasn't happy with the methods I employed.) Celia, on the other hand, considered the entire experiment a colossal failure.

"You'll just have to write it that way. That you tried and failed. Maybe the readers will enjoy the human touch." She pursed her lips to show her disappointment. I was a failure. I was a (fat) loser to her. The idea of a *La Vie* girl being on the same footing as humans was repulsive in Celia's world. We were better. We were the elite in every way. We didn't age, we didn't get fat, and we sure as hell didn't have body issues. Evie, whose idea it was to begin with, smirked gleefully at me, her bony porcelain shoulders taunting me. She leaned in to whisper something in Sarah's ear, and they both giggled. Those bitches. What would it be like to take a hammer and smash Evie's pretty collarbone to pieces?

Despite my exhaustion, I had to admit, I looked fan-fucking-tastic. So I wrote the story, "How to Lose Two Dress Sizes in Less Than Six Weeks—We Tried It!" And I dished on all my cravings, my failings, the weigh-ins, the planks. Instead of photos of me, I ran shots of my food. It wasn't the highest moment in my career, but the piece was a success. The commenters were all rather sympathetic to my cause, even expressing concern over what I'd had to endure. Diana said we were "crazy" to make me do it. (Thanks, babe! I knew we'd be friends.)

* * *

"Dammit! Lisa's flaked again!" It was Tuesday morning, and Sarah was pouting at her phone. "She's gone M-I-A on me. W-T-F, right? Like, Jack hasn't heard from her either. Ugh, I hope she's not mad about not using my beach house."

I hid my smile. "Maybe she choked on that pearl necklace of hers," I suggested.

"Not funny. I wonder if she's mad at me."

"Why would she be? You know how she is. Such a bitch."

"She is not!"

I only nodded in reply. I'd wait for her to come around. It would happen, and I'd be there when she realized her friends were jerks.

* * *

"At least your outfits are less embarrassing now that you're a normal weight," Sarah said coldly as we hopped into our car to Spring Studios on Varick Street. "Just try not to make a horrible face in photos." She was wearing a leather fringed Valentino dress in lilac. (She got caught in the door twice.)

We weren't getting closer. She was sulking over Lisa. And taking it out on me. Or maybe she had Fashion Week mood. Everyone was extragrouchy when shows were on. I mutely looked out my window as we inched through traffic.

I knew what else was bugging her: Greg. Our publisher was causing a major rift between us. He had decided that our audience needed me to blog every up and down of this week. I was the "voice" of the people. Somehow, using Diana's account to post happy comments made him think I was in sync with our readers.

"The readers *get* you. We need that, build some brand loyalty!" Brand loyalty. As if brands were ever loyal back. "And, Sarah, work with Anya to improve reader reaction to your stories. She has it down."

She'd turned around and walked away.

Between Lisa vanishing and Greg's attention, Sarah downright loathed me. But I didn't get it. She was without a bestie; the trinity was down a member. (They just didn't know it yet.) And Jack didn't go to women's shows (though he met Sarah at after-parties). Which meant she needed me, her friend, more than ever this week. Instead, she sulked and ignored me. She was *this close* to making me pick up her dry cleaning as penance. It was going to be a long week.

So far, the shows were not going well, and it was just day one. We sat snarled in New York City traffic. We should have taken the subway, but, as Celia liked to remind us, *La Vie* girls show up in black cars. Escalades if you wanted to be specific. Evie and Dalia had their own cars; their schedules were too crazy to ride with us. Evie had to work backstage with the beauty teams, and Dalia had to rush from accessories appointments to runway shows. Sarah's schedule overlapped with mine, so I spent the better part of an hour stuck in traffic with her, as she alternated between ignoring me and whining that Greg was ignoring her.

"I mean, why don't I have a blog? I'm, like, so much more interesting than you."

"I don't know, Sarah. You'll have to talk to Greg."

"But, Anya! It's not *fair*!"

I wondered what would shut her up the fastest: smashing her head through the glass window or agreeing with her. I decided to go with the latter. Why ruin her pretty face?

"Why don't you come up with an idea and pitch it to him and Celia? I'm sure they're open to it."

"Right, like you haven't told them to not let me do anything. And, like, I don't get why the readers have such shitty taste."

"Uh, paranoid much? You're my boss. Why would I work against you? And I do think you should have a blog or diary too. It's only fair."

"You're right, I should. I want my own thing!" She nodded, wiping her nose.

"Then ask for it. Jeez, I didn't ask for this blog, but I'm doing it."

She did her bobblehead nod. She whipped out her phone and began texting angrily, no doubt to Greg. She was wearing her Diana necklace today. I stifled a giggle.

By the time we got to the venue, we were thirty minutes late, which meant right on time. (All fashion shows start at least thirty minutes behind, except for Marc Jacobs, who, after years of being hours behind, now started two minutes ahead of schedule.) We ran to check in.

"Name?" the Lauren-bot asked, clipboard in hand. They were multiplying despite my best efforts.

"Anya St. Clair. Here's my invite and seat."

"You're not on the list."

"Um, but I'm holding my invite and seat assignment. So obviously I am."

"Hold on."

I looked at Sarah, who shrugged and walked in, leaving me to deal with the robots.

"Sorry, you're not on the list. Which outlet are you with?"

"*La Vie*," I ground out. I wanted to take her headset and wrap it around her neck until she turned blue. I was having déjà vu.

"Oh. Oh! Sorry, let me see what we can do. We can put you in standing—"

"I have a seat assignment, and I'm going to use it. The rest is your problem," I said, moving toward the seating area. Standing would be social suicide.

"Wait, sorry, we double sat, it's our fault. We have a new seat for you. Lauren, can you walk her in?" The Lauren-bot looked expectantly at her intern, a young girl who was holding a cup of coffee. A bot in training, baby Lauren guided me to my third-row seat (kill me) and then spilled her coffee on me when she tripped on her way back out. Disaster. I got up and walked out. A few eyebrows raised, but there's only so much one girl can take. This was not the best start to the most glamorous week of the year.

I sat in the car, driving around the block over and over until the show was done.

"There you are!" Sarah exclaimed, climbing into the back seat. "Why didn't you wait for me?"

"Because that idiot intern spilled coffee all over me, and I needed to dry my dress."

"Stop! She didn't!" Glee filled her eyes as she giggled helplessly. My face was burning. Sarah was laughing at me. She snorted with glee, her eyes tearing up. I was a joke to her.

"Kill me now. Thank God I'm wearing a cape—it covers most of it."

"Why are you wearing a cape? Aren't you hot?"

"We all have to suffer for our style, Sarah." I sniffed. *Keep it together, A. Never let them see you upset.* I wanted to scream, but I didn't.

The PR firm sent me a bouquet to make up for the show, but the damage was done. Someone was going to have to pay for this. I hated when Fashion Week started on such a bad note.

Tomorrow would be better.

* * *

It was just one week. I could get through this. I could deal with Sarah's moods and tantrums, the seating snafus, and the relentless pace. I could do this. I was even wearing more comfortable shoes, now that block heels were in for the season. I'd learned my lesson on proper shoe attire from Diana. (See? We both learned something that night. And wasn't that the point to life? Dr. M would agree.) But the constant pushing and shoving to get into a venue, the catty comments about what the audience was wearing, and the seat stealers were all getting to me. I was drained, and it was only day two.

On the bright side, Greg was loving my blog posts.

"They're just so real." He'd jumped into the car with me and Sarah, wanting to chat about our coverage. Sarah was forced to sit up front with the driver. I could feel waves of hatred emanating from the passenger seat.

"Well, you wanted vérité."

"Awesome. Just awesome." His hair didn't move as he spoke, slicked and gelled into a black dome. I stared in fascination, all the while digging my nails into my palms. The pain was freeing. Greg continued talking, but I didn't hear him. I felt only relief as the pounding in my head eased.

"Don't you agree?"

"Hmm? Oh, yes."

"Great, then let's do a photo diary for Sarah. That will be a perfect addition."

Sarah beamed, thinking she had stolen an opportunity from me. But this was, as Greg said, perfect. The last thing I needed was to have my photo splashed all over the site. Not all attention was good attention. Not everyone wanted their every nail color, outfit choice, and hair part posted for posterity. What if one of Mariana's old friends recognized me? Disaster, that's what.

"I think that's a fantastic idea!" I raved.

"I'm so glad you agree. I was so worried." Sarah reached back to pat my knee. "I didn't want to steal your thunder. I mean, your little blog is doing so well."

"Oh, no, I don't mind. I hate having my photo up. Besides, the idea suits you better. Fewer words for you since you aren't much of a writer." There were two methods for dealing with Sarah: compliment her or make her feel insecure. Negging was a totally appropriate workplace mode of conduct. If she felt like a loser, I could control her. If I made her feel lame, maybe she'd forget about anything Lisa told her. Then Sarah would see how great I was, and we could start hanging out seriously. The idea of hanging at Sarah's apartment, playing dress-up, was almost overwhelming. I wanted her to say to me that I was perfect, I was everything she wanted in a friend. There's nothing wrong with that. Nothing. Besides, I didn't exactly have time to write her diary on top of my own work this week.

"I can write, but—oh, hey, are you bleeding?" She recoiled.

"What? Oh, I cut myself. Paper cut." I had recut my palm.

"Oh. On what, your invite?"

"Um, yeah. My invite. You should totally wear your new necklace in the photos. It's such a unique piece."

She brightened. "O-M-G, you're so right!" I had already seen three copies of her Diana necklace at the shows. Whatever Sarah wore turned to gold.

Sarah was getting more attention from the photographers than I was at the shows, which was dandy. Today she was wearing a shirt that looked like it was made from every crystal Swarovski had and a leather skirt paired with Uggs stiletto boots up to her thighs. It screamed, "Please take my photo!" She was vying with the bloggers for a coveted street-style shot. Sometimes she won, but often they did. I'd opted for a more sedate look—my usual all black, this time a Vivienne Westwood. And after shows, I ran quickly to the waiting car we'd ordered instead of standing with Sarah, which annoyed her every time.

"Um, that was so rude," she said after the Mary Ann Mark presentation.

"You were having your photo taken, Sarah."

"So? You could have waited and held my purse."

"I'm not your assistant, so no."

She glared at me. I had said the wrong thing. Besties shouldn't make friends do grunt work. It never works out. Just look at Paris and Kim. Sarah was going to have to see me as on her level, and she would. Soon enough.

"Whatever, I'm your boss." She sniffed.

Her mood soured even more when she was forced to sit second row on day three. (I'd lost track of which day of the week it was. Time only moved ahead according to Fashion Week days.) I was next to her and loved it. For a brief moment, I had what I wanted. Sure, it wasn't front row. But Sarah and I were *together*. At the finale, I was planning on grabbing her arm. Like friends do.

Directly in front of us was the new blogger *du jour*: Zhazha. She was Russian royalty, from Siberia, so the story went. And she milked her persona for all it was worth. Zhazha was wearing a giant fur hat, despite the eighty-degree temperature outside.

"W-T-F. I can't even see anything!" Sarah muttered loudly enough for the Russian girl to hear. "Why does she need that giant babushka hat anyways?"

"I think it's a fur kubanka."

"How do you even know that?"

I shrugged. "Do you want to trade seats?"

Sarah glanced at me with disdain. "No, I want *my* seat. Excuse me. Excuse me!" She tapped Zhazha on the shoulder. The hat turned. "Could you remove your hat, please? It's impossible to see over it."

Zhazha glanced at Sarah before turning to look at me. I half smiled.

"No. It's my outfit," she replied, her accent thick and luscious.

"Are you serious?" Sarah's jaw had fallen open. She wasn't used to being told no.

"Sarah, just switch with me. It's so not a big deal."

"No! Um, fur lady? Do you even know who we are?"

I dropped my head into my hands.

"Yes, you're second-row person. I'm first," Zhazha said. Her voice made me dizzy. I wanted to spread it on toast and eat it. She flashed a grin at me.

"Ugh, whatever." Sarah stood, deliberately bumping into Zhazha. She stomped her way over to a PR girl. You could see her gesturing and waving her arms wildly. The Lauren-bot nodded sympathetically and then took her to a new seat across the catwalk.

"Your friend is a real bitch," Zhazha said.

I snorted. "She just likes to get her way."

"For you, I take my hat off," she offered. I declined. I liked the fur outline. Besides, the clothes on the runway wouldn't be half as exciting. "I'm Zhazha."

"Oh, I know! I mean, I've seen your blog. I'm Anya from *La Vie*. And, um, that was Sarah Taft."

Zhazha wrinkled her nose in the most adorable manner.

"She's a real bitch," she repeated.

She laughed. I tittered away with her. Fashion Week rules dictated that we gossip, we mock. Even about Sarah. The best way to communicate was to laugh at someone. So I giggled along with the Russian as she made fun of my bestie. I caught Sarah's death glare from across the runway. I was going to pay for my treachery. I shrugged back at her. What was I supposed to do? I had to laugh. It was required of me. She had laughed at me first, so fair was fair. But I quieted down and tried to look forlorn and upset. See, Sarah? I'm with *you*.

The lights dimmed, and the music began pounding. I smiled at Sarah once more and glanced down the row from her. I swore I saw Mulberry von Gratz sitting no more than ten seats from Sarah. With that horrible shoe smashed into her head. That bitch! Assistants don't sit front row, ever. I waved to her, to be polite. It was that or kiss her after the show, and no way was I going to cheek-cheek shoe-face. The music was loud enough to drown out the buzzing in my ears.

* * *

"That fucking foreign bitch!" Sarah yelled as our car pulled away. "Can you believe her? And you. What were you doing talking to her?"

"I was informing her of who you were." Not a total lie. "But you have to admit she has style."

"Goddammit, Anya, you have the worst taste. That's why you didn't get the promotion, you know." Sarah wasn't happy, and it was my fault. "I can't with you. She's a roach! All bloggers are roaches!" Her eyes were wild as she repeated our joke. I just shrugged. The blogger had been nice to me. "You *would* like her. You're a phony like her," she hissed under her breath. I felt like ice-cold water had been dumped on me.

Sarah held her phone a few inches from her face, using it to block me and everyone else out. I bet Zhazha would be nicer to work for.

I should have lavished Sarah with all my love and affection. But my phone buzzing distracted me. Detective Hopper. Didn't he know it was Fashion Week?

"Hi, Detective."

"Ms. St. Clair, we've been trying to reach you."

"I know, I'm so sorry. It's Fashion Week, and I'm running around like a crazy person. Is something the matter?"

"We need you to come in."

I grimaced. Now? Was he fucking kidding me?

"Today? Because I have more shows and presentations to do."

"Yes." That's all he said. No, sorry for fucking up your schedule, Anya. Nothing.

"Fine, text me the address. I don't have it in front of me. I'll be there as soon as I can."

Sarah ignored me and my conversation. She was busy clack-clacking on her phone. I'd have to read it later.

* * *

Detective Hopper was wearing a suit. I wondered if he ever got hot and sweaty through his crisp white shirts. He glanced at my outfit, which was a bit much for a precinct visit: I was wearing a Saint Laurent minidress with ankle boots. It would have to do.

"It's for Fashion Week," I hastened to explain. "You have to dress up." He just nodded, then led me into a meeting room. He didn't even compliment my dress. Or my legs—and they looked really good.

"Thanks for coming in; I know you're busy."

"Um, sure. Is this about Mulberry? Have you found someone?" It had been a month and a half. The police had interviewed anyone and everyone who had ever interacted with Mulberry and come up with nothing. Mulberry's parents were furious and writing editorials blasting the NYPD.

"No, I wanted to ask you about Lisa Blitz."

"Lisa? What about her? You don't think she did it?"

"How well do you know Ms. Blitz?"

"Not well. Just from around the industry. You know, we go to the same events. She's really good friends with Sarah and Jack Archer. Sarah could probably tell you more. Although . . ." I paused a bit for drama. It was so important to take breaths. "I think they were having some sort of fight. I don't really know, but you should def talk to Sarah."

Detective Hopper nodded. God he was pretty. The thought barely formed when I heard Sarah laughing at me in my head, calling me a phony. My shoulders tensed.

"Have you seen Ms. Blitz lately?"

I frowned. "Actually, no. Sarah's been complaining that she hasn't seen her since before Labor Day. And I haven't run into her at shows."

"When was the last time you saw her?"

"Me? Huh. Let me think. It was either an event or . . ." I opened my calendar on my phone. "It was at a party two weeks ago, at the Gramercy. Why? Is something wrong? Did something happen to Lisa?"

He looked at me. That same look he gave me when we first met, like he thought I'd tell him everything. And weirdly, I wanted to. I wanted him to know I'd killed three people this summer. A fucking personal record. I wanted to see the awe and admiration on his face. Shit, what if he could read minds? What if he could know everything I was thinking right now? What if he could see into my brain?

"Detective, you have to tell me. What happened to Lisa?"

"She was found in her apartment yesterday. Dead."

About time.

I gasped. "Wait, like suicide?" I managed to ask. Always ask details about a death, but not too many. Be interested but not creepy.

"We're considering it suspicious for now. Why didn't anyone report her missing? She'd been dead for a few days."

A full week, actually. But who was counting?

I opened my mouth and closed it a few times. I call it fish mouth, but it's good for emulating shock. Innocent people who have nothing to hide went into shock.

"You'd have to ask Sarah. I think they were in a fight or something," I repeated. This is what you did during Fashion Week: you talked shit.

"Can you think of anyone who'd want to hurt her? Was she dating anyone? An ex-boyfriend, perhaps?"

I shrugged. I didn't know Lisa's dating schedule. "No, not really. I mean, she wasn't the nicest girl, but who is around these parts? But I don't know who'd want to kill her. That's just so . . . extreme."

"What about you? Did you have a thing for Lisa?" Me? Had I heard him correctly?

"No, I'm not into girls."

He nodded. I knew why he was asking me about Lisa fucking around. The crotch lace. Cops are so unimaginative sometimes.

"I heard you two didn't really get along." Silence. Bomb dropping. Who was talking about me? Who even knew about me?

"It's fashion. No one really gets along." I shrugged. "Lisa wasn't nice unless you had something she wanted. I didn't. But beyond that, we tolerated each other."

He eyed me, and I was positive he could read my thoughts. Fuck, if I had to start wearing a tin foil hat, I was going to be pissed. Not a good look at a fashion show.

"Neighbors saw a blonde woman going into Lisa's apartment a few days before. Does that remind you of anyone?" My wig. They had mistaken me for Sarah. That was the best thing I'd heard all week.

"Sarah," I whispered. He raised an eyebrow at me. "Sarah said Lisa was upset she couldn't crash at Sarah's beach house for Labor Day." It came out in a rush. "Shit, Lisa's dead. That's so messed up."

"We'll be talking to Ms. Taft as well. She just hasn't called us back."

I helpfully gave him her fashion show schedule. What are BFFs for? Sarah couldn't be mad. I had to help the detective. It'd be weird if I didn't. Still, I silently prayed to the fashion gods that she'd laugh this off. I also crossed my fingers and hoped he pulled her out of Marc Jacobs. In front of everyone. That would be amazing.

* * *

News of Lisa's death spread like wildfire at the shows. I couldn't help myself. I told everyone and anyone next to me, even if I didn't know them. Gossip was a staple at shows, and for once, I had something juicy no one else knew yet.

"Um, you heard about Lisa Blitz, from Cartel? She's dead! The police are asking about her. They want to talk to Sarah Taft. Crazy, right?" And then I'd sit back as a very stylish game of telephone was played. By the end of the day, Sarah was rumored to have killed Lisa in a pre–Fashion Week meltdown.

I snorted when I heard the latest tale. Sarah was the talk of shows, which was impressive even for her. (She could get a few murmurs about her outfits, but this was something else. All eyes followed her more than usual.) She should thank me. Lisa never got her this kind of attention.

Sarah posted a selfie of herself crying, mascara running down her face. It was touching. On the bright side, she now had an opening for a BFF. This was my big break. I was going to console her. We could mourn Lisa together, talk about her ridiculous veils, and cry. And then I'd hug her, and she'd realize that I was her one true friend in this world. Who said the fashion world was heartless?

* * *

Sarah wasn't dragged out of a show. Bummer, I know. The spectacle would have made my day. Instead, she willingly went to talk to the detective before her morning appearances the next day.

"I'm taking the car so find your own way around," she said coldly. She hadn't spoken to me in a full day. Almost twenty-four hours of silence. I was miserable. I wanted to go with her, to hold her hand. To tell her it would all be okay. That Zhazha meant nothing to me. I wanted to know what she told the detective, whether she said I was a fake. If he knew, then they'd all know. It'd get in the papers or something. My panic was overwhelming. I took off a brooch I was wearing and stabbed my thighs repeatedly. Relief.

* * *

Sarah reappeared at the office a couple hours later, dressed in her best funeral attire. Head-to-toe darkness. Celia caught her and screamed. Actually screamed. This was not the look she wanted for Sarah at Fashion Week.

"You cannot wear all black to the shows. You are not Anya! What will it say about us?" she yelled.

"Um, my bestie died. I can't even."

My heart hurt. *I* was her bestie. Not Lisa. When would Sarah realize that?

"We need to present a united front after Mulberry. We can't look morbid. So you can and will *even*. I'm having some new clothes called in, and you will wear them. Or else."

Sarah just stared. Maybe she *was* mourning? I patted her hand later in the car. She pulled it away. I had no idea how to comfort her, but I had to try. Why was she so upset? When Meredith died, I got over it. Now it was Sarah's turn.

"Lisa would be really touched by this, but even she wouldn't want you to give up your sense of style. She'd totally make fun of you for it." She would.

"What would you know, Anya? She hated you. So does Jack. Everyone hates you. Just look at you. You're so not a *La Vie* girl." The comment stung. She had learned from Celia. "You know what everyone is saying about you, right? That you totally faked your way here. Lisa told everyone what her little detective found."

It was a lie. It had to be a lie. I'd checked all of Lisa's emails and scoured her apartment. He hadn't found much. Still, I wanted to throw up. Sarah was lashing out, Dr. M would say. Don't take it personally. (Whatever, everything was personal.)

"Okay, then dress like an idiot and lose your job." *Fuck you too.* Tough love. I couldn't win with her.

I ignored her sniffling for the rest of the day. How could she be this sad over someone who wore veils? If she wanted me as her one and only BFF, she had to realize I was awesome and that no one else mattered. If I could get over the whole betraying me thing, she could too. (I hadn't, but whatever.) Dr. M told me I needed to value myself more. Besides, Sarah had to get it together. This was life; shit happens. You either dealt with it and went back to wearing Gucci, or you curled up in a ball and waited to die. Only the strong survived.

9

I waited for it. For that moment when Sarah would want me to comfort her. To tell her she would be okay, that Lisa's death was ultimately good for all of us. But it didn't happen. I didn't even get to pet her hair.

Instead, she turned to Jack. Not me.

I couldn't blame her; he was in the trinity. Or what was left of it. Since he only covered menswear, he wasn't attending shows, but he rode in the car with us, forcing me to sit in the front passenger seat. He was her moral support. I needed a friend like that. I needed someone who would support me.

I heard them whispering behind me.

"I can't stand her. She's a fraud."

"Oh, come on. You know Lisa was a jealous bitch."

"Ugh, Jack, if you only knew." What did that mean? "She's the worst. God, look at her clothes," she snickered.

I glanced down at my outfit. I was wearing a denim jacket with Gucci splashed all over it. With a little black dress of course. What was wrong with my look? *Don't react, Anya.*

"I do know. I told you. But do you really think she did it? I mean, look at her." I felt eyes on the back of my head. Don't turn around. I pretended to be busy on my phone. I was texting Dr. M. *Help me! NYFW is a disaster!* He didn't reply. It felt like the world was against me today.

"You're right. I'm just really sad about Lisa."

Jack made comforting cooing noises at Sarah. I should have been doing that.

"When's the funeral?" she asked. I wanted to pipe up, tell her I put it on her calendar for her. But didn't. All I could hear was Sarah saying I was the worst.

"Uh, while you're in Europe. But there's going to be a memorial after, don't worry." Sarah strangled out a sob. I wanted to turn around. I wanted to join in. But I wasn't welcome.

Worse than that, she was blaming me for Lisa's death. Me? As if. She should be blaming Lisa. No, she should be thanking me—Lisa wore veils. I couldn't believe Sarah was acting like this.

It couldn't go on. I had to distract her from it. How do you make someone forget her so-called friend was murdered? *You know how. You have to get her to focus on her favorite person: herself.* I like to call these lightbulb moments because, hello? Flash of genius.

After all, Sarah was still seething over Zhazha. The blogger was everywhere. At every show, front row. And more incredibly, she wore a new outfit to every appearance. Zhazha went from Saint Laurent to Balenciaga to Gucci in a flash. I had no idea where she changed, but in one hour, I saw her wearing two very different outfits.

The street-style photogs grew in number exponentially each season. They had started with one or two, and now an entire horde of them clogged the sidewalks outside each venue. And yet not one was paying attention to Sarah, despite her best efforts. Not when Zhazha promised them new looks at every show.

"God I hate that Russian bitch," Sarah muttered as we exited the car. Not to me, to Jack. I didn't exist in Sarah's world right now. I was, at best, her employee. I had to change that. I had to show Sarah how much she really did care for me. Her love for me was there, deep down. Like, buried in a hole, covered in cement deep down. She and I were kismet, meant to be.

Dr. M would tell me I had an insane need for approval. Um, duh? My entire life was about getting teachers and doctors to sign off on me. To say I was doing well, following the rules. You don't just turn that off once you're in the real world.

So Sarah would see how perfect I was, how well I did actually fit into her life. I'd make her see. I straightened my shoulders and very deliberately walked over to Zhazha. The blogger would be my friend, I was sure of it. At least until Sarah came around. We even chatted like old pals. I caught Sarah glaring. We had four shows that day with Zhazha. By the third show, Z and I had exchanged contact info and a promise to do drinks with Dalia, who was my new seatmate. (Sarah refused to sit with me as long as I was "buddying up with that Russian whore.") Sarah wouldn't even look at me. Was she telling everyone I was a fake? That I didn't belong there? Each second she ignored me sent me deeper into panic mode. If she didn't start paying attention to me, loving me soon, I was going to lose it. And that's a major *don't* during Fashion Week.

"Her accessories are amazing," Dalia said. She meant Zhazha, not Sarah. And she was right. Dalia glanced at my own bag, a vintage Dior saddlebag. "Oh, chic." Approval. It wasn't from Sarah, but I'd take it. I beamed. I had winged my eyeliner just like Dalia did. I wonder if she noticed.

By the final show, Sarah had had enough. I watched with fascination as she shoved her way to the center of the photographer throng. We were just outside the Cedar Lake stage, with cobblestones everywhere. Not my favorite place to get to, but the catwalk inside was fabulous.

"Out of my way!" Sarah bellowed before breaking out five different poses. She was so engrossed in the flashes going off that she didn't notice Zhazha walking her way. Blinding light, photographers yelling. The buzzing sound was roaring in my head. *You're a phony, Anya. A fraud. Do it now. She'll expose you. This will make her need you. She'll finally love you.* I tried to shut out the intrusive thoughts—that's what Dr. M called them—but it was too late. *Look at her outfits*, I heard Sarah sneer. Her taunting laughter echoed in my head. I had to do it. I had to shut the noise out, to refocus. To show Sarah how much she needed me.

Sarah was already flying through the air.

People around us gasped.

Sarah screamed. I froze. What had I done?

Zhazha claimed innocence. It was maybe her giant bag that had done it—was Sarah okay? She cooed her concern, trying to help my boss up. It wasn't Zhazha's fault. No one noticed me. They never did. That's the good part of wearing all black. I blended in with everyone. Who looks at the ugly chicken when peacocks are around?

My blog that night included shots of a resplendent Zhazha in a fur cape and, next to it, a shot of Sarah sprawled on the stone steps. She'd wanted her photo to appear on the site more often, didn't she? Her wish was my command.

I did feel a teensy bit bad when I saw Sarah wearing a cast and sling later. But it wasn't my fault. Intrusive thoughts weren't real; they couldn't hurt anyone. Except maybe mine were taking over? The whole scene had been like an out-of-body experience. I saw myself push her, and I couldn't stop it. I made a note to talk to Dr. M about it. BFFs don't trash each other's outfits like that. I had to do it. I had to make Sarah refocus, from dead Lisa to me.

Back at the office, Celia was loving Zhazha, despite the thrashing Sarah took (or because of it; Greg was tripping over himself to take care of our little wounded dove, and it was pissing Celia off).

"She's wearing fur in this weather. That is so damn chic," she said approvingly. "Anya, get her in here, ASAP."

"Of course. Though I did see Annie from *Mince* taking her away in a car. And it didn't help that Sarah cursed her out. I had to do a lot of apologizing."

"Dammit. Should we send her flowers?" Celia asked.

I smiled. "Better. Send her caviar."

"Brilliant." It looked like I had just made friends with *La Vie*'s newest star.

* * *

Zhazha was my new ally. And she'd managed (without trying) to make Sarah look like a fool, which made Sarah need me even more. Sarah was practically useless with her broken arm.

I sent a couple ounces of Petrossian to Zhazha's rooms at the Gramercy Park Hotel, along with several bottles of champagne and a note that said, *We adore you. Let's talk more? xx Anya.* If I didn't already hate myself and everyone else, I'd probably vomit over the "xx," but that was how it was done. At least it wasn't as bad as *Kisses!* or *Love you!* or *Oh my gosh, you're amaaaaaaaazing!*

Still, I poked my finger with a staple until it bled to punish myself for the shitty note. It reminded me there may be a soul in there still. I watched as the blood kept pooling and pooling, a deep crimson circle—

"What are you doing? Are you bleeding again?" Sarah screeched, interrupting me. She winced slightly as she shifted her arm. She looked like a bird, standing there in front of me. Her blazer was draped over both shoulders. We were at the office before the day's shows started. She was talking to me again. See? It had worked. A broken bone was the perfect distraction from grief.

"What? Oh, yeah, my hand slipped," I muttered.

"Well, get a Band-Aid, you freak. Why do you always cut yourself?"

"How's the arm, Sarah? Still broken?"

"Ugh, yes. That stupid commie bitch—"

"Is getting a spread in the magazine." I grinned. Zhazha was new, hot, and so very in.

"*No!* She can't be!"

"She's the new *it* girl. Dalia's working on her accessories as we speak."

Sarah's face reddened as she processed the news. For a moment, I thought she was actually going to cry. Good. Let her. I felt a twinge of joy at the thought. You always hurt the ones you love the most.

"I'm going to tell Greg."

"You do that, but it won't help."

"Yes it will! He'll stop it!"

"Zhazha will lure in new advertisers and younger readers. So good luck."

I enjoyed watching her face as she realized I was right. The blogger was going to be huge, and *La Vie* needed in on her momentum. Sarah pouted. I should have hugged her, told her how cute she was. But I had had enough rejection from her this week.

"Ugh, just get a Band-Aid, would you?"

I put my finger in my mouth.

"You are so gross, Anya."

I bared my blood-covered teeth at her and winked before heading out to my next show. She flinched. She hadn't said a word about missing Lisa.

I started my Zhazha mood board that night.

* * *

I needed total silence. Why I thought I'd find that in New York City, I'll never know. But those rare moments when the roar of the traffic sounds like waves at the beach, the jackhammering has ceased, and your neighbors have stopped fucking too loudly are the closest to bliss any of us will ever get.

White-noise machines. Calming music playing. Deep breaths and ohhmmming until you are too zen to care that a toddler is jumping up and down one floor up. None of that worked for me. Each and every sound was an assault on my senses.

To properly make a mood board, to have it magically come alive, you needed quiet. Not really come alive. That's crazy. But to bloom in your head and heart. To take over, to channel your ardent wishes, you needed to focus. How could I focus when my neighbors kept screaming? (She was obviously faking it.) I had to shut out everything screaming inside my head. Lisa's taunts. That pitying look Mulberry gave me. Diana's stupid comments. And the detective who kept leaving me voice mails.

I shook my head. *Not now. Focus on Zhazha.*

My Russian friend (that word again, *friend*) was so easy to be inspired by. Photos of her filled slideshows on every fashion site. She was the new girl to watch, the Russian czarina pouting just so at the camera in head-to-toe red. A shot of her carrying a bag that was just on the runway and not available to purchase yet. (God, that was hot.) And then her holding a bottle of vodka in her hand for a not-so-subtle moment of sponsorship.

She was perfect.

But she wasn't my BFF.

Look, just because had a small tiff didn't mean Sarah and I had broken up. She needed space to grieve, and while in that dark hole, she'd finally see the light. The Anya light. Sarah would realize I was the only way forward. That what happened in the past—in *my* past—didn't matter.

Ever since her promotion, Sarah had been ordering me around, and Fashion Week made her extrabossy. I'd even gotten her lunch for her, carrying it like a pathetic assistant while she whimpered about her arm. I didn't even spit in it. I wanted to. (Imagine watching her eat something that came from inside me. Oh, heaven.) *Anya, get this. Write that. O-M-G, fix your hair.* I love-hated every second of it.

I set the two boards together. Zhazha versus Sarah. Who did I want more? Did I really have to choose? Couldn't I have it all?

I can usually tell when it's time to move on from BFF-dom. You just don't care about the person anymore. You feel nothing. They're an annoyance. My first BFF, Meredith, was like that. I couldn't wait to be rid of her. That's the thing with kids. It's so easy to move from group to group. But even then, the idea of Meredith having a bestie after me really made my stomach hurt. That wasn't possible. I was the ultimate. I was everything.

I didn't want to get rid of Sarah. She was my everything. Dr. M said I was merely infatuated and that this would pass. Eye roll. Sarah and I were destined to be BFFs. But, she needed to step up if we were going to make it, or she'd end up like Meredith. Why Mer had to play with matches like that I'll never know. Doesn't mean I tried to stop her. No, I watched her burn.

Everyone whispered about me back then, like they were now about Zhazha. Maybe she and I were soul sisters? I drew a big heart on Zhazha's board in red glitter. It was so her. On Sarah's, I drew a mustache on her photos in black. We were going to have to talk this through. Until then, I had a new distraction: Zhazha. I took my gloves off and threw them in the trash. Why make a mood board if you're going to smudge it with fingerprints?

* * *

Finally, the longest week ever was over. The team was headed to Europe—without me. Celia, Sarah, Dalia, and Evie were hitting London, Milan, and Paris. The gloating was insufferable. Despite missing Lisa's funeral, Sarah was happy again. Europe did that to people. She was going to be attending the Burberry, Gucci, and Valentino shows, and I wasn't. I tried to not let the idea of three weeks without her get to me. This would be good for us. Sarah had to learn to miss me. Absence made the heart grow fonder and all that shit.

"I can't wait to go to Selfridges! And Harvey Nichols! And . . ." Sarah droned on for a while. "Anya! Are you listening?"

"Not really."

"Don't you want to know where we're going to go? I mean, while you're stuck here?"

I didn't bother replying. I couldn't go to Europe even if I wanted. And I didn't want to go. Really, I didn't. I swear.

Fine, I was seething with envy. But all that schmoozing was too exhausting to maintain. The European shows were on top of one another: London bled into Milan, which bled into Paris. I didn't know how Sarah did it. Maybe she was better at this world. This life. But no, I didn't want to go to Europe.

Besides, there was that issue with my passport. Dr. M handled it all for me. The name change, the new identity. He swore the papers were filed. But sometimes I ran into issues. Better to just avoid the whole mess. London and Paris were on my "one day" mood boards.

"I mean, Riccardo Tisci is just so dreamy! Aren't you so jelly?" Sarah asked excitedly.

"Mmhmm."

"Anya! Admit it!"

"Sarah, one of us needs to hold down the fort. Have a lovely time."

"It must be sad that you're just not cool enough to go to Europe with us." A saw was going off in my head.

"Is Greg going to be here alone? I hope he doesn't get bored."

"What's that supposed to mean? Whatever, he's meeting me in Paris." Sarah rolled her eyes, as if I were stupid for even mentioning him. She was going through a large box that had been delivered. She jumped up and down and, with one useful arm, carted it to Greg's office. I didn't ask.

At least she'd be in Europe with a broken arm. A broken yet still nearly perfect arm in a chic sling. She'd walked around the final New York Fashion Week shows as if she were in a Helmut Newton spread. Her slings (she'd rotated a few different ones) were made from black leather, fur, and even Swarovski crystals. By the end of the week, copies of them had started to appear. I even spotted Mulberry all slung up.

"Oh, bee-tee-dubs, I assigned Cassie a story. So she could get a byline," she said later as she left the office. She grinned at me. She had done it to fuck with me, I knew it.

"You did? Oh, great!" Kill them with kindness and enthusiasm if you can't kill them at all. And killing Sarah was not part of my plans. A dead Sarah couldn't give me what I needed most: her. I didn't bother asking what she'd assigned. Knowing Sarah, it was something like, "Oh, write a story on clothes."

I was determined to leave the office and watch more SVU. I had missed the team, and I was sure they missed me. That lovable Detective Munch. Ice-T. Benson and Stabler's solid asexual partnership. I wish Sarah and I had that relationship.

Once the Fabulous Four (their words) decamped, I took pleasure in knowing Sarah had no real friends with her. Jack stayed in New York, and Lisa was dead and buried. Her funeral hadn't gotten the red carpet treatment Mulberry's did. Lisa was self-made, trying to become someone. Sort of like me. You'd think we could have bonded over that. What happened to sister solidarity? (I wondered if the police had any leads. I made a note to call Detective Hopper.) Now Sarah had only Dalia and Evie.

The office was downright pleasant with everyone gone. Even Greg stayed on his side of the floor, sulking for lack of attention. Cassie would go visit him, which made me gag on my lunch. I was working weeks ahead, our calendar filled with stories. I got so much done. I opened my mail and Sarah's mail and filed for her. I emailed Sarah anything important that came.

Thanks, babe, she replied. *Also, why do you keep calling me Meredith?*

Cassie was, sadly, the only distraction I had. Zhazha was in Europe; a few brands had paid for her airfare and hotels.

She began sauntering in later and later, much like Sarah. She wore similar outfits to Sarah's (as seen on Instagram). Cassie even started wearing lip gloss like Sarah and responding to me in acronyms and abbreviations. She had highlighted her hair so it was a touch blonder. She was like a Sarah doll come to life, only not as perfect as the real thing. Cassie didn't have the bone structure to be Sarah. She was the fake sugar version, SarahLite.

And she was outdoing me in her devotion. I hated her and myself at the same time.

"Did you file your story yet?" I asked the Monday after everyone had left. Sarah and the team had been gone four days.

"O-M-G, totes forgot! I'll get to it. But first I need to walk Frou-Frou." Frou-Frou was Sarah's albino Pomeranian. Dogs had been a key accessory at Fashion Week, so Sarah had run out to buy one—just in time for her to fly to Europe without it.

Every day brought a new mini-Sarah into the office. Soon Cassie's clothes seemed to come straight from Sarah's closet. And maybe they had. She did have a key to her apartment. I had to tell on her. Sarah had to know.

Um, did you know Cassie's raiding your closet? I emailed.

What? LOL!

That was it? No outrage? Had Sarah been won over by the social-climbing intern? I sat completely befuddled. Was Cassie better than me? No, that couldn't be. I was her boss.

* * *

Cassie finally turned her story in—one week later—and it was awful. No, worse than awful. It wasn't real. I picked up a pen and debated stabbing my leg with it. Wait, ink poisoning was a real danger. Instead, I decided to cull Cassie from our ragtag herd as soon as possible.

"What I Wore to My First Fashion Week" was the easiest type of bullshit piece anyone could write. I could whip it up in two seconds. Hell, Diana could have written it in our comments, and it would have been hilarious! (I should have hired her as a writer. Hindsight.) A quick intro, some photos, a few comments on each image, and some vague bullshit about what you learned. It wasn't rocket science. I had expected spelling errors, copy mistakes. I was even ready for poorly lit photos.

What I wasn't prepared for was Cassie submitting the exact same story that Lisa's site, Cartel, had run—literally the *exact* story with the byline swapped out for her own. (The site had continued on even without its illustrious leader. Ad dollars were all that mattered.)

The photos weren't even of Cassie; they were of the original writer—who was a guy. You had to commend her balls—and marvel at her stupidity. *Deep breaths, Anya. Deep breaths.* Frantically, I mouthed WWMKAAD (What would Mary-Kate and Ashley do?) to myself over and over until the rage subsided a bit. Then I called Cassie over.

"Um, Cassie, I'm not sure I like the post you wrote."

"Why not? I thought it was great." She pouted, dropping her chin. Sarah's chin dip. Did the girl have an original bone in her body? She was so obvious, it stunned me that Sarah, *my* Sarah, would fall for her tricks.

"Oh, did she? When it ran on *Cartel*? Because you didn't actually write this, did you?"

"Yes I did. See? There's my name!" She pointed to her byline, grinning.

"Changing the byline doesn't make it yours. You do know that, right? This is full-on plagiarism. Explain to me why I shouldn't fire you."

"I-I didn't—"

"Save it. If you want to succeed here or anywhere else, you need to put in some effort. This is a very small industry. If people find out you steal anything, you will be *so* ruined. Understand?"

"Except it's too late to get a new intern, so even if you say something, you'll be down a body." She smiled triumphantly.

A body. No, there were always bodies.

I tried a different tactic. "This will make Sarah look bad."

"No, it won't." She sounded unsure. She straightened her spine. "Besides, Sarah loves me. She's going to give me a recommendation."

"As what? Her dog walker?"

Cassie blanched. She nervously tugged at her highlighted hair. "Whatever, Anya. Sarah wants this to run. And she's your *boss*. But you should hear all the things she says about you when you're not around. It's hilarious." She giggled.

Sarah was confiding in Cassie. She was talking shit (the fashion way!) about me—to the intern.

I've always wondered what a nuclear blast would feel like. Sound like. Would the roar block out everything, be so loud that you heard nothing but silence? That was the sound in my head. So much buzzing and screaming, I heard nothing.

"Go to the fashion closet and see what they need you to do. Now." I sounded out each word slowly.

Sarah emailed to check in.

Things are good. Except Cassie was carrying a fake bag. I lied. But there was no point in telling her about the plagiarized story. Sarah wouldn't care. I added, *She's always with Greg. What's that about?*

SHUT UP! Fire her! She replied.

* * *

By week three, I found myself at the dessert station in the cafeteria, staring at the cakes: cheesecake, coffeecake, chocolate cake. I wanted them all. I took the cheesecake. Cassie was driving me to stress eat. All that hard work losing weight was going to be wasted because that moron couldn't do her work. I spooned the creamy cake in my mouth, the blissful richness taking over. This was better than sex. Fuck orgasms, I just needed more cake. Maybe it was time to move on from the fashion chapter of my life and just fill up on daily desserts.

No. I threw my fork down. I caught a few stares as it clattered on the plate. I spat out whatever was left in my mouth. I would not let Cassie do this to me. I would not get fat because of her. She would not derail me. I had my goals. I had my plans. I was going to stay thin. I had to, or I'd be out of a job. I was going to be Sarah Taft's BFF if it killed me. Life was going to be really fucking awesome, Goddammit. I was one of them. I had to act like it.

I went back upstairs, disgusted with myself. I needed to see Dr. M. He'd know just what to say.

"Anya, you just need to be firm with your intern."

"I know, Dr. M. But she only listens to Sarah."

"Did you ever think that this might be Sarah's way of testing you? To see if you have what it takes to get ahead?"

Was she testing me? Was I failing?

He sighed. It was my cue to calm the fuck down.

"Why is this Cassie girl getting you so upset? What's really the issue?"

"The issue? She's a fake!" I spit as I said it. Okay, fine, I was worked up.

"Anya, are you really the one who should call others fake? Your background isn't exactly bulletproof."

"Cassie and I are not the same! How dare you? I'm trying to improve—"

"By being like Sarah. And like Cassie."

Have you ever wanted to shove your Stella McCartney mesh heels into your shrink's mouth to make him stop talking? I couldn't believe he was saying such hurtful things.

"We're not the same. I help Sarah. Cassie is using her. There's a difference." It was like talking to a brick wall. We weren't the same. We weren't.

He sighed. "You know none of this is good for you."

"I know, Dr. M. That's why I need to fix it."

"Why don't you set up to-do lists for the girl and see if that helps." I did as instructed. I always did. I typed out Cassie's to-do list every morning for four days. They weren't too in depth—I didn't want to overwhelm the girl. But every day, she all but ignored them. Frustrated, I tore the paper to shreds at six PM daily. I could feel the fury building. The only way to calm myself was to suck on the strips of list strewn about my cubicle, chewing them like gum. Chew away the unperformed tasks, *chew chew chew*. And then swallow. Dr. M called this internalizing.

With every strip swallowed, I felt the burden lift. It was like taking Holy Communion. I hadn't shit in four days from my paper-eating habit. I was going to have to put an end to this. Cassie was bad for my health. At this point, it was her or me.

In NYC, the fashion party circuit had quieted down as everyone waited for the European shows to end. But there were still a few events here and there: bourbon and barbecue at a menswear store; a beauty launch at the Ritz Spa. I saw Jack at both. He hugged me like we were old friends.

"Girl, I love running into you!"

"Sames! Isn't it so great to have some chill time with everyone gone?"

"*Yes*. And now I get to hang out with my new friend!" He smiled. Did he have a new Lisa?

"Oh? Who's that?"

"Um, you?" Jack laughed as he said it. Did he mean it? He looped his arm through mine and spent the rest of each event whispering in my ear. "Have you seen the cameras Sarah put up?"

"The cameras?" Sarah had cameras? Was she spying on me? Was everyone watching me? My heart jumped into my throat.

"O-M-G, yes! She hid them in Greg's office while she's away. Isn't that hilarious? She has a guy who makes them or something." He guffawed, wiping a tear from his eye as he laughed.

I didn't ask why he was telling me this. Why he tattled on Sarah. That's what Jack did. He gossiped, he traded on it. Tell him something and he'd give you juicy details back. But there were two things I learned. One: Sarah was craftier than I thought. And two: I didn't trust Jack. Not one bit.

10

"I mean, can you believe how much weight I've gained? I was such a pig in Paris!" Sarah laughed, poking her jutting hip bones. "Look, it must be at least two pounds! So much *vin rouge* and croissants!" She beamed, waiting for the obligatory compliment. It was early October, and the team had flown back the day before. (They had spent an extra weekend soaking in the sights and shopping.)

"I'm sure Celia and Evie can help you drop the weight," I suggested helpfully. I could hear her teeth gnashing. She had yet to hug me.

"Well, what did I miss here? How's the good old fort?"

"Oh, you know, the usual. Oh, before I forget, here are your keys."

"My keys? Why do you have them?"

"Cassie got sick"—after I'd dropped some ipecac into her green juice—"and couldn't walk Frou-Frou."

"And you did? How sweet of you!" She practically cackled, likely imagining me doing the menial task of walking her dog.

But walking Frou-Frou had been my idea. I'd wanted to go to Sarah's apartment, alone. Smell her clothes, steal hair from her brush, make copies of her keys.

"Have you seen Greg?" she asked.

I shook my head. "No, but he was with Cassie earlier." Her face went a gorgeous shade of red. "But tell me more about Europe! What happened? How was Celia? Did you see Zhazha?"

"That commie is a style whore. I don't know what everyone sees in her."

"Well, she's thin, rich, European, and was born to wear fur." She shot me an eyeful of daggers. "What's not to love about her? I adore her accent, don't you?"

"She's rude, crude, and nothing but a Russian hooker."

"Jealous much?" I taunted.

"Of that? Never. You can find chicer girls in Brighton Beach."

"As if you even know where Brighton Beach is."

"Whatever, I've heard of it. But I barely saw her."

"Weird because she was all over the street-style blogs."

"Ugh, who would shoot her?" Sarah rolled her eyes.

"We would." I pulled up twenty photos we'd just run, a slideshow of Zhazha's outfits. "Our audience loves her. The comments are insane. She and I are having dinner together next week." Before Sarah could finish pouting, I fished out my present for her. "Before I forget, this came for you. I think from Greg? There wasn't a card." I handed her a teddy bear, my eyes wide, waiting for her reaction. She was either going to love it or hate it.

"O-M-G, Anya! Why'd you wait so long?" She hugged it, burying her face into the stomach. I turned my face away, trying to contain myself. "It smells kind of funny."

"Oh, probably the packaging. You should spritz it with something. Some Santal 33?"

"Totes. I'm going to go say thank you!" Off she ran, still hugging the bear.

At one of my special schools, there was this girl, Susanna Jennings. She was paranoid and delusional—and a total legend. If you think it's easy to make a name for yourself in a school for troubled kids, you're nuts. She thought everyone was out to get her and retaliated in what I felt was an entirely appropriate manner. You know, look at her funny, she'd poke your eye out. That sort of thing. Once, she thought her room-mate was messing with her things. Moving her toiletries, her photo frames, cutting up her mattress. To get even with her, Susanna cut open her roomie's teddy bear. After shitting into the bear, she sewed it back up using a bobby pin and dental floss. For weeks, no one could figure out where the stench was coming from—until the sewing job unraveled.

Frou-Frou pooped a lot for a small dog.

Sarah left early, her bear in her bag. She was going to meet Jack, who she hadn't seen in "like forever." They didn't invite me.

"That's cool. I'm having drinks with Z," I lied.

"Z? You can't mean Zhazha?"

"Of course, who else?" I shrugged. See, Sarah? Two could play this game. "Oh, tell Jack he owes me drinks!"

He didn't. But I wanted her to see I was moving up in the world.

* * *

Sarah was furiously texting again. All day long, I heard the clack-clack of her nails. I tried to act cool, but I had to know if it was about me. I couldn't wait until the end of the day. I read her texts in the bathroom.

Sarah: *OMG, last night was banz.* (Her new way of saying bananas.)

Jack: *Right? So fun.*

Cassie: *I feel soooo hungover now.*

Sarah: *LOL, you shouldn't have had so much wine, you lush.*

Jack: *Drunky.*

Cassie: (Kissy face emoji.)

Cassie had gone out with Sarah and Jack. Cassie. Not me. How had I not seen this coming? Even with the hints I'd dropped about Greg, Cassie had wormed her way into the trinity. I'd stupidly thought Evie or Dalia might try for the spot. It didn't matter that neither wanted it. Well, maybe Evie did. But our intern? That's what all the Sarah doppelgänging was about. Cassie was trying to steal Sarah, to have her all to herself. And worse than that, she was fucking succeeding! Sarah was choosing her over me. I let it sink in. All my work was for nothing. My face burned with fury and hurt. I felt my eyes water. *Deep breaths, A. Keep calm. You can't cry at work. Pull it together and fix this mess.* Was Sarah so damaged that she wanted to befriend Cassie? Of course not; she was perfect.

I argued with myself in a bathroom stall. I had known. No, I didn't! This was bad. Wait, could this be good? I heard a flush and covered my mouth in horror. I thought I was alone. Someone had heard me. I froze. I waited until I heard footsteps go to the door and leave. Then I waited even longer in case anyone was outside, ready to ambush me. Trust no one, especially not at a women's magazine. After twenty minutes, I decided it was safe.

"That was a long break," Sarah said. She was in boss mode, eyeing my time away.

I shrugged. "Had a meeting."

"With who?"

"None of your biz, babe." I winked at her. It was my new thing. I wanted it to say, *See? I'm easy and cool and so much fun. I'm a winker.*

"Well, it couldn't have been an interview, because that outfit is such a don't."

End of conversation as I stared glumly at my leather-and-denim jeans, silk blouse, and Helmut Lang blazer. Was she right? Of course she was. Sarah's taste level far surpassed mine. But I couldn't let her know she had wounded me. That would be like giving up. I had to play it cool. Chill.

"Totes!" I winked again, this time also flashing a thumbs-up. Nailed it.

* * *

I wasn't procrastinating dealing with Cassie, I swear. Considering how small the suspect pool would've been if I'd done it while everyone was away, I had to wait. Timing really was everything. So you see, I had to let this happen. I told myself that several times. I had to let her become Sarah's new Lisa. I had to. Yes, this was part of the plan.

Still, I was seething. But to pass the time that night, I watched and rewatched footage from Greg's office. Sarah had set up her oh-so-secret cameras to send feeds to her email. I tried to watch them sooner, but seeing that much of Greg made me nauseous. (I breathed a sigh of relief once I checked the camera locations while Greg went to Paris. There weren't any aimed at me.) They were bulky and large, comically obvious. A binder cam sat on Greg's desk, a plug snaking out underneath. Another protruded out of a plant. How he hadn't noticed them yet was beyond me. But Sarah must not have seen the feeds yet, because there Greg was, fucking Cassie on his desk while his so-called girlfriend was in Europe. I needed Sarah to see it. I needed her to unleash her wrath on Cassie.

But she didn't.

Instead, the worst thing ever happened: Sarah walked down the hall holding Cassie's hand. They were planning a weekend away. To Miami. Just them and Jack and not me. That seeing-red thing happened again. Like, literally, everything was coated in red. As if a layer of blood was dripping everywhere. Have you ever felt that mad? It's overwhelming. Even my fingers were angry. My chest hurt. My head was pounding. Was I dying? Was this the way it all ended? Popping arteries over Cassie-fucking-Sachs? I had to calm down. Dr. M was right. He said I was transferring my frustrations onto the intern. But, like, she *was* my frustration.

It was time to fight back. I started small. Over the next week, I stole a few key items from Sarah's apartment (a pair of Gucci boots, Jennifer Fisher jewelry, and a new Chanel bag) while she was at showroom appointments and left them in Cassie's desk. I also sneaked in a few times to mess up her bedroom (after lying on the bed for a bit, inhaling the smell of her hair lingering on the pillow) and flood the bathroom.

I hinted again that Cassie and Greg had seemed close while she was gone.

"Yeah, she mentioned," Sarah said. "They just talked about me."

I wanted to scream, *Look at the video!* But I managed to hold it in.

When the entire office heard Sarah yell at Cassie later, I was relieved. Some of my sabotage was working. Sarah's stolen items had appeared magically in Cassie's desk. Sarah threw her (iced) latte at her. It was glorious.

"What's that about?" Celia asked, stopping by my desk to drop off some approved stories.

"Oh, just intern drama. Sarah's learning to not use them for personal errands."

Celia raised an eyebrow—or tried. Her Botox habit was back. "Does she not know we have an intern lawsuit cooking? What the hell is she thinking?"

Interns demanded payment and to be treated like humans now. Things sure were changing.

"I know! I'll ask her to handle it, Celia."

"You girls are going to ruin us. And did you just scrap your diet entirely while we were in Europe? You could have at least tried, you know." She tapped her foot expectantly. Damn those cheesecakes.

"I was busy dealing with a few things, but I'll be sure to get back on the wagon," I said, gritting my teeth.

"Great, let's not have this talk again, Anya."

Cassie and Sarah made up. I don't know how or why. But they were back to planning their weekend. My sabotage had been ineffective. I had been ineffective, only managing to bring them even closer together. I hid in the computer closet and sobbed.

"Fucking failure! Goddammit, do better! Anya the Asshole."

I wouldn't be disturbed here, and if anyone heard me, they pretended not to. Everyone avoided the Murder Hallway still.

There were rumors of it being haunted. Mulberry was the only one around to comfort me. She was sweet. She didn't have any dirt on the intern, though. Sweet but useless. I was sick of seeing that damn shoe in her face.

To make myself feel better, I did some online shopping. Retail therapy always worked. Some jewelry, a vitamin C serum, and a new hunting knife. I couldn't wait to put my new toys to use. A sharp knife could handle anything, even a plagiarizing intern. I know, I should have just asked Evie for some serum, but she was the worst.

* * *

Cassie was a squirmy little thing. Thankfully, the park closed at night so no one was around to hear her thrash about. It was one week before Halloween, and if anyone saw us, they'd think this was a weird prank. Cassie was stronger than I expected. I really wish those boot-camp classes would go out of style—they made my life so much harder.

But do as many push-ups as you like, I will persevere. I parked the rental van in a field past Avalon Park outside the city. Hikers would find her in a few days—I was counting on it. I dragged her out and threw her on the ground. She groaned through the duct tape.

I sat on top of her and slapped her. "Cassie, wake up. Wake up."

She was groggy from the bump on her head. I would use chloroform, but it takes more than five solid minutes of inhaling to knock someone out. (TV shows are so misleading about that.) I picked up my hunting knife and carved a two-inch slice into her right cheek. She bucked under me, her eyes opening wide. She wanted to scream, but her lips couldn't move through the tape. I had bound her arms too. Better to be careful, right?

"Hello, princess! Good, you're up." I glared at her. Usurper. I watched the blood drip down the side of her face and into her hair. Her dyed-blonde locks looked muddy with the blood.

"Did you know that in 1982—way before you were born, I know—there was a serial killer here? Well, not here. But in Long Island. Anyways, he liked to call himself the Raptor because he hunted his prey like a bird."

She blinked at me. I was counting on her confusion from the head bump to chill her out. She couldn't move anyways. I had triple-taped her arms. Try squirming now, intern.

"Anyways, his real name was Joseph Landon. And like so many pathetic male killers, he'd leave a calling card. Isn't that the stupidest thing you've ever heard?" I laughed.

Cassie's eyes searched for help.

"He'd carve the word Raptor into girls' faces. What a nut-job, right?"

Cassie nodded. Finally, she was getting me. We were on the same fucking page.

"He finally got caught, but he'd killed, like, way more women than anyone ever found." She made a noise against the duct tape over her mouth. "Don't fucking rush me! What is your damage, anyways? Like, you're my intern—you work for me. And you're going to stay still and keep quiet until I'm done. Got it?"

She nodded her head slowly. Ugh, she was so annoying. I put the knife down next to her head.

"The reason I'm telling you all this is because you are a total copycat. All you do is copy people. You copy Sarah, you copy stories. You even copied Lisa by joining the fucking trinity. And the whole Greg thing. Gross! You're so damn pathetic!" I wanted to laugh, but listing each of her offenses enraged me more and more. Cassie was a shitty intern.

Her eyes opened even wider, pupils dilated. She was gearing up to fight. *Bring it, bitch.* She tried to shake me off her, but my hands were already around her throat. Her arms were still tied, but even if she could free them and scratch me, I wore long sleeves and gloves. For added fun, I was wearing my blonde Sarah wig.

"I wish you'd put this much effort into your work! Do you know how far you'd have gone?"

I slapped her hard just to punctuate my sentence. Body language really helps get the message across. She was crying now, just as we were starting to have some fun. Cassie always had to ruin things. I had never loathed another human as I did Cassie Sachs.

Do you know just how much pressure it takes to choke the life out of someone? More than you realize, and at the same time, so much less. It's almost shocking, like that moment you're holding an egg and it breaks in your hands. Or squeeze a glass too hard and suddenly you have shards everywhere. It's so easy to extinguish a life this way. It's a wonder we all don't do it more often.

Watching her eyes bulge only pissed me off more. Who the fuck was she to make faces at me? This was who Sarah wanted to take to Miami? Ugh, I couldn't even. I let go and grabbed my knife again.

"You're making me do this." I raised my arm and brought the knife down over and over again. "Why [Stab!] did you [Stab!] have to be [Stab!] such a loser? [Stab! Stab! Stab!] You're not Sarah's BFF! [Stab! Stab! Stab!] I am! [Stab!] You're never [Stab!] going to work [Stab!] in this industry [Stab! Stab!] again! [Stab! Stab! Stab!] Fucking intern. [Stab! Stab!]"

I was out of breath by the end. Between lifting her and killing her, Cassie was working me out. At least I could skip the gym now.

"You'll never take my place with Sarah again."

I felt relief when it was done, when she was more blood than person. Her torso was riddled with wounds, her head nearly decapitated. I was finally getting rid of one giant problem in my life. No more idiotic intern not following my rules. No more bullshit. No more sucking up to Sarah, trying to be her bestie. Sarah had only one BFF, and that was me.

"It's me!" I screamed. No one heard me. I heard Dr. M's voice in my head, suggesting I was only trying to hurt myself by doing this. Transference or some shit. Ugh, I was not looking forward to our next session.

Killing Cassie was over so fast. I wanted it to last longer, to feel the endorphins for as long as I possibly could. I breathed in deeply, trying to make it last, feeling a wave of bliss wash over me. This was everything. I felt calm and content. No more seeing red, except for the blood. No more panic at being found out (for the time being). My head didn't hurt. Chest pains gone. And then, like most happy moments in life, the euphoria was gone. Disappointing and yet satisfying at the same time. Like a quick fuck done well.

I carved *Raptor* into the left side of her face. On her forehead, I added the word *Intern*.

I sat back, looking at my work. It wasn't bad. Her outfit was covered in blood. What a waste. I was pretty sure she was wearing Wes Gordon for Carolina Herrera. Chic. I stripped her naked, took her clothes, and pulled out her nails for later. I poured bleach all over her, making sure she was clean. Purified. Then I posed her with arms spread like wings.

Satisfied, I took a photo with a burner phone and then drove to the beach. No one ever notices a bonfire on the beach. Watching her clothes burn reminded me of Meredith. I wondered what she was up to now, all charred and dead. I wish I had marshmallows. I wiped the car down and left it in the city. I wondered if it was too late to kill Frou-Frou and bury them together.

Steps taken: 8,276. Calories burned: 2,200.

11

My eyes cracked open. Last night's workout with Cassie had left me sore and exhausted. Muscles I didn't know existed hurt every time I moved. I wanted to stay in bed. Sleep it off. But not today. Today was fashion Christmas. It was the Manolo sample sale.

The line already stretched down the block, but *La Vie* girls never wait in line. I went up to the door. Jack and Sarah stood two people front of me.

"Um, we don't know her," Sarah muttered to the Lauren-bot with a clipboard. (Jack still waved.)

"Where the hell is Cassie? Wasn't she meeting us?" he asked. Sarah only shrugged.

The Lauren-bot in charge smiled at me. "Good morning! The VIP room is through there. Just show me your ticket, please."

I waved my sacred golden ticket like this was a chocolate factory and breezed in, ready to begin piling up my treasure. My idea of pure heaven: shoes everywhere. I closed my eyes and inhaled the scent of leather. I love the smell of freshly made shoes. This was zen.

I decided on a pair of black suede pumps and another pair of blue ones (to replace the ones Diana ruined); patent ones in red, aubergine, and black; a pair of loafers; and two pairs of boots. All things in moderation.

I waved at Sarah, who was giggling with Jack. *Go say hi, Anya. Stop being a weirdo.* I took a deep breath, psyching myself up to spar with Jack when the ankle boot I was holding was snatched out of my hand.

"Oh, were you going to buy that?" A tall glamazon was waving my precious shoe in the air. She had almost a whole foot on me. I'd never be able to reach. She looked all of nineteen and chock full of attitude—an assistant.

"Yeah, I was."

"Too bad. It's mine now."

Was there no etiquette left in this world? I couldn't believe it. She turned to keep browsing, her bag full of shoes. The buzzing was back. Every second she held my boot, it grew louder. Sarah would never tolerate this shit. I glanced to make sure no one was watching before kicking the back of Glamazon's knee with my sneaker, sending her tumbling down, howling in pain. She was lucky I wasn't in boots.

"Oh, I'm *so* sorry! My bag must have hit you!" I said in a loud voice, leaning down to help her and snatching my shoes from the ground. Quietly, I added, "No, I think it's mine now. Learn some fucking manners."

As I turned to leave, I spied Mulberry filling up her bag, her Marc Jacobs shoe popping out of her head like a fascinator.

"Well, that's one way to get what you want." Jack smirked at me. His perfect eyebrows waggled, as if they were laughing at me. "Who knew you were so vicious, Anya?"

Where had he even come from?

"I don't know what you're talking about." I continued browsing. Fuck. I needed to be more careful. My lust for boots made me sloppy.

"Yeah, okay, babe. But, like, that was hardcore. I approve." He did?

"Approve of what?" Sarah asked.

"Of Anya turning shopping into a contact sport. Is that girl's knee broken?"

"No, but she'll be limping for a while." I said it without meaning to. I covered my mouth.

Jack looked at me shrewdly. "Interesting. You know, there's a lot more to you than I thought."

"Oh, please, Jack. Hey, hold my shoes, A." Sarah dumped four more pairs on top of what I was already holding. "But she's such a good minion. Right?" She grinned.

"I dunno. I wouldn't push her." Jack knew. I looked at his face. His eyes. He was grinning at me. "I mean, she did just kick a girl's ass for stealing her shoe. That's so *maje*." He winked at me. "I knew I liked you for a reason."

"Come on, she's a teddy bear. Right, Anya?" Then as if to demonstrate my cuddliness, Sarah hugged me. She actually hugged me. I froze. She had never hugged me before. I knew it was for show, but it still felt heavenly.

"I'm gonna go pay," I muttered, turning my fiery face away from Jack's all-seeing eyes.

"Don't hurt anyone, Anya!"

"Oh, I have to pay too." Sarah trailed behind me. "Don't you just love Jack?" she asked.

I shrugged. I wasn't feeling love at the moment. Panic, fear, annoyance, and anger, perhaps. But love?

"Sure, he's great. We ran into each other while you were gone."

"Yeah, I heard. Wouldn't it be great if he worked with us?"

With us? At *La Vie*? No way.

"We don't cover men's." It was the most diplomatic answer possible.

"But maybe we should. I think it'd be fab."

"What would?" I jumped at Jack's voice. He was like a cat. I needed to put a bell on him.

"You joining us at LV."

"Right? It'd be to die for, girls. But not literally. Especially after the Mulberry sitch." He looked around, likely to see if there was anyone else he had to say hi to. Jack was the king of networking.

"Whatever, it's totally safe there."

"Well, yeah, if you have body-slamming Anya with you!" Jack snorted. "Seriously, is that girl's knee okay?"

"She's fine," I muttered.

Jack reached out and grabbed each of us. "Girls, aren't you freaked? There's a killer in your office. Or he, like, came to your office. Whichever. Still creepy as fuck."

Sarah nodded in reply. I shrugged.

"What if," Jack continued, dropping his voice, "what if the killer is someone we know? Like in the biz?" Sarah and I both gasped, but for different reasons. "Mulberry gets offed. Then Lisa. What if some sick serial killer has a hard-on for fashion girls? O-M-G, that means you two could be next!"

He clapped his hands. I don't think he wanted us dead, but the excitement of it all was too much.

"Gross, Jack. No. That's not what's happening." Sarah rolled her eyes. "We're so beyond safe. Right, Anya?"

"Of course. Besides, do we even know if Mulberry and Lisa are linked? I mean, let's wait to hear from the police." My head hurt. The buzzing was getting louder. I wanted to rub my temples, but my hands were holding all the shoes. "Anyways, there's a thirty-three percent chance the murders won't be solved." They both stared at me. "I heard it on NPR. Just, like, statistics." Crime shows make you think every homicide will be solved thanks to a stray hair, a random skin cell. It wasn't real. Nothing was as advanced as what we saw on TV.

"Dark, Anya," Jack said. "I'm just saying something is really messed up around here. I still think it's someone we know."

A hysterical bubble of laughter came out of me. I didn't mean for it to. But it did. Sarah and Jack stared at me.

"Oh, come on! Who is smart enough to pull that off? Obvi not one of us." I laughed again, to show how absurd it all was.

Mulberry waved from across the store.

Sarah glanced back and forth between me and Jack. "You know, Anya's right. A fashion girl could never pull this off."

Jack shook his head. "Y'all aren't giving yourselves enough credit." But he dropped it.

* * *

I paced my living room. It wasn't really a full room. My apartment was one big box with a closet splitting it down the middle. I walked from my front door to my windows, which faced the East River. *Walk and breathe.*

Jack knew. I don't know what he knew, exactly. But he knew a little. He saw me kick that girl, and it clicked or something. Shit, what if he had followed me to Lisa's? Seen me leave her apartment? What if he'd gone to the police? He wouldn't be able to resist Detective Hopper's dreamy eyes. I could barely resist them. Hopper would get to him, force Jack to dig up dirt on me. I couldn't even blame Jack for it. Ugh, Detective Hopper could get *me* to spy for him if he asked nicely enough.

I was suddenly positive that Jack was recording each and every conversation we'd ever had. I called Dr. M.

"Don't you think you're being a bit paranoid?" he said slowly, cautiously.

"Paranoid? Dr. M! He said one of us was the killer. What kind of person says that?"

"Maybe Jack's trying to rattle you. Or is it possible he's the one the police are looking for?"

"Huh. I never thought of it like that. He could be the prime suspect. He never cared for Mulberry. And Lisa was one of his closest, but you never can tell." Was Dr. M onto something? Did the police think Jack was the root of all fashion evil?

"What if, and hear me out, what if he just wants to be friends with you? It seems like so far he's been on Team Anya."

I tilted my head. Was Dr. M right? In the loud clutter that filled my thoughts, Jack's smile and wave from the High-line party jumped out. Jack defending me in the car. I didn't know if I could trust him yet. You couldn't let your guard down with anyone in fashion. But maybe, just maybe, I could get Jack to be my friend. Then Sarah would fall in line. The trinity needed a third.

"Maybe. I mean, that would be great. But it's so hard to know who to trust in this industry." There was an awkward pause.

"Are we going to talk about Cassie?" he finally asked.

"Ugh, no. She won't be a problem anymore." I could hear him sigh. He was not happy with me. I was going to get a failing grade for everything this week.

"Anya, do I need to point out that you're transferring your feelings onto your intern?"

See? Told you so.

"That maybe you realize how unhealthy your obsession with Sarah is?"

"No, Cassie was just annoying. We're nothing alike. I did Sarah a favor. Cassie was screwing her boyfriend. I gotta go." I hung up.

Transferring. Pssh. Shrink jargon was such bullshit. Why do psychiatrists always try to force some big breakthrough on you? Didn't they know it had to be organic? But he was right about something—Jack was confusing. I had zero idea what his intentions were. And until I did, he was majorly suspect. Jack complimented me a lot this morning. It made me feel warm and confused. Did he want to be friends? People only say nice things when they want something from you. But what could Jack possibly want from me?

He texted Sarah for my info. He called me crazy and chic. Sarah stopped replying. The parental monitoring app had paid for itself. I felt happy and strangely nauseous.

* * *

Sarah was sulking at her desk the next morning.

"What's the matter, Sarah? Don't like your shoes?"

"No, it's Jack. He's being weird, is all. Sometimes his taste level is really low." She grimaced. She meant me.

"Oh? What's he going on about now?" *Play it cool, Anya.*

"Ugh, you. You're all he talks about. Can you believe it?"

I laughed. "He hates me, so whatever."

"He doesn't. He just didn't know you before. But now he thinks you're like super-goth-fighter girl. Isn't that hilarious?"

"That's so funny!" I laughed.

"I think he needs to get his meds adjusted."

"Well, I don't care much about him. Except—who does his eyebrows? Because they look so good."

"O-M-G, right? Ugh, I hate when the gays are better browed than me." We both sighed. We were the same, me and Sarah. We were one.

I started my Jack mood board when I got home. He was with Sarah in every single photo. I drew skulls, unibrows, and giant Xs over some of their smiling and kissing faces. Except for one where they looked exceptionally pretty. They were flawless, and it killed me. I stared at my face in the mirror for comparison. I needed a new one. Face, not mirror. Something that was Sarah approved.

Dr. M always says I need to vent my emotions or I'll have a toxic buildup. That probably explained going to town on Cassie. I didn't realize I was so upset with her. But it's good to get it out there, hash it out. Then you can make up and be friends. I didn't even hate her anymore.

I took a deep breath and let loose a wail. It started low, but then all I could hear was my own scream filling my apartment. I wanted the world to hear it. To hear me. I stopped when my throat hurt. My downstairs neighbor pounded on his ceiling. My doorman, Travis (he was my favorite), called to ask if I was being murdered.

"Every day, Travis."

I had all weekend to do some recon on Jack. His email password was HediSlimane1. Like it was hard to figure out. He clicked on a link in a spam email he shouldn't have. (I'll admit, if I got an email that said I was getting free La Prairie skin care, I'd click too.) One click is all it takes for any kind of malware to get on your computer. Keylogging software was the best. Jack was going to a showroom the next day at nine. Funny, so was I.

* * *

I dressed with care Monday morning. Head-to-toe the Row, giant sunglasses, nude lipstick for a washed-out look, and I carried a venti coffee from Starbucks. (I hated the taste of their coffee, but I did as the Olsens did. They were my spiritual masters.) I swanned into the showroom. I didn't say a word, just looked around and snapped photos with my phone. My goal? To get Jack on Team Anya.

"Anya?" I turned to eye my target, my (freshly tweezed) eyebrow lifting in mock surprise to see him.

"Oh, hey." Deadpan and slightly hoarse. Just like the Olsens.

"That's a look. Hungover?" He leaned in to stage-whisper the last part.

I laughed. "You know how it goes." I was cool, I wanted him to see that.

He nodded emphatically. "This place is such a disaster, right?"

I didn't know his game yet. I couldn't give anything away. So I continued our conversation about nothing. Chitchat was always a must at fashion appointments. I couldn't come right out and say, "Jack, ditch Sarah. Be my friend." *Wait, could I? No, be cool, Anya.*

"Oh, sweetie, this is so amazing!" he lied to the publicist who came by. Fucking Lauren-bots, always in the way. At least this one didn't have that stupid shard in her eye.

"Let's go get brekkie. I'm famished." And then Jack Archer grabbed my arm and marched me out the door into a waiting Uber. "Cafe Cluny on West Twelfth. Lemme put in the address for you." He rolled his eyes at me as if to say, *Can you believe this shit?*

I sat, frozen. He chattered the entire car ride. This was most definitely a trap.

"I'm just saying, I don't think Sarah gives you enough credit. I mean, look at your outfit. Just look. Total MK and Ashley realness."

He got it. He understood what I was going for. Was this what friendship was?

"We might need to Insta this. Oh, just up here is great." We jumped out, and he stopped me. "Okay, let's pose this, bitch."

If you've ever had a superchic gay man order you to pose, then you understand how awkward I felt. I tried to summon every bit of inspo I could. I dipped my chin slightly, angled my head, crossed my ankles, and clutched the coffee cup with everything I had. I had taken notes on Zhazha's pics. Jack murmured appreciative comments.

"Ahh, got it. So good. Come on, I'm starving."

Inside the restaurant, I peered around the dining room. Only the coolest boys and girls in fashion convened here. I hadn't made the cut before now.

"Isn't the avocado toast here the best?" Jack said.

"Totally."

"We should totally get some and split it."

"Sure," I said. He wanted carbs. That was a diet no-no. But we were having such small amounts.

He ordered us coffees, the toast, and oatmeal. I sat back and pursed my lips in my best imitation of Celia.

"I'm *so* glad I ran into you. You're, like, really blossoming, Anya."

"Am I? I'm just the same old me."

"In the Row. Whatever, *bish*. So, okay, can we discuss what's happening?"

I shrugged. Whatever could he mean?

"Like, Mulberry," he said. "Do you know who did it?"

"Who killed her, you mean?" I was thankful for my dark lenses. I didn't want to give anything away. Not to Jack. "Honestly, no. The police are still digging, but . . ."

"But, like . . . who else hated her, you know?"

"No one hated her. I mean, Sarah didn't love her. I think she was jealous of Mulberry, to be honest. Shit. Please don't tell her I said that."

Jack grinned at me. "I'd never."

He would.

"And Celia wasn't a fan of hers." There. See? I wasn't blaming Sarah.

"I bet Celia is bitchy enough to smash a shoe into someone's face. I mean, doesn't she throw shoes already?" He barked a laugh, even snorting. I was fascinated. He didn't seem to care that he sounded ugly. Was this the gift of being attractive?

"So, like, did you kill her?" he said suddenly.

I jerked my head back and blinked behind my sunglasses. "God, no! I liked Mulberry, even when she fell down in her shoes. How can you even think that?" I paused. "Did you kill Lisa?" Tit for fucking tat, right?

He gasped. "Hell no! Look, we both know Lisa was a see-you-next-Tuesday, but I would never. She was so fixated on you. It was awkward. Is the detective as hot as Sarah said?"

"Oh, so hot." I nodded enthusiastically. The topic shifted.

"What are you going as for Halloween?"

I shook my head. "I wanted to dress up, but it's two days away, and I totally left it all to the last minute. What about you?" Really, I hadn't done anything all weekend but obsess over Jack. And Sarah. And Jack with Sarah.

"I have three costumes." He counted off on his fingers. "Gaga in the meat dress, obvs. Wonder Woman—Gadot style, because so chic. And I think my next one will be Adam Rippon. He's my guiding light."

"You have the eyebrows for it!" He did.

Jack's face lit up. "You are so sweet. Did I tell you I *loved* your NYFW diary, bee-tee-dubs? It was so real. Oh, god, are you in love with Zhazha too?" He shot me questions faster than I could answer them. I was unnerved and charmed at the same time. Jack was dangerous that way. He could interrogate you, and you'd love every second of it. If he did team up with Hopper (and I wasn't convinced he hadn't), I was so screwed.

"She's incredible. You should hang out with her sometime. I think Sarah will learn to love her."

"After the arm incident? Though I saw the photos, and Zhazha wasn't close enough to push Sarah. You know who was?"

I shrugged.

"You." He smirked, popping a piece of toast in his mouth.

"*As if* I'd hurt Sarah. Besides, it made for more work on my end. She couldn't carry anything."

"Huh, that's true. That'd be like you shooting yourself in the foot!"

"Did I tell you I saw Cassie hanging all over Greg while Sarah was in Europe?"

"Shut the front door, you did not! Does Sarah know?"

"Well, sure, I told her. But didn't you say she put up cameras? I dunno, I'd check them if I were her."

He grabbed my hand. His eyes were wide. Then Jack grinned, avocado all over his teeth. Gross. Maybe Jack wasn't as handsome and charming as I thought.

"You know, I just don't get why Sarah doesn't like you."

Sarah didn't like me?

"You're pretty, and sure, you're a bit bigger, but you wear the clothes well. O-M-G, brillz idea! Let's all hang out. You, me, Sarah, and Zhazha."

What would avocado toast vomit look like? I was going to find out soon. Hanging with everyone, together, would never work. Friends colliding. All those mean things I'd said about Sarah to get Zhazha to like me. Fuck. This could only backfire.

"Just imagine the fireworks!" He slapped the table.

"Maybe. Listen, I need to get back to the office—"

"Okay, I got this brekkie. Next one is on you."

I nodded. *Smile, Anya. Smile at him.*

"This was fun," I managed to say. Then I ran out, hoping to get a cab.

Avocado toast vomit is green, in case you were still wondering.

* * *

Sarah gave me the silent treatment at the office. Had Jack told her what I said? Probably. But when I checked their texts, he had only compliments: *Anya is way more fun than you give her credit for. Can we all hang? Oh, PS, have you looked at your spy cams?*

It wasn't what he did or didn't say that upset Sarah so much; I think it was the photo of me he posted and the caption *Anya St. Clair is so damn chic. Channel the Olsens, boo.*

I grinned. I couldn't help it.

Sarah must have noticed. "Jack is a slut with compliments. It doesn't mean he likes you."

"I know, Sarah. But at least I don't look too ugly, right?" Silence. She hated me today. But if her friend was my friend, then we were totally friends. BFFs, almost. Just like I wanted.

My phone buzzed. *Hey, girrrrl. Loved hanging. Let's do it again. Don't kill anyone.* Was he joking? My stress level hit a ten. That's when Dr. M said it was overload time. Did Jack really think I was the killer? Could I not trust him?

I texted back, *LOL xx.*

Sarah remained distant with me for the next couple days. I pored through her Instagram for any details. She had gone as a geisha for Halloween, hugging Jack's Adam Rippon. I alternated between being horribly depressed and full of glee over how jealous she was that Jack liked me. But really, I wanted to hug her and tell her she was my one and only. Her hug the other day had left me wanting more. Jack continued to text us both separately. I wasn't in the trinity yet.

Since Cassie had all but disappeared, we had to hire a new intern. A pile of résumés were on my desk. I skimmed through, putting the best ones on top for Sarah to review.

"Ugh, no, not this one." She held up the offending paper as if it were a dirty diaper.

"She's perfect. Why not?" She was, too. A Parsons student who knew design and had interned already at several fashion houses. She even had her own blog.

"Her name! What is that? Like, what language? Does she even speak English?"

I stared open mouthed. The candidate's name was Maria.

But Sarah, and by extension *La Vie*, preferred their girls to be pale. It was the fashion way. If you had melanin and were hired, you were the token girl, shown off for diversity. But there was a hierarchy. And Celia would never let you forget it. She much preferred to hire blondes from "good families." But you could get around that, if you really wanted to. I had a strike against me for not being blonde and, okay, another for not having the right background, not that Celia would know. But the family part was the easiest to fake. Photoshop some pics so it looked like you were a WASPy dream come true. Pearls and teacups and ham in the background. A "good family" coming right up.

Sarah shrugged. "*La Vie* women need to uphold certain standards." Rich, white, thin standards. "And we used up our diversity card with—"

"Don't say it."

"—you." She smiled triumphantly. "Because you're, like, the crazy one. All that muttering to yourself you do. And your clumsiness has got to be a disability. And you have that ugly scar on your arm. So between you and Dalia, we're the most diverse staff anywhere." No mention of my background. I prayed she'd forgotten. Manifesting really did work.

"And there's all that weird info on you."

My heart thundered. Fuck.

"Weird info?"

"Yeah, that Lisa was gathering. With that guy she hired. She had a whole file on you. You, like, appeared out of thin air. She even said your name wasn't real." I can usually read Sarah's face like a gossip blog, but her smile didn't tell me anything. Did she think Lisa had been crazy obsessed? Or did she believe her?

"Ha, hilarious. It only feels that way because I was a big nobody before I got to *La Vie*." Shrug, smile, easy breezy. "I still don't get Lisa's big obsession with me."

"With you? She was obsessed with me. And anyone near me. That's how it works. Oh, and you still are a big nobody." She laughed at her own joke. "But did you know Lisa was looking for your birth certificate? She was convinced you were a fraud." A pause. "Are you, Anya? Or whatever your name is?" I could confess it all to her now. *Hail Sarah, full of grace, forgive me my sins.* But I didn't.

"Of course not. Do you need a copy of my paperwork to feel at ease? You sound so paranoid."

"Whatever, I asked Greg to run a background check on you all the same."

I clenched my jaw.

"He should have done it years ago. We'll know soon enough! I can't look at any more résumés. Let's just get Jack in here and let him handle finding an intern."

I put my head on my desk. What if Sarah did try to make Jack work for us? He said he didn't want to, but would he say no to Sarah? (As if.) He was too observant. He'd find out the truth if he were here in our office. I closed my eyes, willing myself to have some great epiphany, a moment of genius that would fix things. Distract everyone. It hit me while Sarah clack-clacked on her phone.

Zhazha.

I ran to Celia's office and knocked. I couldn't wait to share this idea.

"What is it, Anya?"

"Let's hire Zhazha. Or, rather, get her to write for us. A contributing editor. She has such a huge audience, and we need someone with her street-style cred." I bit my lip waiting for an answer.

"Huh." She tilted her head. "That's actually a good idea, Anya. Do you think she'd do it?"

"Oh, totally. She mentioned it when we had drinks last. I can set up a meeting for you."

"Do that. Check with Bronwen on my availability."

"Will do. Thanks, Celia."

Bronwen was under her desk. She said something about hiding from ghosts. Her crown was made with sage. Maybe she was seeing Mulberry too. She said she'd email me times Celia was free.

I crossed my fingers that Zhazha was into my idea. I had lied. We'd never discussed her coming on board. We were supposed to have drinks, but shit got in the way. I had Cassie to deal with; she had to Instagram her life. But if I had to choose between her and Jack, I'd pick her. There was no way Celia was hiring both of them. That would take the pressure off me a bit. I wouldn't be watched all day, every day. Unless I already was being watched.

I left early to check my apartment for bugs and spy cams. You can never be too careful.

12

"What is *she* doing here?" Sarah spat as Zhazha catwalked into the room. She was meeting us for drinks at Balthazar and was doing her best fashion walk and pose. Walk, pose, look around nonchalantly. Zhazha had it down. Jack had the brilliant idea of uniting the two over vodka shots. I was on pins and needles and Xanax.

"We invited her, dummy!" Jack stood and waved. "Over here!"

"What? Anya, is this your doing?"

I shook my head weakly. "Jack thought you two should get to know each other."

"I'm leaving." Sarah stood up in a huff.

"Stop being such a drama queen and sit your ass down," Jack said. And shockingly, Sarah did as Jack ordered. She listened to him. How did he do that? "Z! Darling! So glad you made it. You look *amazing*!"

Zhazha permitted a kiss on both cheeks before sitting in the empty seat next to me. "Anya, so good to see you again, my friend." *My friend.* It sent delicious chills down my spine. Her accent only made it more tantalizing.

"Zhazha, so good to see you." I felt stupid as the words stumbled out of my mouth. She looked like a princess. She even had a tiara on. Sarah glared more.

Drinks progressed at a glacial pace. The conversation mainly consisted of Jack fawning over Zhazha, me smiling like a moron, and Sarah adding mean snippets here and there. Our favorite blogger added in fun bons mots that made Jack erupt in laugher. It was delightful.

"You are a treasure," he said. "Isn't she, Sarah?"

"Whatever." Sarah crossed her arms.

"Ugh, just hash it out, you two. Zhazha, were you the one who pushed Sarah during Fashion Week?" His face was serious for a moment.

"No. I would never."

"See, Sarah? It wasn't her. Now let's move on."

Zhazha reached out suddenly, grabbing Sarah's hand. "I would not hurt anyone. And I want us to be friends, Sarah. Especially now."

"Now? Why now?" Sarah demanded as Zhazha and I exchanged looks.

"She doesn't know?"

I shrugged. "She does now. Um, Sarah, Zhazha's going to come work with us. As a contributing editor. She's your new coworker." Sarah's and Jack's faces made me want to giggle. "Ta-da!" I added. I held my hands up like a magician's assistant.

"You bitch," Sarah spat at me.

"Oh, well played, Anya," Jack added admiringly, holding his vodka up to salute me. "Guess you won't need me there after all!" He wasn't mad? "Cheers, Zhazha. Congrats, girl!" Everyone but Sarah downed their vodkas.

"Does Celia know? Greg?" she demanded.

"Who do you think approved it? Now you guys are going to have to work together, so—"

"Fuck all of you." Sarah grabbed her bag and left.

Jack sighed. "Let her go. Ugh. Okay, so this is so major. Seriously, *La Vie* just got so chic, you guys." Jack nodded his head as he said it.

Zhazha smiled. "It was all Anya's idea. She's been such a good friend." Friend. Again. She kept saying the word. It made me feel strange. Warm and tingly. I had a friend. A fabulous friend. And her name was Zhazha.

"Anya, I'm so impressed. I knew there was more to you than what Sarah said." Jack winked at me. See? Winking was cool. But what did Sarah say about me?

"Should we go get her?" I asked.

"Nah, let her throw her tantrum. She'll be fine. Let's order fries!" Jack could eat carbs and never gain an ounce. My envy levels were through the roof.

"Brillz," I said, grinning at Zhazha. My friend.

* * *

Lists, according to Dr. M, were supposed to be used like a cheat sheet to help me move forward when I got stuck or overwhelmed. He made me do them so I could focus. Realign, he said. He'd been reading too much hippie wellness shit. Next he'd have me playing with Sarah's crystals. But I dutifully made my list of everything I had to deal with. All the stresses in my life. He was right; it did help.

Realign. Change what you can, ignore the rest. The shard wasn't my problem anymore. Lauren would have to deal with it herself. Mulberry would eventually stop getting invites to things—I hoped. Diana was on #TeamAnya and helping me out in the comments section (thanks, girl!). Cassie was no longer an issue, but I did need a new intern. I was fetching our mail myself. How sad.

That left Zhazha, Jack, and Sarah. One of those intrusive thoughts crossed my mind. What if they became the new trinity? Without me? I bit my tongue while thinking of it. Not in a figurative way. Blood filled my mouth. Was I supposed to swallow it? No, wait, I'd read that was bad for you. My debate was interrupted by Sarah screaming in her cubicle.

I rolled my eyes, swallowed with a grimace, and drank more coffee. It tasted metallic.

She popped up to peer over my cubicle wall. "Oh my God. Oh my God!" Her shriek resonated through the office. It had to be serious. She was saying the actual words for once.

"Calm down. What, did you miss a party or something?"

Her face paled. "Cassie!" She gasped.

"Is she still not here? Have you called her apartment?"

"No, she's dead!"

"What do you mean she's dead?" I spit by accident, spraying bloody saliva at Sarah. She impatiently wiped her face, glaring at me. *Smile.* More coffee was needed.

"She's dead."

"You said that. Sarah, tell me what's going on."

"It's in the *Post.*" She waved the paper at me. There on the front page was Cassie's photo and the headline, *"Intern Slain!"*

"Holy shit." I grabbed the paper and read everything: her dreams to work in fashion, her life at *La Vie*, and the possibility of a copycat killer. I had a feeling Detective Hopper was going to want a date soon.

"Wow, Sarah, that's messed up."

"I know. Now we *really* need a new intern."

* * *

Celia made us meet and talk about Cassie, just so she'd have something to say to the press.

"Was she liked? Was she pretty? Who was her family?" she demanded. Sarah said nothing. I gave Celia the necessary info, and we went back to our desks. Before reaching them, Sarah suddenly grabbed my arm, shaking me. It was not a pleasant feeling—but she was touching me!

"Oh, God, Anya, do you think we're, like . . . next? I mean, Mulberry, Cassie, Lisa—what if someone's after us? What if it's someone in fashion like Jack said?"

"I don't know. I don't see how they're connected."

"Well, they were in fashion, with us, and now they're dead!"

"But they didn't die in the same way. The police haven't said anything about them being connected. They seemed to think an ex killed Lisa." They hadn't. It was all, "We can't comment on ongoing investigations."

"But what if they *are*?"

"I dunno. There are, like, two thousand active serial killers in the US right now. So it could be." Sarah's jaw dropped. I hadn't helped. "Well, um, I could call that detective and find out what's going on, if that will put you at ease."

I dialed Hopper's number while she watched. My heart skipped a beat when he got on the line. "Detective Hopper? It's Anya St. Clair."

"Hi, Anya. What can I do for you?"

"Is it true about Cassie Sachs? She was our intern." He was quiet for a moment. I didn't know how to interpret that.

"Yes, we identified her body."

Took them long enough. She'd been dead for almost two weeks. Benson and Stabler would never let corpses rot this long. Someone gets killed and *bam*, they're on the scene. Maybe Hopper wasn't as good a detective as I thought. I felt both relieved and disappointed. I wanted a smart boyfriend.

"Oh, God. That's awful! Is there anything we can do, or any information you need from us?"

"We'll be coming up to your office tomorrow to ask some questions."

"Okay. Um, well, we—that is, Sarah and I—were a little nervous. Two people from our office are dead. Are we being targeted, do you think? Should we be worried?"

"These are ongoing investigations, so we can't comment." Eye roll. "But it's not a bad idea to be extracautious until we catch the perpetrators." The perpetrators. Did he have any suspects? Was it me? Was I on his list?

He hung up quickly. No "Bye, Anya" or "Please don't die, Anya." He needed to work on his wooing just a bit.

* * *

We were on pins and needles waiting for Detective Hopper to arrive the next day. I'd changed my outfit three times that morning already. I needed a look that said innocent but hot.

"The police are here! They're here!" Sarah waved her hands around excitedly.

"Did someone steal jewelry again?" Evie asked, testing out some new nail polish.

"No, they're here to talk to us about Cassie," Sarah snapped. "What if they want to question all of us?" She began pacing.

"Calm down, Sarah. What do you have to worry about? I mean, unless you did something?" I asked pointedly.

"No! I didn't! They're just scary. The police are, I mean. God, why does this always happen to me?"

"As opposed to Cassie, the girl who's dead?"

Sarah turned to glare at me. "You know what I meant. Who could have wanted Cassie dead?"

"Probably some psycho. I read that her body was totally disfigured. Only a real crazy would do that," Dalia chimed in. All eyes shifted to her. "What? It was in the *Post*."

"This is why she should have gone to Europe with me. No one would kill us there," Sarah said unconvincingly.

"Unless the killer *also* went to Europe, in which case . . ." Dalia replied.

Sarah gasped, clutching my arm again. I should definitely hug her.

My phone rang. "Hello? Yes, okay, I'll be right there. Well, looks like it's my turn to talk to the police. Let's get this over with."

"Tell me how it goes?"

I looked at Sarah and then at my arm before shrugging her off.

"Of course."

* * *

Detective Hopper's team had taken over the larger conference room. Greg wanted to give the appearance that we were
doing everything in our power to help find the killer of our
dear, beloved intern. (#SavetheIntern was trending on Twitter, incidentally. I might have started the hashtag. Who knew
it would take off?) He'd even had a catered cart sent up with
sandwiches, salads, low-calorie yogurt, sparkling water, and,
of course, Veuve Clicquot. ("They may get thirsty!" he pro-
tested after I pointed out it probably wasn't a good idea to
offer champagne to the police.)

I knocked on the glass door. *Be calm. Be cool. You're only
upset about Cassie. And worried about your friends. That's all.
This has nothing to do with you.*

"Hi, Detective." Could he hear my heart pounding?

He didn't look up from the file he was reading. Two other
policemen sat in the room, eating from the cart. Officers,
both in uniform. They seemed to be enjoying the spread,
though the bubbles were untouched.

"Hi, Anya. Have a seat." He still hadn't glanced up at
me. I needed him to notice my outfit, a black DVF dress that
was superflattering. I needed to see him look at me. Then
I'd know how he felt about me. Whether he thought I was
a killer. "You know, it's strange that three women you know
have been murdered." He lifted his head as he said it, staring
at me. Daring me to admit I had done something.

Challenge not accepted, Detective.

I nodded, eyes wide. Only innocent people opened their
eyes this much. "I know, and it's terrifying. Any one of us
could be next. Is this a serial killer thing?" He raised his eyebrow at me. It wasn't overplucked, but it was still perfect.

"We can't comment on that. Can you think of anyone
who would want Cassie dead?"

"Well, she wasn't the best intern here. There were . . .
issues."

He didn't say anything. I knew that trick. Stay quiet so
the suspect babbles and incriminates herself. They tried that

when Meredith died. I hadn't said anything then. I was the only person I could really trust.

The silence was getting uncomfortable. My skin felt like it was crawling with bugs.

"She and Sarah were having problems," I finally said.

"Sarah Taft? Really? Because I heard *you* weren't happy with her."

Fuck me. Who was his source? Jack. He *was* spying on me! I opened my eyes wider. I felt like my eyeballs were going to pop right out.

"Well, no. But I don't want to speak ill of the dead. I mean, her parents don't need to hear bad things, do they?" I pasted on a concerned frown.

"No, but we need to know who had it in for her."

"Just because I didn't love her work doesn't mean I had it in for her. At worst, I wasn't going to give her a good recommendation. You know how it is. A young nobody gets a toe in fashion, and all of a sudden they think they're Kate Moss or something. Demanding this or that. It happens to the best of us."

"And that was happening with Cassie?"

I nodded, pacing each bob. Too quick and it was sketchy. Too slow and it seemed like I was making shit up.

"Yes. Instead of doing her assigned work, she wanted to get into the good graces of some editors here by becoming a personal assistant of sorts. You know, cleaning their apartments and getting their dry cleaning. Even walking dogs. We don't encourage that at *La Vie*. Internships are supposed to teach you, not make you a slave. It kind of goes against labor laws, and we've had our hands slapped for that sort of thing. We're already in the middle of a lawsuit, so we have to be really careful with our interns." I had practiced this for hours last night.

"I see. And Sarah Taft was one of her side gigs?"

"Um . . . yeah, except Cassie wasn't being paid." I grimaced. *Please don't make me say more, Detective. I can't point the finger at my BFF.* I wasn't betraying Sarah. I wasn't! I was merely refocusing the police's attention anywhere but on me. Self-preservation should be number one on anyone's must-have list. And if they did suspect Sarah, well, that'd be a damn hoot. Sarah Taft, socialite and murderer. Couldn't you just die?

"It's important we have all the facts. I know you don't want to stab anyone in the back, but this is about an innocent girl dying." He reached over to cover my hands as he said this. It was just for emphasis, right? What if he meant to tell me something more? Was he asking me out? Telling me he really liked me?

"Well, Sarah *was* yelling at Cassie the other day. You know what? It may have been the last day Cassie was here. That's probably a coincidence. But I did hear through the gossip mill that Cassie was getting really close to Greg Davies, our publisher." I paused. "He and Sarah have been dating." I leaned forward and dropped my voice. "Jack Archer said Sarah was filming Greg. Like spy cams."

"There are cameras?"

I shrugged. "I haven't seen them myself. But that's what he told me."

"What else can you tell me about Cassie and Sarah?"

I wanted to touch his forearm.

"Well, things had gone missing from Sarah's apartment. They reappeared in Cassie's desk. It was all so weird."

He nodded. He was with me.

"And is Ms. Taft here today?"

"Yes, she's waiting to speak with you. But please don't tell her I told you. She isn't someone you want to cross." If I had to choose between Sarah and Hopper, who would I choose? The question made my head hurt. It's like choosing between Valentino and Gucci. You just don't.

"I see. Anyone else have issues with Cassie?"

I shook my head but stopped suddenly. "Not that I can think of. Maybe Greg? I don't know what was going on with them personally. But there was something."

"You seem to know a lot about Cassie's life."

"I like to know who's working for us. I think she had some money issues too," I lied. "Like, her family was cutting her off? You kind of need to have money to intern here."

"And you? Are you wealthy? Your clothes look expensive." He had noticed! Finally.

"I have some family money."

He sat back and crossed his arms in front of him, watching me. It felt like forever.

"You know," he finally said, "we ran background checks on everyone at *La Vie* after Mulberry von Gratz's murder. Do you know what was on yours?"

Fuck.

This went beyond my Google hits. He had case files at his fingertips. *Don't panic. Shit. Do not panic.* What would Dr. M say to do right now? *Breathe. But don't look like you're breathing. Be normal. Just fucking be normal.*

"Um, no? I've never seen what's in one of those, to be honest." That was the God's honest truth. I'd never seen my police files. I'd run background check after background check—on me, on me as Mariana. But whatever the detective was reading was beyond my sleuthing skills. Shit, this was bad. What did it say about me?

"Nothing. Absolutely nothing. Like you don't exist. Why is that?" He wasn't smiling. His eyes were cold but curious. That hand touch earlier hadn't meant anything. It was a trick. It always was with them. "Unless you had a mafia run-in, something isn't right here. Or did you steal your identity?"

Tell him! Tell him your story. You'll be okay. No. If he knew, he'd suspect me for everything. Trust no one. I shook my head. "I can't say why it's blank. That's weird." *Keep going, be normal. You can do this.* Sarah's voice echoed in my ears: *You're such a freak, Anya!*

"Did you kill Cassie?"

There. The big moment. The police like to drop the accusation, hoping to catch you off guard. Hysteria rose in my throat. He could do it now. Arrest me. Take me away. Lock me up. I'd forever be known as the psycho who killed people at *La Vie*. No, that couldn't happen. I had to take control. That's what Dr. M would say. *Take control. Don't be a victim, Anya.*

"God, no!" I raised my voice. *Indignant, be indignant.* "Look, she was a pain in the ass, but killing her would be a bit extreme. She was only going to be here for a few more months. That's how these things work."

I felt dizzy. Was I going to pass out, right here in front of everyone? Would that make me look more guilty or less? I couldn't decide.

"I'm keeping an eye on you, Ms. St. Clair. Or whatever your name is. If you've committed a crime, like identity theft, we will find out."

He was majorly displeased with me. But did you hear what he said? They didn't have any proof of anything. Whew. I was dismissed. I walked out, waiting for one of the officers to tackle me. No one did. I was safe. Free. For now, at least. My heart was beating so hard, I thought it would pop out of my chest.

I had survived my first real interrogation by Detective Hopper. Sure, he'd asked me questions before. But that was different. I was maybe a witness before, someone with info. Now he was looking at me. Watching me. He probably had spies everywhere. But I had passed the test. Hopefully, he'd look into Sarah next. I didn't want to put her in the line of fire, but I needed to deflect attention from myself. She'd get it. It's what you did for friends. Shit, I should have expected the background check. What was I supposed to tell him? Dr. M would know. He knew how to handle everything.

"Well?" Sarah pounced on me before I even made it to my desk.

"Well what?"

"How did it go? What did they ask? Do they know who did it?"

"Sarah, take a fucking Xanax already." She pouted and looked genuinely crestfallen. It was like kicking a (mean and gorgeous) kitten. I sighed. "It was fine. They aren't sure who did it yet. But we talked about Cassie, what her duties were here, and her work with you—"

"With me?"

"Well, yeah. They knew she already worked with you, idolized you. So they wanted me to elaborate. Don't worry, it was nothing bad. She adored you."

"Oh, yeah, that makes sense." She nodded.

"*And* he said it was gruesome, the way she died," I said, embellishing a little. I loved having all of Sarah's attention on me. I could talk like this for hours.

"Shut up! You're serious?"

"Yeah, but New York is full of crazy people, and bad things happen all the time."

"Is this supposed to make me feel better?"

"I guess not. But the point is that it could have been a completely random attack."

"Anything else?"

"Well, the detective is the same hot one from before."

"Now that I can work with!"

It killed me when Sarah went to talk to Hopper. Would they talk about me? What would she tell him? Why hadn't I thought about this before? *Stupid, Anya. You're fucking up left and right. You're such a fucking loser.*

I didn't have a mantra for this moment. So instead, I sank deeper into my self-loathing. It's what kept me going.

By the time lunch rolled around, rumors were flying. The story was that Cassie had been murdered by an ex-boyfriend, and it had something to do with Mulberry. It was all over Twitter, and once again, #FashionVictim was trending. The wave of hysteria the office was riding was delicious and contagious. Celia was starting to break. She had security escort her to and from her office and check her car for any intruders.

Evie actually ate carbs in her zest for life. "If I need to out-run a maniac, paleo just won't do it!" She had a point, though her six-inch platform stilettos weren't going to be much use either. Which of course meant I had to do a utilitarian fash-ion story for the website: "Combat or Couture: Twenty-Five Pieces You Can Rock From Bootcamp to the Boardroom."

All these extra murder-related blog posts were adding to my workload. Granted, it upped my profile, but I was now writing three stories a *day* (including Sarah's), compared to everyone else's three a week.

Greg was ecstatic over my sudden newsiness. "It's so timely! We need more of these. Is there anything we can do about getting out of bondage or duct tape?"

"Um, I don't think so, but perhaps the beauty and fitness departments will know?"

"Genius idea, Anya." He high-fived me. I washed my hands.

* * *

The following Monday, Celia decided drastic steps had to be taken. She walked out of her office, looked at me and Sarah, and said, "Let's go." We followed her to a waiting car. Once we were in the back of the Escalade, Sarah asked where we were going.

"To see Henri." Henri was Celia's psychic. Everyone in fashion had a psychic, astrologer, tarot reader, or some sort of spiritual adviser that we took with us to dinner parties, a cov-eted accessory that told your future or the state of Mercury like a clock. I myself had two astrologers, a medium, and a spiritual fêng shui master. So far, I was winning the psychic race. (Though not one of them had foreseen death or murder in my life, so I wasn't sure what I was paying them for.)

Henri lived in Sutton Place in a second-floor walk-up. It was a nice building, but with his clients, he could no doubt afford better. He excelled in fashion matters, deftly help-ing Celia pick her wardrobe, her assistants, the new trends, and more. For this, she bought him a new Mercedes. She explained just how big a deal he was in the car ride over. "He helps me with everything."

"Henri!" she called, swooping into the door. "We need you." She sat on a chaise lounge, her coat taking up the entire length of the piece. Sarah perched on the edge while I stood near the door. Faded, floral wallpaper was covered up by photos of Henri's customers. Like at a dry cleaner's, there were framed and signed headshots everywhere. On nearly every flat surface were piles of crystals. Sarah's mouth dropped seeing them all. They were so shiny, so pretty. Just like her.

"Darling! I knew I'd see you today." Henri was wearing a silk kimono with feathered mules. His movements were so graceful that I wanted to ask him to teach me his ways.

"And this is Anya and Sarah," Celia said.

"A pleasure!" He held his hand out. His brown hair was delightfully bouncy. Was it a wig? Where did he shop?

"Lovely to meet you," I replied. *Don't read my mind. Don't read my mind.*

"So what can I do for you ladies today?"

"You must read them!"

"Celia, you know that's not how it works. Let's first have tea, shall we?" His voice was that melodious tone older gay men in New York have, though I wasn't positive he was gay, simply dramatic. Henri's divining process involved making us drink hot tea with heaps of sugar. "It makes us sweeter," he said with a wink. Somehow this would tell him which of us he could "read."

Watching Sarah ingest carbs was worth everything. We held our teacups (mismatched sets that only added to the charm). She grimaced, chugging back her cup. I slowly sipped mine, gritting against the overwhelming sweetness.

"Her. I'll read her." He pointed at me.

This could not end well.

"Give me your shoe."

"My what?"

"Your shoe."

"Don't be difficult, Anya. Just give it to him," Celia said wearily.

I took off one Stella McCartney mesh pump, hoping my foot didn't stink. He waved it around and then stuck his face deep inside the arch, inhaling as if his life depended on it. I glanced at Sarah. She sat transfixed.

"Okay, I know." He set my shoe on the table. "Give me your hands now." He held both hands and put one on his forehead, one on his chest. My skin prickled. I needed Purell. "You are up against many things now. You fight now—for love, maybe? But there is something else. Maybe you're fighting for . . . life? No. Yes. I see danger around you. Death. Someone wants to do you harm."

Celia gasped. "Oh my God, Anya. What if you're next?" she shrieked.

"You must fight if you want to win," Henri continued, ignoring her. "You can have what you want. Okay? You will win. Can I keep your shoe?" He let go of my hand and nodded to my pump.

"Uh, no, I think I need that."

"Pfft, fine." His voice shifted. Gone was the musicality, replaced by the cold and flat New York accent. "That's all I'm reading today. Next time, honey, bring me a pair of shoes. Size twelve. Celia, darling, ciao." She dropped a couple hundred dollars onto his table, and we filed out, completely silent. What had just happened?

None of us said a word in the car ride back. Sarah and Celia eyed me like I was about to fall to pieces. But had they missed the part where he said I'd win? I was wondering if Henri would have to die and if he knew it. Fucking psychics.

It didn't take long before Sarah told all of editorial that I was next on the kill list. It was ordained, she said. The stars wanted it. I just rolled my eyes whenever someone mentioned it.

"Anya, you really should take this seriously!" Sarah scolded me as she moved a lock of hair behind my ear. By becoming the next target, I was suddenly cool and chic. It was as if I was her perfect friend: short term and trending. I'd take it. BFFs—as long as forever was a few weeks, at least.

13

D r. M decided I needed an emergency session after the Henri show. He didn't like the "direction" things were going, whatever that meant. He was such a worry-wart. He even made a house call, which was, like, so rare for him. He only did it for me. I was his favorite patient.

He held up a photo of Sarah at some gala I wasn't invited to. She was looking off camera, her face angled so you saw more than a mere profile and wearing what I called her inflamed vagina outfit: a fuchsia dress with hood by Valentino.

"This is who you've been freaking out over?" He shook the photo. "This girl?"

"Woman," I corrected him. He always called us girls.

He took off his glasses and cleaned them. "Frankly, Anya, I'm concerned that you're heading into a level of obsession beyond my help." I opened my mouth to argue. He raised his hand. "This fashion world that you've wanted to be a part of, well, it's messing with your head. Don't you see that?"

I stared at him.

"Anya, I care for you like you were my own. But you need to stop. Stop thinking you're not good enough. That another pair of shoes will change your life. It won't. This Sarah isn't better than you. Enough is enough!"

"That's not fair!" I yelled. "You've always told me to bet-ter myself. Well, I am. I have goals—like you wanted. I want to be better and perfect just like Sarah! Look how far I've come. From reading the magazines to working for one. Come on, Dr. M. You have to see that I'm achieving what I always wanted." We stared at each other for what seemed like ten minutes. (Try thirty seconds.) Then he sighed. White flag waved.

"Fine. You're right. You've come far. But let's discuss what you need to improve. What is it you think would make you 'perfect'?"

Sometimes I swore he was blind from a head injury. What did I need to change to be the chicest girl in Fashionlandia? Everything. But he'd hate that answer.

"I have to lose weight, be more popular. Show Sarah that I'm amazing."

"But, Anya, you are—"

"By your standards, sure. But this is *fashion*, Dr. M. Everything is different, harder. You only get ahead if the powers that be like how you look!" I was whining. "I need to look like I belong in a photo shoot! That I'm cool and chill and don't care. I need to affect—what's that word? Not boredom . . ."

"Ennui?"

"Yes!" I jumped up and clapped. "I need to ennui the fuck out of my life. You're brilliant, Dr. M." If I acted blasé and like nothing affected me, I'd be cool. I'd be someone Sarah wanted around her.

He gave me an F for the week; my self-esteem issues were out of control.

* * *

I wore my Rick Owens jacket over leather pants and a silk blouse. My shoes were the yellow Pradas. It was a look. Sure, the police had just been to our offices last week, and yesterday a shoe-loving psychic said I may die, but parties still needed to be attended. I had changed my outfit in the women's room so I was fresh and perfect for my after-work event. I had no idea what this party was for, but I was going with Sarah and Jack. *Together.* My mood boards were working.

"Anya, don't you agree?" What was Sarah talking about?

"What?"

"Weren't you listening?"

"Not really." I shrugged. I was doing my best to be too cool. Above it.

"Ugh, you're the worst!" I didn't reply. "Jack, did you hear what Celia's psychic said?" He turned to face us. "Anya is going to die next."

"Ha!" he said. "Didn't think suicide was your thing."

I narrowed my eyes. "Better watch out, Jacky. You could end up on my list." We both snorted at that. Murder, it was hilarious. How edgy of us.

"Okay, but just make sure I look good in the autopsy photos. My left is the better side."

"Obvi. I'll talk to the coroner. We've gotten *très* close."

"Can you two stop it?" Sarah threw her hands up in the air. "You're both so ridiculous. People are dead. People we know. Knew. This is so not funny."

Jack and I exchanged guilty glances.

"You're right, boo," Jack said. "Gallows humor. It's easier to joke about it than to worry who may be next." He put his arm around her. I should have been the one comforting her.

"If we die, we die, Sarah. Stop acting like you care." I caught a glimpse of her hurt face before turning to scan the crowd. Had I gone too far?

"Meow. You are such a bitch, Anya. I approve!"

"Thanks, Jack. That tops the list of my accomplishments. Your approval." I rolled my eyes to show how much it didn't mean to me. Ennui it.

"God, what crawled up your twat and died?" Sarah pushed me out of her way to go to the bar. There were waiters with trays at this event, but apparently she needed her time away from us.

"She's so sensitive lately." Jack frowned. "Do you think she's taking the Cassie thing personally?"

"Only because she needs a new servant."

He laughed. "How am I only just now discovering you? Seriously, Sarah never told me you were like this. I wonder if she's jealous of you."

Jealous? Of me? My head started spinning. Maybe I'd keep Jack. If only to get more dirt on my true BFF.

"Please. She's got everything. What is she jealous of? My extra cushioning?" Self-deprecation was a way of hiding pain. But it also made you cool. (But being ugly *and* lame was not actually cool.)

"Um, she's not as smart as you. That really bugs her. She gets way jealous. Hello, the cameras? Wait, does she know that Cassie was, you know . . ."

"Fucking Greg? She didn't believe me. But who knows?" I was trying to be nonchalant, totally easy breezy. Sarah was jealous of me. Me! "Besides, being smart isn't that chic. Fashion girls aren't smart." We giggled. "Why are you telling me this, anyways? Aren't you her friend?"

"You're *both* my friends. Anyways, I think she's scared one of us might die next."

"Oh." One of us, meaning me. Thanks, Henri. That psychic fraud had worked wonders. "Maybe we should go to her and—"

"Group hug!" That wasn't what I was thinking, but the idea made me giddy. A hug? The three of us? Oh-em-gee. We walked over to Sarah, who was a whole twenty feet away. She was talking to some girls we didn't know. They stepped back as they saw us approach.

"*Babe*, we *love* you!" Jack cooed, motioning with his head for me to join in.

"Yeah, we do. Sorry for being so facetious back there." There. Not too much. Jack grabbed my arm, and together we enveloped Sarah in the only threesome I'd ever had. To my surprise, she hugged back.

"Thanks, guys. I'm just, like, really freaked out. Cassie worked for us. We should be scared."

"We are, and we get it. The humor is just a way to deal. Right, Anya?"

"Um, right." We linked arms with Sarah in the middle. I felt like I was going to faint.

"But the three of us are in this together. The fucking musketeers! The three amigos!" Jack shouted the last part. Eyes swiveled to us. The party was watching us, watching me link arms with Sarah Taft. This had just become the best night in history.

"Yeah, totally." I felt stupid even speaking. "Anyone who wants to get to you will have to go through me first." Sarah smiled at us both.

"You guys are the best." And we hugged once more. "Oh, hey, Anya? Babe, will you get my dry cleaning tomorrow? I just can't."

It was so perfect, I wanted to throw up.

* * *

My ennui mood board had spreads of models looking balefully at the camera, old Calvin Klein ads with Kate Moss (vintage!), and even a cutout from *The Gashlycrumb Tinies*. I was going to be so perfectly nonchalant that everyone would adore me. I wanted to draw glitter hearts everywhere, but that was the opposite of what I needed. Instead, I put my own photo up, a shot of me smiling. Then I crossed out my face in black sharpie.

Jack's board got an update too. God, there was always so much work to do. Update this, kill so-and-so. I wish people understood how hard we worked in fashion—all to make it look effortless, easy.

Jack was my friend now. Or was he? Did I have friends besides Sarah? I should have asked Dr. M about it. It was all so confusing. I made a new pro/con list, all things Jack:

Pros: He was bringing me and Sarah together. He liked my outfits. He told me secrets. He defended me against Lisa.

Cons: He could take it all away any moment. Whenever he wanted. If I didn't keep entertaining him, it would be over. I'd have to keep him happy forever. What if I couldn't do it?

"I'm not a fucking dancing monkey!" I shouted. I was alone. The only response was my downstairs neighbor pounding on the ceiling. He sucked. I wished he'd fall out of his window or something.

Someone was knocking loudly on my door. Was it Detective Hopper? Was this it? Had I gone one too far? I looked through the peephole. An irate man stood before me. My downstairs neighbor.

"Yes?" I opened the door slowly.

"Keep it the fuck down, lady!"

"Excuse me? I don't know what you're talking about. I'm working, in silence."

"I hear you yelling constantly. You're fucking nuts!" He moved forward, and I slammed the door shut. He screamed. I'd gotten his finger. Shit. He was going to make trouble. I had to do something. I called Travis, the doorman.

"Hi, there, it's Anya in 29D. Frank from 28D's pounding on my door and trying to get into my apartment. What should I do? Can you get the police here?" I sniffed.

Frank left after a few minutes, with the encouragement of Travis, who knocked lightly on my door. "Miss St. Clair, everything should be okay. I'm sorry about the disturbance. He's been told to leave you alone from now on."

I nodded. "I mean, if I'm being at all loud, come and talk to me. But he was screaming and trying to get in here. Is he on drugs? He is, right?"

Travis shrugged. "Couldn't say." He could. The doormen knew everything about our lives. "But he has had some issues. If he bothers you again, please let me know." I thanked him, handing off a fifty-dollar bill. He deserved a good tip. His eyes lit up. "I think his girlfriend left him or something. It's why he's always home and in such a bad mood."

I nodded. "Of course. That makes sense. Poor guy. He needs some cheering up."

"And a life." Travis grinned as he said it.

Travis was right. Frank did need a life. Why did I attract these bitter weirdos? First Diana, now Frank. I didn't make a mood board for him. There was no point. I didn't want to get that involved. But I did want him out of my life. Plus, he gave me something to ask Sarah about the next morning. People love being asked their opinions. It makes them think you love them (I did). She'd know just what to do about Frank.

"Can you have him evicted?"

"I wish. I think he's just bummed over a breakup. Or so my doorman said."

"O-M-G, you know what you should do? Pretend to be a secret admirer. Send him chocolates or something. It totally works."

I nodded. Sarah had the best ideas.

* * *

"More champagne," Zhazha said to the woman next to her, who scrambled to grab a glass from the trays wandering the room. "I love champagne," Zhazha declared to applause around her. The Lauren-bot by her side smiled cheerfully.

"Everyone does, babe." Jack laughed. We were all at a dinner for some new product launch. An intimate dinner, meaning twenty people. Three of those people were us. Sarah wasn't here. She was invited, of course. But she couldn't make it. She was resting, she said, after last night's "emo party." (Her words.)

Jack worked the room like a magician. He was even better at schmoozing than Sarah. He remembered names, and when he didn't, he called everyone *babe* or *boo*. It worked. The room loved him.

We didn't know anyone else at the dinner. There was the girl whose name I could never remember. It was floral, and she based her whole look on a different plant each month. This month's theme was cherry blossoms, and she wore cotton-candy pink. Next to Flower Power was the drawing guy. His shtick was to scribble a few lines and call them fashion illustrations, even though his images looked like squiggly smudges, fashion Rorschach tests. I called him Simon, after the kid's show. You know the one. It was always on reruns. He did all those chalk drawings. Like body outlines for tots. At the other end of the room, Jack was talking with two girls. One was Mulberry. I would have to ask him how he could stand the shoe in her face. So distracting.

Zhazha was next to me, talking to a Lauren-bot and Flower Power.

"Oh, Anya! You're little Z's friend?" the bot cooed. She'd set her sights on me, and now I was doomed. This was my third event where Zhazha had appeared, and every time, I was her friend. Not Anya St. Clair, *La Vie* editor. But Zhazha's pal.

I bared my teeth at her. "Is that angora?"

She nodded.

"Did you know that when they get the fur from the bunnies, you can hear them scream?"

She gave me a confused look, not sure if she should keep smiling.

"It's amazing, really, the screams. They almost sound human. All so you can wear a fluffy pink sweater. Cute."

I caught Jack's maniacal grin. He loved it. He loved me. The Lauren-bot frowned, confusion flashing across her face. Her programming must have been on the fritz.

"What is this dinner for?" Zhazha asked me, loud enough to make the Lauren-bot flinch.

"Fuck if I know. I hope the food's good at least. Is there anyone here worth talking to?"

"No." She shrugged. "But they want to talk to us."

"Correction, they want to talk to *you*." I wasn't jealous. I swear. If they ignored me, I wouldn't have to make conversation. Besides, I was used to it.

"Anya, don't hog all of Zhazha's attention. You get her all the time. Time to share!" the Lauren-bot admonished.

"What's this dinner for?" I asked her.

"It's for the launch of a new capsule collection of vitamins," she said proudly.

"A capsule collection of vitamins? Seriously?"

"Yes, they're great. And we had designers create the outer casings. So very chic."

"Is the formula at all different or special? Will it make you live longer or fight disease or anything?"

"No, we can't make those claims. But they're really pretty!" She beamed, as if waiting for applause. A waiter walked around with a tray of pills, and I had to agree they were pretty. One was Rothko inspired, another went for Jackson Pollock. There was a square-shaped vitamin that I imagined was hard to swallow.

"That one's very editorial," the Lauren-bot said, nodding enthusiastically, the go-to phrase for when something was heinously ugly but a good stylist could fit it into a magazine shoot. It'd never sell.

"Well, anyways, you all should try the vitamins! And have more drinks," she chirped. More alcohol came out. We were toasting health supplements by guzzling booze, eating hors d'oeuvres of pâté and caviar, and then having a heavy dinner.

"Give me, I'll try it." Zhazha reached out her hand, each finger covered in at least two heavily bejeweled rings. She made it work. Zhazha puckered her lacquered red lips and opened up to swallow the skull vitamin. Dry, no water needed. "Now I'm healthy."

I imagined she was beaming. I couldn't tell for sure because Zhazha was wearing sunglasses despite being indoors and it being evening.

"Oh, that was chic," Jack noted. "Dry swallowing. *Girl.*" I wasn't sure what he meant, but I nodded along. *Go with it, Anya. Pretend you belong.*

"Anya, what are you working on lately?" he said. "Sarah said you were buying chocolates for someone . . ." They had been talking about me again.

"What? Oh, no. She suggested I do something like that for a nasty neighbor I have. He's such a pain in my ass. But really, he doesn't deserve chocolates."

"Oh." Jack made a face. "That's not nearly as exciting. I was hoping you had a hot affair we could discuss."

I was boring. I bored Jack.

"I wish. You?"

"Ugh, like Death Valley over here. Z? What about you? Who are you dating?"

She grinned at us both. "It's a secret."

"O-M-G, dish, now!" Jack grabbed our hands in excitement.

"I can't. It's a secret," she repeated. "We will work together soon." They were going to work together? But that meant . . .

"O-M-G." I was horrified. "Tell me you're not."

"What? What did I miss?" Jack asked. He glanced at each of us.

"You're seeing Greg?" I whispered it so only the three of us could hear me.

Zhazha grinned again and flashed a thumbs-up at me.

"Holy shit." Jack dropped our hands. "Isn't he with Sarah?"

"*Was* with Sarah," Zhazha corrected.

"Goddammit. That's just . . ." I glanced at Jack. He nodded. He got me. It was gross. Wrong. Mean. "I hope Sarah knows."

"She will now." Jack texted her.

I closed my eyes. This was going to be bad. Sarah would be devastated. It was bad enough Greg slept with every intern he could. But Zhazha? She was Sarah's sworn enemy. Somehow it would all be my fault. I would be to blame, and Sarah would hate me for the rest of her life. Or this week. Her newfound devotion to me courtesy of Henri would be over. Dead and buried.

We were saved by a literal bell.

"Okay, everyone, let's all find our seats!" The Lauren-bot called out, a silver bell in her hands.

We walked into the dining room, where a gorgeous table had been laid out. I had to give them credit—the space and venue were fabulous. It was in a not-yet-opened hotel near the far west side of Midtown. No one came here; it was impossible to find. And yet, stunning. The table was laid out in all white with crystal. I guess the vitamin biz was lucrative.

We all found our seats. Jack plunked down next to me, ignoring the seat assignment. Zhazha was farther down the table.

"What the fuck do we do about Zhazha and Greg?" he asked quietly.

"Nothing we can do. Did you text Sarah?" He nodded. "So I guess we wait and see what she wants." I felt nauseous. There was going to be drama, and we were going to be pulled right in the middle of it. If Sarah's personal life was going to implode, I preferred to be out of the line of fire.

"Anya, tell them about the intern," Zhazha demanded from her perch four seats away.

Oh, God, make this evening end. Please, just kill us all. I want it to be over.

"What?"

"The intern, who died."

"Zhazha, that's not appropriate."

"Wait, your intern was the one who was butchered?" Simon asked, his face red with excitement.

"Well, it's an open investigation, and we really aren't allowed to talk about it."

"But, like, do they know who did it? You can tell us!" Flower Power gave it her best shot.

"No, not—"

"I heard it was Sarah Taft," she continued. "Didn't she lock the intern in her apartment to work like a slave? Can you imagine? So bananas!"

Jack gasped in horror. "Take her name out of your mouth! Sarah is the sweetest person ever," Jack hissed.

I nodded along. *No laughing, Anya. Be serious.* Sarah, a murderer? It was hilarious, right? It was one thing to point the police in her direction (hello, self-preservation) and another for the industry to think she was a total psycho. I wanted to clap my hands. Bloody Sarah, fashion killer. God, it sounded so good. Sarah could make anything sound good.

"Well, I mean, I heard she killed Mulberry von Gratz too," Simon said.

Now everyone gasped.

"And Lisa. Wasn't she your other bestie, Jack?" Flower-Power said.

Jack blanched. "You have no idea what you're talking about," he said stiffly. "Anya, maybe we should leave. This place blows."

The Lauren-bot made a mewling noise. "No, please stay. Guys, we should talk about more appropriate things," she said. The crowd seemed to listen.

Jack grabbed my hand under the table and squeezed it. Hard. What did that mean?

As we were tucking into dessert (kale sorbet), there was a commotion at the door. We all glanced up, ready to be entertained by some new bit of gossip or outlandish behavior. Anything could happen tonight. It was a full moon.

Sarah Taft stormed into the room.

Flower Power nearly fainted at the sight of her.

"Anya! There you are!" Sarah swooped in, kissing me on the cheek. I heard a few gasps behind me as the table grew silent. "Jacky!" She sat in his lap, ignoring everyone around us.

"Sarah, what's up? Are you okay?" he whispered in her ear.

"Fabulous. I got your texts, honey. I was celebrating being single. It turns out my boyfriend was dating some Russian hooker. Oh, hi, Zhazha." She waved.

You could hear a knife drop.

"Anyways, I figured I'd come get you two so we could blow this joint."

"Yeah, um, we should go." Jack hopped up carefully, holding Sarah so she wouldn't fall.

"Good. I'm worried you might D-Y-E," she said to me.

"Dye? My hair?"

"No! Die! Like Henri said!"

"Wait, you came here drunk because you thought I might die?" Was she actually worried about me?

"Yes! Is that so hard to believe? Anya, we're like sisters. That, and you shouldn't hang out with hookers."

We were like sisters. Dr. M would be thrilled to hear this news.

"Who's Henri?" Simon asked in a whisper.

"Henri is almost the most *amazing* psychic!" Sarah said, slamming her hand on the table. "And do you know what he said?" The table shook their heads in unison. "He said Anya was the next to die."

And cue the gasps.

I groaned. "It's not that dramatic. Come on. He said I just had some battles to fight, that's all. And then he tried to steal my shoe. So pardon me if I don't believe him."

"Whatever, Anya. I'm here to escort you home."

"But . . ." Flower Girl piped up. She was still splayed in her chair, blinking with confusion.

"*Yes?*" Sarah swiveled to her.

"How do we know Anya's safe with you?"

The room fell silent. Sarah's eyes narrowed before she picked up my half-empty glass of champagne and tossed it back.

"Are you fucking serious? Who even are you? Like why are you even talking to me? Anya, Jack, let's go."

"No, Anya, I take you home," Zhazha offered.

"Listen, you commie bitch, Anya's my friend. If anyone's going to watch her back, it's me." For a moment, Sarah looked like a banshee. A gorgeous, blonde shrieker, ready to bring ruin to her foes. But really, she needed to comb her hair and redo her makeup.

Jack shrugged. We got our coats and left. I mouthed *Sorry* to everyone, but inwardly, I was jumping for joy. What the hell had just happened? Was I dreaming? Was this a hallucination?

We climbed into a waiting taxi outside.

"Sarah, are you okay?" I asked.

"No, I'm not okay! Greg and I broke up because of your friend! *And* he was sleeping with Cassie. Why didn't you tell me, Anya?" I opened my mouth, but nothing came out. How many times did I warn her? "And then, there you two were. With Zhazha! What kind of friends are you?"

"She was invited to the dinner. I had nothing to do with it."

"It's going to be fine, Sarah. Let's all go home." Jack rubbed her back.

"I know. We can make voodoo dolls of Greg. That would be fun, right?" I offered.

Sarah sniffed, wiping her nose. "I think I want to be alone after all." She got out of the car at the next light. "Maybe tomorrow you two will start acting like my friends. Oh, and Anya, my dry cleaning isn't going to pick itself up."

We said nothing en route to Jack's apartment. He hugged me as he got out.

"You did great, Anya. Seriously. You're a great friend to her. To us." Was this what having friends was like?

* * *

There was an ambulance and fire truck outside my apartment. Part of First Avenue was blocked. Was everything on fire? My life was crumbling into a pile of ashes. I got out of the cab and walked over to a crowd of onlookers.

"What happened?"

"Someone's dead," one person said. "Overdose maybe." She shrugged. She was clearly enjoying the spectacle but didn't care too much about the details.

I moved toward the building.

"Hold it, miss." An officer held his arm out to stop me.

"I live there. Can we go in, or is there danger?"

"Which floor?"

"Twenty-nine."

He radioed in and then waved me through. Only one elevator was working. On the way up, it stopped on twenty-eight, and when the doors opened, I saw a gurney with a sheet-covered body. I pushed the "Door Close" button and went to my floor. I needed to decompress. The night was too much. I was certain the moon had done all this. An eclipse or something was bringing the crazy out. Henri should have warned us.

Whenever I felt deeply unsettled, I showered. It was the only way to stay sane. Wash away everything. Don't worry about anyone else. Wash my makeup off, scrub myself clean, and smother my skin in rejuvenating serums. And then I could begin again. Refreshed. Renewed.

Tomorrow would be a new day. I didn't ask what horror it would bring. But I knew something bad was going to happen. I said a prayer to the fashion gods and went to sleep.

14

woke up in the best mood imaginable. Sarah Taft was worried about me! She'd come to get me (and Jack) last night. I had done it. I had manifested and aspired my way to this. To her. Now I'd be part of Sarah's royal court.

I jumped out of bed and kissed my Sarah mood board. These things totally worked. I should do a YouTube how-to on them. They were like serious voodoo or something. Now what to wear as the new bestie of Sarah Taft? I wondered if she wanted matching necklaces. I'd always wanted one of those and found some supercool crystal skull ones that would be amazing to wear. I'd buy them just in case.

I opted to wear my work uniform: leather leggings, a cashmere sweater (the Row), and Isabel Marant motorcycle boots. All black, all the time. I had to pick up Sarah's dry cleaning and three pairs of shoes from the Leather Spa. It's what besties did. By the time I got to work, Sarah was already at her desk, sucking down an iced latte. It was always a latte (iced skinny vanilla latte), never a coffee.

"Hey, Sarah."

Silence.

"How are you feeling today?"

Crickets.

"I have your shoes and clothes." I felt stupid carrying everything. She pointed to a chair, and I dropped everything in a heap.

The buzzing in my ears started up. It was like a saw going off inside my head. If I gave in to it, it'd take over. It would be all I could hear and be. The sound screamed to me that I had failed. I was a failure. I couldn't even make Sarah love me. I wasn't worthy of her. I sat at my desk, closed my eyes, and counted to ten. A coping mechanism courtesy of Dr. M. It didn't work completely, but now the roar was a dull noise. I popped a barbiturate just in case. You can never be too careful. Or medicated.

* * *

Celia made two big announcements during our weekly meeting: First, Zhazha was coming aboard. And second, we had to do some major outreach to Cassie's family and put on a good public face. She looked at me while she said that last part. I groaned inwardly.

"But where will Zhazha sit?" Sarah asked.

"Wherever she wants," Celia snapped. "Now, Anya, I want you to spearhead the Cassie situation. Reach out to her family, see if there's anything we can do. Send flowers for her funeral, that sort of thing."

I made a face.

"Ugh, what?" Celia demanded.

"It's just a bit late for all that, don't you think? The funeral was last week—"

"It was? Why didn't anyone tell me? Mulb—Bronwen! Did you know?"

Bronwen nodded, her face so dewy, it looked like she'd just splashed water on it. "Yes, but it was in California. I sent flowers already." She was wearing an orchid in her hair.

"Oh. Good thinking." Celia nodded at her assistant. "Anya, can you call your police buddy and see if they need anything from us?"

"Sure thing." Detective Hopper was not my buddy. He made that clear on Monday. He was watching me, waiting for me to slip up. Well, screw that. I'd go on the offense.

Celia looked me up and down and sucked her breath in. "It pains me to say this because we've had a difficult few weeks, but you really need to get back on your diet. I'm going to have you go see my doctor. He's a wonder. He can get you anything you need to help you lose weight."

"Um, I don't think that's necessary, Celi—"

"Nonsense. We can't have you talking to the press looking like that."

"I'd rather not—"

"Just do it, Anya, or heads will fucking roll, okay?"

And with that, I was dismissed. *Do it or die.* She and Greg didn't manage us so much as threaten us.

"I can't believe that!" Sarah said as we walked to our cubicles.

She was speaking to me! Relief melted through me.

"I know, me dealing with the Cassie sitch?"

"No, like, W-T-F, Zhazha gets to sit wherever she wants? And she's fucking Greg. Just gross." She shuddered.

"Didn't you used to fuck him too?"

"Anya, don't be so disgusting." Had I imagined her and Greg?

"Anyway, it was really sweet of you to come get me last night." I had to show her I cared.

She smiled. It was cold, cruel. Only Sarah could make a smile terrifying and thrilling. I should have taken the warning. But I didn't. I wanted to ignore what was about to happen. I had aspired. This should have been my moment.

"I came to get *Jack.* You were just . . . extra. I wish you'd stop being so desperate. You work for me; we're not friends. Jack and I laugh about it, you know. How pathetic you are. God, look at you. Leather leggings? That's so two years ago." She snorted.

"I thought—"

"You thought what? That we were friends?" She threw her head back and laughed. "Please. I could never be your friend. You're my *employee*. I was being nice so you'd do things for me. You're so not one of us. All those lies you told. How long did you think we'd let you be here?" She gestured to her desk. She meant *La Vie*. They were *letting* me work here. "God, Lisa was so right about you. What, did you think we'd let that go?" She cackled. "That private eye is still working for us. I thought you knew?" She grinned triumphantly. "And if you don't do everything I want, I'm going to tell the world."

Her face had that maniacal glee that comes from jumping headfirst into your anger pool. I'd seen it before, done it myself. She had become one with her fury, and no one would survive. Too bad I was her target. And she'd hit the mark. Bull's-fucking-eye.

I picked up a stray, unopened box from Sarah's desk (yet another package for her) and brought it down onto her head as hard as I could. Her glorious mane muffled the noise, but you could hear it. The thud. She jerked forward. I dropped the box and grabbed her hair. God it was pretty. And then I shoved her face first into her computer monitor. Over and over again, until Sarah shut up.

I blinked. She was sitting there grinning at me still. Her mouth looked grotesque for once. There was no blood, no smashed computer. None of it was real.

"Lol, what a waste of time and money," I said finally. How did my voice sound so normal? I calmly went to my desk.

I'd learned a lot in my years away at school. But the most important lesson was to never, ever let anyone see how much they hurt you. They're not allowed to win. Only you are.

Do I call Dr. M? I know what he'd say. That sometimes, you hurt the ones you love. That you lash out and make them miserable because you feel sad. I nodded. It made sense. Dr. M was a genius that way. Numbness set in. Maybe this was a heart attack after all. Aren't you supposed to go numb? Reject.

You're a reject. No one loves you. Sarah and Jack are together forever, and you're all alone. You're not one of them. They know who you are, Mariana.

I wouldn't cry. Not at work. Not with Sarah there. I'd do it after I finished running more errands for her. I had to do whatever she wanted. She held true to her word (for once) and ordered me to do every menial task she could think up. She even made me get her lunch.

"I said sashimi, not sushi. Go back." She threw her miso soup at me. It landed all over my sweater. Now I'd have to dry-clean it. Goddammit. Mulberry shook her head, pity in her eyes. I needed Dr. M before I had a full meltdown.

I called him as I got lunch number two for Sarah. He was going to be so displeased with me.

"Anya," he said, "you need to stop putting so much effort into people who aren't worth it. Sarah's a taker. You need someone who will give you love. You can't make anyone love you, you know."

"I know, Dr. M. But I thought this time, just this once, it would work out. We were supposed to be *destined*. What do I do now?"

"Is it possible she feels betrayed by you?"

By me? I scoffed. I got her dry cleaning. I wrote her stories. I cut my hair the way she wanted me to. If anyone was betrayed, it was me.

"By bringing Zhazha to work with you," he added. He knew I needed his clarity.

"But I didn't know she'd steal Greg. Because, ew. It's not my fault!"

"Be that as it may, she's hurt and acting out. You need to grieve for the friend you thought you had. A true friend wouldn't care if you fudged your background. She wouldn't threaten you with it. She'd understand your reasons for it. The way I see it, you have two options: Move on . . ." He laughed at this. He knew me. I would never move on. "Or show Sarah what she's done. Make her see how much she hurt you. Make her *feel* it."

I smiled. He was right. Dr. M was always right.

"And no more giving in to her threats. She'll stop, you'll see."

"You're so good to me. What would I do without you?"

"Well, my dear, you'll never have to find out."

* * *

Friendship breakups are so much harder than romantic ones. Friends are supposed to be there for you forever. That's what all the books and movies said. In reality, they betray you. They hurt you. They blackmail you. Everyone is out for herself. Your friends will all knife you in the back eventually.

Sarah was not my friend. I saw this now. Clarity was a painful gift. Sarah had been pretending to be my friend. She only liked me when I had an expiration date. She wanted me to do things for her, run errands. It was a fake office friendship, the worst kind. Inane chatter and coffee breaks and nothing else. How could I have been so stupid? How could I think she cared about me at all? She was just using me. (I could hear Dr. M going on about how we used each other. I chose to ignore him.) I felt like my world was splintering apart. Sarah and I had been together since we were fifteen. That was over a decade of me wishing upon her photos, crossing my fingers, and sending a nightly prayer to bring us together. And it was gone. All of it. She didn't love me. My manifesting didn't work. I had failed.

Meredith tried this same shit, you know. She told all my secrets to another group of girls at school. And then when I told her we were through, *poof*! Up in flames. She was such a fucking drama queen.

Dr. M was convinced I picked the same girl over and over to live out some karmic lesson. Whatever. I just liked pretty girls who liked me. There was nothing wrong with that. Not one thing. Pretty girls—and by extension, their friends—had easier, better lives. It was a scientific fact. We're born like this, born wanting to be near attractive people. There are studies with babies that prove it.

I had to focus. I had to be better than her if I wanted to win. (It was always about winning.) I had to make Sarah feel it, feel what she had done to me. She'd be crawling on her knees by the time I was done with her. I let out a harsh laugh. It was me or nothing, and Sarah had made her choice. She was going to become nothing. Dr. M called this a major breakthrough.

I dropped Sarah's sashimi on her desk (I didn't even get a thank you). And then I set my Sarah setting to ignore.

"Anya, I need a green juice!"

Crickets. *I can't hear you, Sarah.*

"Anya! Go get me some."

My body pulsed. Part of me wanted to give in, to make her happy. But I couldn't. I had to bury this friendship.

"If you don't do what I want, I'll—"

"What, Sarah? Tell people you think I'm a phony? Do it. I dare you. See if anyone cares. You couldn't even keep Greg interested in you. No one likes you," I hissed it at her. It was a lie. A bluff. Of course people cared about Sarah. About her every decree. But the biggest fear the powerful have is that they'll end up just like you and me.

She stared at me. And then silence. She stopped speaking to me after that. We had broken up.

Once she left for a showroom appointment, I hid a present in her drawer: Cassie's ten fingernails, painted in Sarah's favorite colors. Like Dr. M said, I had to make her feel this.

* * *

Flowers sent and a memorial scholarship fund set up, Cassie's family was crossed off my list. God, I loved that feeling. See, Cassie? To-do lists are wonderful tools. You should have used yours.

Up next, I called Detective Hopper. I wondered when, if ever, I'd call him by his first name. "*Stephen. Stephen. Stephen.*" Nope. It sounded weird. It was Detective Hopper, Detective, or Hopper. Or nothing. No one called Elliot Stabler by his first name. Except for Benson, but hello? She'd earned that right.

"Hi, Detective? It's Anya St. Clair."

"Hi, Anya. How are you?"

"Good, good. The magazine asked me to reach out about Cassie Sachs and see if there's anything we can do to help. Any details I can help go over or if there are interviews you may need set up."

"I see. How thoughtful of them."

"Well, we just want to make sure we're doing everything we can to catch whoever did this to her."

"Actually, I do have some questions. Do you have time to stop by?" At the precinct?

Chills.

"Of course. What time?"

"Now is good." And with that, he hung up.

No need to panic. He was just an in-person kind of guy. I quickly checked my hair and makeup, eliciting a slew of questions from Sarah. We had gone two blissful hours in silence.

"What's with all the primping?"

"Nothing, Sarah." *Like you care.* Ignore her. Ignore her. Ignore her.

"You have a date, don't you?"

I shrugged.

"Well then what's with the gloss? Fine, be a baby. But you need more concealer. Like, a lot more." Her tone was taunting.

That was as nice as she was going to be today. I'd take it, even if I was over her. (I wasn't.)

* * *

Half an hour later, I found myself in an interrogation room. Detective Hopper sat in front of me. Two coffees were on the table. The walls were gray and boring. I smiled. Guilty people didn't smile.

"So what can I help with?" I asked. Being proactive was good. I'd offered to do this. Guilty people didn't volunteer.

"Well we now know when Cassie was murdered."

"Oh, gosh. That's so *CSI* that you can tell!"

"Where were you the night of October twenty-fourth?"

"Um, let me check." I opened my phone and flipped through it. "I had a couple parties I popped into, nothing major."

"And people can verify?"

"Yeah, I'm sure they can check the guest list. Am I a suspect?"

"We need to rule people out right now. Can you send me the contact info of who threw the parties?"

"Of course." I had made an appearance at two events that night while Cassie was passed out and tied up in the van. Drive-bys, in and out. Enough that they saw me.

He shifted slightly in his seat. "We need to talk about your history, Anya. It's the big red flag here. Are you ready to tell me why you don't seem to exist?" He was doing the good cop thing, being nice. Asking gently. They'd tried this before. The police were not my friends.

"I do exist. I'm right here, aren't I?" Now who's the crazy one? But he kept that intense gaze on me. I cleared my throat. "Fine. But I'd really like what I tell you to stay between us. It's not something I need everyone to know. My old name was Mariana Evans." I paused, waiting for him to get what that meant. *Hello? Mariana Evans, who killed her best friend as a child? And who caused the crash her parents died from?* But nothing. He didn't know who I was. My voice trembled as I continued.

"When I was younger . . ." I paused for dramatic effect. "I was friends with this girl. Meredith Burgess. She was troubled. Like, a level of crazy you can't imagine. Like, killed her cat and made me watch kind of crazy. And then she told everyone I had done it, that I had strangled Mr. Meow."

I had.

"Looking back at it all, I think she was abused. But I didn't know back then. One day she did something horrendous, and unfortunately, I was there."

"Go on." He leaned forward. Five more inches and we'd be touching. My heart skipped a beat.

"Meredith would get so mad when she didn't get her way. You know, acting totally spoiled. But she was an only child—like me. So we bonded. But if she got upset, you had to hide. Or she'd kick and hit you. And this one time she threw a huge fit." I wiped my eye. "I'd never seen anything like it. My mother wouldn't let us be friends anymore. She thought Meredith was a bad influence." I picked up the coffee in front of me and took a sip, grimacing. "And when I told Meredith . . ." Pause for effect. "She set herself on fire. I don't think she meant to, but the flames went all over her, and I couldn't do anything. It traumatized me so much, my parents sent me to special schools to deal."

He nodded as if he knew those schools, the kinds of kids who went there. How they came out.

"Anyways, my shrink thought a new start would be best. You know, with Google and all. New name, new history, nothing to follow me into adulthood."

"And your parents can verify all this?"

I shook my head. "They died in a car accident. Not too long after Meredith. We were all in the car. I broke a few bones, got a concussion. Got this scar." I showed him the weird spotted scar a few inches above my elbow. "Glass cut through that part of my arm, but I survived. I'm still not sure how. My mom was in a coma for a few days, but she passed eventually. Dad died instantly."

I pulled a tissue out of my purse and blew my nose. Gross, I know. But it's the little details that really help.

"Sorry, it all still gets to me. I just don't know how Mer could have done that. And then my parents . . ."

He patted my hand. "Thank you for telling me that. That must have all been very traumatic."

I nodded. It was. I took a gulp of air.

"Can your doctor verify this info? Just the history, nothing about your health." He wanted to talk to Dr. M? Was that even allowed? The idea sent me into mild panic.

"Um, I guess so. But I'm not waiving my patient confidentiality." I watched *Law & Order*, bub. I knew my rights. "But he can tell you the basics. Don't you have, like, case files too? That you can reference, I mean?"

"We have some info, but we'll be looking at everything." That meant what really happened with Meredith too. God, that spoiled little brat was always ruining things for me.

I nodded. "You have to know, after what I went through, I'd never hurt anyone. I can see the damage it causes. To make anyone else go through what I did . . ." I shuddered.

"I appreciate your honesty. Do you know where Sarah Taft was the night Cassie died?"

"Hang on." I pulled up her calendar on my phone. "Um, doesn't look like she had anything that evening. Which is weird because she usually does. But maybe she didn't put anything on her calendar? Did you check her social media?" He shot me a look that translated to *Duh*.

"Hmm, okay. And can you think of anyone else who would have it in for Cassie? Anyone at all? Any leads we may not have pursued yet?"

"No, I can't." After a pause, I made a face.

"What is it?"

"Well, there were the cameras. Did you find them?" He shook his head. He hadn't taken it seriously. "Sarah hid cameras in Greg's office. She'd have to have seen Cassie and Greg . . ."

He looked at his notes. "Right, Jack Archer told you. Someone was supposed to check it out. I'll find out what happened."

"I figured Jack was just talking shit, but better to be safe, right?" I held up my hands in an emoji shrug. "But also, I saw something in her desk the other day. I was looking for a stapler, and instead, I found these nails. Like, fingernails? I thought they were fake, but they were kind of gross and bloody."

"There are fingernails in Sarah Taft's desk?" He looked excited. I nodded. His eyes became round and huge, and his cheeks flushed. He licked his lips a few times. It was kind of sweet-hot.

"Why didn't you tell us this before?" He started flipping through Cassie's file, her whole life reduced to one manila folder. That was the best any of us could hope for. "Here." He pulled out a photo of Cassie's body. Her hands. The nails were missing. I gasped. And turned my face away.

"I can't—" I strangled out.

"Cassie's nails were pulled out. Luckily, after she died."

I shook my head. "I don't even know if they're real. But I figured you'd want to know."

"Where are the nails now?"

"I have no idea. Her desk, most likely?"

He looked grim. Detective Hopper was disappointed in me for not telling him all this sooner. Dammit. This was supposed to help me look good.

"Let's go."

He escorted me back to *La* Vie. It was like a minidate, except a few officers followed us in their cruisers. Not exactly romantic.

Sarah wasn't at her desk when we got there, so I started poking around while he stood by. I opened her bottom drawer and found the nails, wrapped in tissue.

"Good thing she's a pack rat. Here you go." I handed it to him. It now had my fingerprints on it—but that was fine. He'd seen me touch it. He opened the tissue (with gloves on) and made a face.

"This smells bad. Definitely something off about it."

"Like . . . dead-thing bad?"

"Yeah. Listen, I'm going to take this to the crime lab, but I'm going to need your statement that you gave this to me."

"Of course. Whatever you need." He handed the bundle to one of the officers chaperoning our outing. He was saying something about chain of custody, statements, yada yada, when Sarah finally skipped on over.

"What's going on?" she asked, blissfully cheerful. She did the hair flip she reserved for hot men.

"Um, Sarah, the detective is here about those fingernails."

She glanced from him to me and back. Confusion colored her face. "What fingernails?"

I wanted to laugh. I wanted to scream in her face that she could have been my friend. My BFF. Then I'd have protected her. Kept her safe forever. But she had to threaten me. Use me. This was what she deserved. No, she deserved worse than this.

An officer left to see Greg. He came back holding two cameras.

"Ms. Taft, are these yours?" Hopper asked.

"What? No. Of course not." Her voice trembled.

"So we won't find a history of you buying these or any of the footage on your computer?"

Sarah's face went ashen. "I didn't mean—"

"Anya, thank you for your help," he said. "We'll take Sarah to the station to continue our questioning." Detective Hopper motioned to the officers, who guided Sarah to the door.

"What?! Oh my God, Anya. What is this shit?" Sarah screeched.

"Um, should I call someone?" I asked him.

"No, she's not under arrest. It's just questioning, for now."

I didn't know whether to laugh or cry. What had I done?

But then relief settled over me. This is what she got. I played out the scenarios that could happen. Sarah arrested. Tried, convicted. Everyone would hate her. Or she'd be a suspect, not arrested. And everyone would still hate her. I smiled. Sarah wouldn't be queen bee anymore. Sarah would be branded a lunatic. Even if she tried to expose me, no one would believe her. Or care. She'd be powerless. Faking a résumé was so quaint compared to killing people.

And best of all, I could make her think about me until the day she died. I would win. She should have just been my friend. But no, she had to threaten me. Blackmail me.

You know what they say—if you can't join them, beat them.

* * *

The media caught onto the story quickly. Do you know what the papers were saying about Sarah the next morning? Poor little rich girl. So bored with shopping that she chopped up her intern and maimed Celia's assistant. *Allegedly*. So desperate for attention, she turned into Bloody Sarah. But rumors were rumors, and despite all the buzz, Sarah came to work like nothing had happened. Like her face wasn't plastered on the front page of the *Post* and *Daily News*. Like no one knew she'd been filming Greg. (The police were still mulling over charging her for that. At best, they could get her for invasion of privacy.) That's poise. I had to admire her for it.

At least until she got to her desk. Or what *used* to be her desk.

Sarah was ready to throw her stuff down, when she stopped. "W-T-F is *this* shit?"

Zhazha didn't bother looking up.

"Anya! Why is this Russian whore at my desk?!"

"You need to go talk to Celia."

"This is so not okay!" She half stomped, half ran to Celia's, where she no doubt was told that Zhazha would be sitting next to me from now on. Sarah needed to keep a low profile: she had to work from home, stay away from events, and not represent *La Vie* in any way until this mess with Cassie died down.

And I might have told Celia I was too frightened to work so closely with Sarah. That it was a safety issue. That she shouldn't be allowed in the office with the whole Greg thing.

"You can't do this!" Sarah whined loud enough for me to hear. And then she got pissed. "I'm Sarah Taft. I'll do whatever the fuck I want!" And out she blew, Hurricane Taft.

"This is not how a *La Vie* woman behaves!" Celia called after her.

Sarah stopped at my desk. "This is your fault, Anya! I bet you put those nails in my desk!" she bellowed.

"And I put the cameras up too? Really? We're supposed to be helping with the investigation, per Celia's orders. I had to tell them everything."

She glared. But I wasn't at fault here, and she knew it. Deep down.

"Well, fuck you! This is all your doing! You—you fake!" She took a deep breath. Maybe she was learning from me? Deep breathing and mantras make all the difference. "Make sure you hold my packages so no Russian prostitutes get ahold of them. And you—" She pointed at Zhazha. "You're just the flavor of the month. Don't get too cozy. You know what happens to people around here who do."

I heard gasping around me. She stomped out of the office. No one commented on the fake bit.

"Well, we knew it was going to be awkward. But back to work, ladies!" Celia clapped her hands like we were all at Miss Mabel's Academy of Fine Manners or some shit.

Sarah was right, this was my fault. I had made this happen. But I didn't feel guilty. This was just the end of me and her and the beginning of me and Zhazha. Why wallow when I could just move on? Besides, Zhazha fit in. Everyone loved her. Best idea ever!

I said all these things to Dr. M that night, but he probably knew I was lying. If I was ever too positive, he knew I was faking.

"I mean, it's totally great having her in the office, don't get me wrong." I paced my living room. Dr. M was sitting in his usual orange chair. He was the only one who used it. But he was also the only person I allowed inside my apartment.

"But . . . ?" Dr. M prompted.

"But I don't think she's ever worked in an office before, so there's an adjustment, I guess. But everyone has a weird trial period. Right?"

He didn't say anything. Why did everyone try the silent trick on me? He stayed quiet, waiting for me to continue, waiting for me to find the answer on my own. I knew the goddamn answer, I just had to "show my work" out loud to him.

"I just hope that everyone else gives her a chance to adjust and learn our ways before giving up on her. Otherwise, it will look bad for me since I brought her in."

"Well, you'll just have to help her, won't you?"

I spent the evening uploading Sarah's videos of Greg online. Sarah never changed her email password. Now the entire world would see our publisher fucking the intern, doing coke before lunch, and (my personal favorite) crying in his underwear after hours. *La Vie*, so chic.

15

Sarah was out. Of the office, at least. Zhazha was the new star, there to take our minds off death, bloody finger-nails, and my now former BFF. But as excited as every-one was to welcome her, it didn't last. Nothing golden, blah blah blah. *La Vie* was cursed. Everyone associated with the magazine became evil. Or died. Ruined. Maybe the ground we walked on had been hexed, salted so nothing, not even friendship, could grow.

I hadn't heard from Sarah in what seemed like weeks. No "Happy Thanksgiving, Anya!" text. No hilarious refrain that I'd eat the whole turkey and gain weight. Well, joke's on her—I ordered Chinese food to celebrate the pilgrims mas-sacring Native Americans.

"Did you have a good holiday, Z?" I asked the Monday after. It had been a week since Sarah stormed out.

She looked up and smiled, her lips fuchsia. "Yes. I went to Belize for some sun." She hadn't invited me. I didn't think she would, but still, it'd have been nice. I smiled and went back to work.

Zhazha was dressed like that old zebra joke, all black and white stripes but with yellow platform Crocs by Balenciaga. (They were a few seasons old but still spectacular.) She had only been with us for a week and already stood out like a giraffe. She was loud and impulsive and wore any brand she wanted. Her hands weighted down with rings and bracelets. Like a run-through come to life. Evie's and Dalia's jaws dropped. I loved every second of their reactions.

"Okay, everyone!" Celia clapped her hands, ushering us into the conference room. "Let's go over the latest issue."

"My photo shoot," Zhazha said once we were seated. It was a statement, not a question. Everyone swiveled toward her.

"What about *your* photo shoot?" Celia asked coldly.

"When we do it?" Zhazha didn't ask permission. I was obsessed.

"Well, if you'd let me speak, I'd get to it. Please try not to interrupt. Just listen and observe, Zhazha."

Zhazha pouted.

"So where was I? Yes, we need to do Zhazha's shoot ASAP and sneak it into the next issue. We were thinking old Hollywood icons."

Zhazha looked at me for my opinion. Maybe I did like her better than Sarah.

"Celia?" I interjected. "What if we changed it slightly?" This was a gamble, but I wanted to go big. "Something darker, as a way to offset all our bad news."

"Like what?"

"Well, we want to highlight pencil skirts and coats, right?" She nodded. "What about Zhazha as Hitchcock's heroines?" Silence. It was almost deafening. No one talked, everyone waited for Celia to speak. The buzzing was starting up. She had to say something soon, right?

Finally, Celia said, "Oh, that could be good."

"There are so many great bags and shoes for it," Dalia added.

"Oh, and the hair and makeup would be on point," Evie chimed in.

Everyone was falling in line. They were here to help me. Me!

Celia nodded. "Okay, let's pull some clothes and see if we can make this work. Good idea, Anya."

Holy shit, she liked it! She liked my idea! I knew she would, but still, a win for me! I wanted to tell Sarah, but she was MIA. Under the table, Zhazha grabbed my hand. But instead of feeling excited that she wanted physical contact, I was repulsed. I bet Dr. M had some clinical term for it like intimacy avoidance. But really, there's nothing quite as unsettling as the feeling of another person's hand in yours. (He later said it had to do with Sarah, that I was mourning our friendship, replacing her too quickly. He suggested I set boundaries with Zhazha and ease into things.)

"I want froyo," Evie said after the meeting.

"Wait, are we doing froyo again?" Dalia asked.

Zhazha had run off, presumably to see Greg.

"Yeah, it's totes okay with my diet," I replied. They both smiled at me. I was finally belonging. "Let's go." I grabbed my wallet.

Without our leader to guide us, Evie and Dalia were looking to me to take over. It was everything I had worked for and also completely fucking terrifying. I was aiming to be a benevolent leader. Make our group whole, an organic assortment of talent, working together. Ugh. I needed to up my meds. Kumbaya shit didn't work in real life.

"Can I admit something to you guys?" Dalia was spooning a berry-flavored yogurt into her mouth on our way back. "I kinda miss Sarah. I mean, I don't miss her bossy attitude, but, like, her. You know?"

Evie and I nodded. Evie was eating chocolate. I stuck to vanilla. Vanilla was the best flavor, hands down.

"Do you think she killed everyone?" Evie grinned.

"No, no way," I said. "Sarah would faint at the sight of blood." She nearly threw up each time I cut myself. "Besides, aren't these things usually done by men?" Fact: 80 percent of violent crimes were committed by men. The more you know!

"So one of us could still die next?" Dalia shivered.

"I bet we're fine," I said. "We can't worry about that. Like, you could have an aneurysm and die this very second." They both looked horrified. Had I said the wrong thing?

"Dark, Anya. So dark. Ugh, no more froyo. Let's do a cleanse tomorrow!" Evie tossed her yogurt in the trash.

"Anyways, with the Greg vids all over the internet," I said, "I wonder if Sarah will even be allowed back." The two of them gasped and then ran to their desks to hunt down the videos in question.

* * *

My love affair with Zhazha burned bright—and then flamed out.

"I told you, you can't jump into a new friendship like that," Dr. M chastised. I hated when he was right. Zhazha had started following me around the office, butting in whenever Dalia or Evie stopped by to chat. It was cute at first. But by the end of her second week, her voice was like nails on a chalkboard. Dr. M broke it down for me that evening.

"You're realizing she isn't Sarah. Anya, I keep telling you, you have to mourn Sarah and that friendship before you can get close to anyone. It's how the brain works. Stop trying to fight it." Each time he struck a nerve, I wanted to stab something. Someone.

"So you're saying I resent Zhazha for not being Sarah?"

"Exactly." He smiled triumphantly, like this was a breakthrough.

"How do I get over this?"

He shrugged. "That's up to you. Maybe have a bonfire of Sarah items. Or just metaphorically. Yes, a symbolic fire. *Don't play with matches, Anya.*"

"You'll never let me live that down. I set one fire. One." He was always on Meredith's side, but he'd never even met her.

But Dr. M was right. Not about the matches thing. But about Sarah. I had to move on so I could give Zhazha a chance.

I was being such an adult. I held up the wig that looked so much like Sarah's hair. If I burned this, would I love Zhazha? I held up the lighter (no matches, remember?) but shakily moved my hand away. No. I'd never get rid of this wig. It was too perfect, just like Sarah. I'd just have to try harder with my new friend.

At work, I smiled at Zhazha every time she spoke to me. I smiled when she wore her jangly new bracelet by Georges Pike. It made noise every time she moved her arm. I used the metal heel on my stilettos to dig into the tops of my feet. We were in an adjustment period. I had to temper my reaction to Zhazha's quirks. But every sound she made, every time she laughed or spoke in Russian on the phone, I felt flashes of disgust and annoyance. I missed Sarah's constant nail filing. Her biting remarks. Her hair flips. I just missed *her*.

I started spying on Zhazha—just to be safe. Never trust anyone at a women's magazine. Or any magazine, for that matter. Everyone is out for herself. Sarah taught me that. It had to be the low pay combined with the lack of job security that made us all ready to take someone out, Gladiator style. Two editors enter, only one leaves.

She left her phone on her desk. Just like that. Zhazha didn't care if anyone picked it up. She didn't even lock it! I could have tweeted how much she hated the latest brand paying her, but I refrained. (I gave myself a cookie for being good.) But her texts were all there for me to see. Love notes to Greg. (Gross.) Shit in Russian I couldn't decipher. And messages to Jack. (He was such a slut.)

Zhazha: *Let's get drinks soon. But no Anya.*

Jack: *Of course, babe! And how naughty of you.*

She sent a winky face back to him.

So Zhazha was already looking to expand her circle beyond me. So ungrateful. At least Sarah was upfront about wanting to ditch me.

* * *

I snuck out for lunch with Jack the following Monday. It was December, and we both needed some face-to-face time. I wanted to know what he'd said about me to Zhazha. And truthfully, I missed him. Without Sarah, we saw each other less and less. We met at a salad place, and the line was down the block.

"Trust me, it's so worth it," he declared when he saw my annoyed face.

"Whatever. How are you?" We hugged like old friends. He smelled like Tom Ford's Tuscan Leather. I wanted to rub my face against his.

"Babe! I missed you. Okay, listen. We have got to sort this mess out. We need Sarah." He said it like she was air. We needed her to live. And he was right. "There's no way she killed anyone. I'm telling you, Sarah is being set up."

"Okay." What the fuck was I supposed to say?

"I think it's Zhazha. All this started when she came on the scene. And, like, I so don't trust her."

"You said she was *amazing*."

"Her style, not her fucking personality! Did you know she texted me bitching about you?"

I did, but I shook my head. I smiled. Smiling says you're breezy and don't care for petty nonsense. (Inside, I was seething. She'd called me a dictator. Compared me to Stalin for not letting her act out at work. Ugh, I was trying to help you, bitch.)

"Do not trust her, Anya." He said it all serious like too, grabbing the fleshy part of my upper arm and squeezing for emphasis. He widened his eyes. "Girthy!" And then exploded into laughter.

Jerk. I made sure to spill my green juice on his Comme des Garçons sneakers. But he was right. I couldn't trust Zhazha. I couldn't trust anyone. Not if they were at *La Vie*. The constant power struggle was exhausting.

* * *

Mornings: Zhazha wanted to get coffee with me. Lunchtime: We went to the cafeteria together. Afternoons: She had to go to Starbucks for a latte arm-in-arm.

Was this my life now?

She acted like we were the best of besties, but I knew it was a lie. Rebounds were so messy. I missed Sarah ignoring me. God, that was totally the best, wasn't it? At least I knew where I stood with her. (At her feet.)

I got up to go to the bathroom, and Zhazha jumped up.

"Dammit, Zhazha, I'm just going to pee. It's called personal space," I snapped. I should have been flattered. The chicest blogger in the world wanted to be with me twenty-four-seven. She needed me. I was like her Beatrice, guiding her through fashion hell. But I couldn't wait to throw her body off a bridge. When I got back to my desk, I found Zhazha on my phone.

"What are you doing?"

"Your phone rang," she said, holding it out.

"Give me that. Hello?"

"Jesus, is that commie whore answering your phone now?"

My whole body melted.

"Sarah! Oh my God, I've missed you." It came out before I could stop myself.

"Of course you have. W-T-F? Why is she answering your calls?"

"Ugh, I don't know. Such a stalker, right?"

Sarah laughed. I felt my stress dissolve. I *had* missed her. Her voice made everything better.

"What am I missing? What's the info?"

"Well . . ." And there wasn't much to tell. Without Sarah, life at *La Vie* was dull. She had been out of the office, working from home, for almost a month. It felt like forever. I needed her back with me. I needed to smell her hair.

"I'm going to ask Celia if I can come back soon."

"Do you think she'll let you?"

"She has to. I'm not really a suspect. I mean, come the fuck on."

"Totes. Well, I hope you hurry back."

"And, Anya, no hard feelings about the nails. You know." She was lying.

"Right. Shit happens."

"Right."

I could feel her cold smile through the phone. She was going to make me pay for my treachery.

"Okay, talk soon!" I hung up, catching Zhazha's eye. She had watched me like a hawk.

"Sarah's coming back?"

"Yes! Isn't that great?"

"Hmph."

"Whatever, Z. You two will have to get along."

"She's an idiot," she said simply. "She got caught."

"Caught? You mean the nails?"

"I know how to dispose of bodies better."

Was she serious? "And how would you do that?" Maybe her methods were better than mine? Sharing was caring. We should compare notes.

"I call my cousin Dimitri. He takes care of it."

"Sounds like you have experience, Zhazha."

"I take care of my problems," she boasted. Was she really saying this out loud? In an office with a killing problem? Should I slap her or kiss her? I wasn't quite sure.

"She's not your friend," she added.

"And you are?"

"Of course."

"No one's really a friend when you work here, Zhazha."

* * *

The papers ran a couple more stories about Sarah, just to remind us all that the murders of Mulberry, Lisa, and Cassie had yet to be solved. There was a sidebar on the Greg videos and the investigation into whether they were revenge porn.

There were rumors of some big exposé on the magazine coming out soon. Celia was pissed. But she was also pleased with the Zhazha photo shoot. So it all evened out.

"Oh, just look at these photos." Celia sighed, sitting back in her chair. She held up the contact sheets from the Hitchcock shoot so I could fawn over them. Zhazha as Tippi Hedren, with birds all around her, including a falcon perched on her shoulder. Zhazha as Marnie, stealing cash while it poured outside. Zhazha in the famous shower scene but shot at the Plaza Hotel adorned only in jewelry. And for *Vertigo*, wearing bold stripes and splayed on a chaise lounge.

"This was a brilliant idea. So glad I thought of it," Celia added.

I bit my lip until it bled.

"Absolutely genius, Celia." I wiped my mouth.

"She's going to do wonders for the magazine."

We were that desperate for better sales. All the murders had scared away advertisers, and we were losing revenue at a terrifying pace.

If we made the deadline, Zhazha was going to be the saving grace of *La Vie*. And looking at the spread, I could see why. If you didn't let her open her mouth, she was lovely. She did well as a Hitchcock girl. Staring at her shots made me happy, not because she looked damn fierce (she did), but because everything was clicking together. I was (finally) a success. I was a magazine person.

"Anya, these are so chic. But I need you to rein her in a bit." Celia's Botoxed brows tried to frown. They failed. "I mean, she's like a giant fucking toddler. 'I want this, I want that.' What is wrong with her? She's been here, what? Three months? And she thinks she owns the damn place."

"One month, actually."

"What? That's it? Jesus."

In that one month, Zhazha had managed to turn the entire office against her. I'm not even exaggerating.

She'd waved her Georges Pike bracelet (from the Zhazha line) in Dalia's face, taunting her that no one had ever made jewelry for her.

"You're the jewelry editor. You should impress the designers more."

Zhazha had set her sights on Evie next.

"Is this good cream?" She held up a bottle.

Evie nodded. "Totally. I use it myself."

"Oh." Zhazha threw it in the trash.

And then there was me. She bitched about me to anyone who would listen. She even emailed Celia to say I was stealing ideas: *Anya steals her stories. She is a thief. Her ideas aren't hers. I can help with this.* As if. I may be a phony, but I've never stolen ideas. I wanted to say I wasn't surprised by what she did, that I knew she was only ever on #TeamZhazha, but her betrayal hurt for a moment. A day. Fine, I had a full session with Dr. M about it. It's hard to fake-like people and not really fall for them.

"Do you know she had the nerve to email me complaining about you?" Celia asked.

"About me?" I aimed for an appropriately puzzled look on my face. *Of course not, Celia. How would I know that?* Zhazha was advancing to full backstabbing *La Vie* girl at an admirable pace.

"Yeah, she said you were stealing her work. The girl can barely write two words." She had loved the blogger just a few moments ago. But the only constant with Celia was that she changed, constantly.

"At least she's helping with traffic. Maybe we should have her work out of the office."

"Maybe. And Jesus Christ, give her a makeover, would you? She's wearing Cavalli today. She's giving me such a headache. Put her in some Jil Sander or something."

"And there's that whole dead-bodies thing . . ."

"What dead-bodies thing?"

"Oh. Zhazha said she knew how to get rid of dead bodies. And then someone tweeted that she had a bloody past? Like, with the Russian mob or something? I don't know. Maybe we should—"

"Oh, great, just what we need. I'll handle it."

I was dying to be in that HR meeting. "So, um, is Sarah coming back? She said she was working on it?"

Celia rolled her eyes. "All of you will be the death of me. Yes, she wants to come back. But only if the team is comfortable with it."

Us? Me? Holy shit, I had power over Sarah's life?

"I think we can make it work." If I was going to have a Judas next to me at work, I'd rather it were Sarah.

* * *

I needed to forget all about my work issues. No Sarah, no Zhazha, certainly no Celia. Just a quiet night watching my beloved Stabler. Except the episodes airing were newer ones. What was the point of *SVU* without Stabler? Annoyed, I threw popcorn at the TV while scrolling through Twitter.

There Zhazha was, subtweeting me. *When your bestie is a fake. [Crying emoji face].* Her bestie? For a second, it felt great; I was flattered. Then I realized, she called me a fake. Did she know somehow? Who could have told her? My mind flashed to the Highline party with Lisa. The trinity, together.

I knew who'd told Z. Jack. He had to. Unless somehow Sarah was going to the blogger behind everyone's backs. That would be surprising; Sarah hated Zhazha. No, it was Jack. Had to be. Maybe he needed to be taught a lesson? The idea depressed me. Jack was fun, I liked him. And now I had to kill him. Why was making friends so hard as an adult?

The next day, I got to the office, and there was Zhazha, sitting at my desk, trying to go through my computer. I wanted to paint a B in blood on her yellow dress. B for backstabbing bitch. Instead, I smiled.

"What are you doing?"

"My computer is not working," she said by way of explanation.

"It looks fine to me. You won't be able to use mine without my password, you know."

Loser. What was I thinking? Zhazha was a social-climbing nobody who would only go higher if I let her. I had traded the queen of the New York social world for her.

It took a few days before I could do anything about Zhazha. I had to wait for Celia to send Zhazha's spread to the printers for the January issue. It was nearly a stop-the-presses moment, but they made it and were being whipped up. Perfection.

And then suddenly, there was Sarah.

I thought I was imagining her. Her hair wavy and cascading just so. Her lip-glossed mouth was open in a snarl. She was wearing a black fitted dress and black heels. Sedate for Sarah; she was like the ghost of *La Vie* past. And she was standing in front of her old desk, her face furious.

"Seriously, move your shit off my desk, whore!" she shrieked.

"I will not move! You go, or I'll call the police!"

"Sarah, are you real?" I whispered.

"What is all this noise?" Celia bellowed. Bronwen stood behind her, covering her ears. Celia looked at me, the one person not making a peep.

I sighed. "Um, where should Sarah sit?"

"Figure it out, ladies. You're adults. And do it quietly, or heads will roll." That was her favorite new phrase these days. She said she liked the imagery it conveyed.

I called the managing editor's office, and the only open desks were with the copy department, one row over.

"The copy department?" Sarah shouted incredulously. "I can't sit there!"

"You can and you will." I grabbed her by the elbow. "Right now, all eyes are on you, and not in a good way. You need to clear your name. Be more agreeable, easier to deal with. Suck it up for a little while, and then we can fix this, okay?"

She nodded mutely. No objection. No yelling. Wow. I needed to be no-nonsense Anya with Sarah more often. I wanted to hug her.

* * *

Sarah was back, but her status in our group had plummeted, thanks in no part to her new neighbors. (The copy department was like hanging with band geeks, or theater kids, or other weird tropes from high school movies. Sarah may as well have dyed her hair purple and worn striped thigh-highs.) I had no idea why she hadn't waited until this was all over to come back. Wait until the murderer was caught (LOL) or at least until after the holidays. Christmas was in one week. Sarah should have been with her family in Connecticut. Instead, she was with us. (Did that make us family?)

Evie and Dalia still came to my desk, forcing Sarah to get up and come along. Worse, she had to spend time with Zhazha.

"Where are we going?" Sarah asked as we all trudged toward the cafeteria.

"Froyo," Dalia answered.

"Oh, but I'm not doing sugar or dairy." We all shot her a look. Pack dynamics insisted she submit to our will, or else. "I guess I can today. Whatever."

Sarah was weak now. We could all sense it.

Zhazha joined us too but would never eat the yogurt. I think she just wanted to keep an eye on Sarah. She waved her party invites in Sarah's face, laughing. (I'd like to say Sarah didn't take the bait, but come on. It's Sarah.)

In response to her dwindling social life, Sarah decided to reinvent herself. Gone was her Valentino and Gucci. She now wore Rick Owens and Isabel Marant. Pieces that could have come from my closet—if we were the same size. I was thrilled and annoyed. That was *my* look. Celia would have thrown a fit if Sarah had tried to wear any of it to our holiday party, but

Sarah wasn't allowed to attend. (The party sucked. The powers that be decided we all needed to keep a low profile, so we had Veuve in the cafeteria.)

Yet outside the confines of our office, Sarah's star was strangely rising. Apparently, being suspected of murder was the chicest thing on the goddamn planet. Fashionlandia loved a good scandal. Forget Cartier dinners; she was headed to underground raves and roving dance parties in subway tunnels. Brooklyn brands invited her to their holiday bashes.

Having Sarah back in the office, even dressed in her most gothic attire, made me jubilant. Sarah was back—for me. She wanted to go back to how we were. I didn't care that she laughed at me before or said we weren't friends. Or threatened me. Okay, I did, but I know why she did it. She was just scared of getting too close to me. That had to be it. I started finding ways to hang with Sarah one-on-one during the day. Lunches, fake appointments, shopping trips to Barneys.

"You know, I heard Zhazha says shit about you to everyone," she said to me over Caesar salad. "Jack showed me the texts she sent him. Anya, you can't trust her."

I waved my hand. No big deal. "Oh, they're just texts." I didn't want to give away how much the Russian blogger's backstabbing upset me. Never let anyone know how you really feel. Never. They'll use it against you.

"No, it's worse than that. Listen to me, okay? I'm trying to help." Sarah looked serious. She looked concerned.

"Since when, Sarah? You've never tried to help me." *Not the way I helped you.*

"Whatever, I care, okay? See?" She held up her own phone. I hadn't checked her texts in a while. Or anyone's. I could offer an excuse that I was busy with the holiday season, but honestly, I was tired of reading mean shit about myself. But there it was. A message from Zhazha: *Let's put the past behind us, Sarah. I want to be friends. Let's get drinks. Without Anya. LOL. Sick of her.*

Now that Sarah was back, the blogger was trying to broaden her reach. If the two of them became friends, they'd be unstoppable. Zhazha had clearly realized that even if Sarah still hadn't. If they became friends, they'd have no use for me.

I glanced from the phone to Sarah, and there it was. The pity in her eyes. I felt my panic, my anger, my overwhelming desire to break something. But I didn't. I ate my salad, drank my Diet Coke.

"Let's go to the fifth floor and look at shoes," I said, smiling.

Sarah nodded, and the topic of Zhazha was dropped.

But I didn't let it go. We shopped, and I thought of Zhazha. So much betrayal in such a short time. She could teach a class on backstabbing at the Learning Annex. By the time we got back to work, I knew one thing: it was time to unfriend my little Russian.

* * *

During Fashion Week, Zhazha got free rooms at a hotel a mere two blocks from her apartment. That was so chic. The rest of the time, she lived in a duplex in Gramercy. The apartment was gorgeous, with a wide, open area for the living room and kitchen. The bedroom was up one of those winding iron staircases that always look so lethal. One fall, and you're done.

I had invited myself over under the guise of exchanging Christmas gifts. Friends did that, right? (I'd gotten her a picture frame and some champagne. I'd left a gift for Sarah in her desk too: handmade voodoo dolls, one for each of us at work, including Lisa.) Zhazha was upstairs changing outfits. Thirty minutes later, she clunked down each step, her platform boots barely fitting on the rungs.

"Okay, now, what did you want?"

"We need to talk." I poured her a drink.

"About what?"

"Zhazha, are you happy with our setup?"

"Happy? I work, I get paid. I live here. What else is there to be happy about?"

"Sure, okay. But is *La Vie* nourishing you? Is your soul being fed?" *Smile.*

She stared at me blankly. I moved farther away on the sofa, keeping a good measure of distance.

"What about dating? Are you dating anyone?"

She gave me a strange look. "Are you hitting on me, Anya?"

"Oh, no. Sorry, I was just wondering what else was going on in your life. With fashion, it's important to have other things to focus on." I kept the idiotic smile on my face.

"Ah, okay, I understand. I see Greg once in a while, but it's not great. The sex is terrible."

I grimaced, nearly gagging on my champagne. What magnetic pull did that man have over everyone? Was it his gelled-back hair? "It can be hard to find good men when you're working so much." I was boring myself. I had to keep the conversation flowing. I couldn't very well ask her why she sucked so much. Confronting her would be pointless. She'd bat her lashes, purse her lips, and pretend all was fine.

"You're right. But that's the price for being us." She laughed.

"Oh, sure. Let's toast! To working women!" I watched her finish her champagne and quickly poured her another glass. But there was no need—her eyes were already getting glassy.

"Anya, I—" And she was out. Even if she had the tolerance of, well, a Russian hooker, enough benzos would knock her out. Thank God for Dr. M and his free samples.

But she wasn't dead yet. I put on gloves for what was coming next.

I felt for a pulse—weak, but still there. I could drop a house on her and she'd still live. The girl was as strong as an ox. Russians were just bred differently, I guess. I grabbed her by the armpits and dragged her into the bathroom. (If you think it's easy to drag a limp body down a hallway, think again. Thank God for Tracy Anderson's arm workout.)

Once there, I stripped her naked. From a purely artistic point of view, Zhazha did have a great body. But I was glad to see she had stretch marks and cellulite too. Some things were universal. I know, I was being petty. But I think I was allowed this moment. I took a deep breath and heaved her into the tub and then propped her up. Angles are always of the utmost importance. Then I turned the shower on—so the blood would be minimal.

I reached into my bag and pulled out my knife: an eleven-and-a-half-inch blade made from balsa wood. Exactly the same make as the one in *Psycho*. Authenticity mattered. I started stabbing. Seventeen stab wounds later—just like Janet Leigh—I decided to add something special. I took out my handsaw (I really should buy stock in Black & Decker; this was the third one I'd bought from them) and sliced through her pretty neck. I had to put some effort into the spine, but finally, her head came off. I placed it in the tub and turned off the water. Using a paint brush I'd brought with me, I wrote a note in her blood on the shower wall: "Heads will roll."

I stepped back to admire my work.

Even disassembled, she made such a pretty corpse, I'd give her that. And though it wasn't quite the same as her spread in the upcoming issue, which was already at the printers and couldn't be pulled, it was similar enough to cause a stir. Yes, it was derivative—the Gucci shows last February already had heads as accessories—but I think it still worked.

I waited for the familiar rush of endorphins to wash over me—but nothing came. I felt nothing. No rush of excitement, no sense of accomplishment. Just nothing. But I didn't dwell on it. Not at Zhazha's. (I'd talk to Dr. M about it. He'd know what was wrong.)

"Maybe next time someone helps you like I did, you won't be such an ungrateful bitch. Oh, Merry Christmas."

Style bloggers were just so impermanent these days. One day they're on top of the world, the next, they're toe up in the morgue.

Steps taken: 11,940. Calories burned: 1,202.

16

Pop quiz: How long can a blogger go without posting on Instagram before her fans panic?

Answer? Seven hours.

Zhazha's loyal legion of followers freaked when they hadn't seen a photo of her jewelry, her bright-red lips, her heavily mascaraed eyes. Comments multiplied on Zhazha's Instagram. Unfortunately for them, it was the holidays. We were all off for a few days, and none of us paid much attention to what Zhazha was or wasn't doing.

It wasn't until January 2, over a week after she was killed, that a photo of Zhazha's head was posted to Instagram. It looked so peaceful sitting in the tub while her body sagged against the corner. I captioned it *Zhazha for Gucci*. It got more attention than the brand's latest campaign. (As Greg would say, "*Engagement!*") People went batshit. You'd think they'd never seen a decapitated corpse before. It was like a boy band breakup, only more dramatic and with far more lip gloss.

We were all back at work when everything erupted. Zhazha hadn't shown up to the office, obviously. I waited for someone else to discover the post. (I may have sent it out to a few people to get their attention, via a spam email account. It was ridiculous how I had to do everything around here.) Finally, I heard some gasps and a few shrieks. Dalia vomited.

Sarah shared it with everyone via text. She wrote, *Ding dong the witch is dead!*

"It's real, right? Tell me it's real!" Sarah said excitedly.

"I don't know," I said. "Maybe it's for a shoot?"

"No, look at that. *Her head's totally off her body.* Even Zhazha couldn't do that," Evie pointed out.

"What about Photoshop?" Dalia asked.

"Ohhhhhh . . ." we all said at once.

"Guys, I think we have to assume it's real," Sarah added, "because, like, we've seen a lot of bodies lately. And this one looks pretty legit. Anya, can you call your boyfriend and ask him?"

"My boyfriend?"

"You know, the one you had haul me out of here." She narrowed her eyes as she said it. I was not forgiven.

"The cop? Whatevs, he's not my boyfriend." OMG, if only he were.

"I wish he was mine. He's hot!" Dalia laughed.

If she went after Detective Hopper, I'd have to cut her hands off and feed them to her.

"You can have him." I shrugged.

"But call him anyways and find out. Because if she's dead . . ." Sarah said.

"Fine. But why would you care if she's dead? You hate Zhazha."

I dialed anyway. I was dying to hear his voice. It had been weeks since we'd spoken. I wanted to ask him if he holidayed somewhere. Foreplay was so much fun.

"Hopper."

"Is it true?"

"Who is this and is what true?"

"Sorry, it's Anya. Is it true about Zhazha?"

"Anya, hi. We can't comment on open investigations." That meant they'd found her body. Of course her freak fans had called the police.

"Oh my God, it is. Oh my God."

"Anya, please stay calm."

"How can I be calm? Everyone around us is getting killed!"

"We're still investigating."

"Tell me it was an accident."

"I . . . can't."

"Dammit! I told you someone's after us!"

"We're waiting on the ME's report, but we'll be coming to interview you guys."

"So more of the same. When are you guys going to actually catch someone?" My voice was anxious. I glanced at the group around me, to see if they were listening. They were eating up every word. Dalia gasped.

"We're working on it," Hopper ground out. He was not happy with me. Was this a fight?

"Okay, in the meantime, we'll all try not to *die*." I hung up and looked at the three sets of eyes waiting for my answer. "It's her. She's dead."

"O-M-G, O-M-G, O-M-G!" Sarah yelled.

"Jesus, why are you yelling? You hated her," I pointed out again.

"Still. Another one of us dead," she said.

"She was not one of us," Evie sniffed.

My head hurt. I needed a nap.

"I need some air," I said and went for a walk.

Detective Hopper didn't care about me. That much was clear. All that flirting, the hand touching, the saying my name? And for what? Nothing. He should be on #TeamAnya, rubbing my shoulders (or just offering to) and telling me everything he knew. He should have called me the second they found Z's body. That's what a boyfriend-worthy guy would do. Until he showed he cared, we were so totally on a break. I didn't know what I ever saw in him.

I kept walking—I needed to hit ten thousand steps today or else. Besides, I wasn't ready to deal with the faux hysterics at *La Vie*. And once Celia found out, well, heads would really roll.

Eventually, I trudged back to work and my desk.

"Have you heard?"

I looked up. Celia stood over me. Bells, I needed to put bells on everyone.

"About Zhazha?"

She nodded.

"Yeah, I heard."

"Awful, dreadful news. Thankfully we have that shoot with her. It will have to be her memorial spread. We can't do anything with the issue, but we can do something online."

Should I tell her about the death photo? How closely it resembled her spread? It passed through my mind. No. Let her deal with it later. A PR disaster. I loved it. Celia should have promoted me. Then we wouldn't be in this mess. It was all her fault. All of it. Celia was the reason all of this happened.

"Um, is Sarah going to move back here now that Zhazha's . . . ?"

"Oh, I guess so. We could always leave Zhazha's desk empty for a bit. To honor her."

"That'd be nice." And surprisingly human.

"Are you going to be okay?" She put her arm around me. I let it stay on my shoulders awkwardly for three seconds before brushing it off.

"Of course. I just need to stay busy."

"I know Zhazha was your friend." She tried to pat me on the shoulder, but I moved deftly away, leaving her hand fluttering uselessly in the air. There was only so much I could go along with.

I liked Zhazha—when she wasn't fucking me over. But she wasn't Sarah. There was only one Sarah Taft, and try as I might, I couldn't replace her. Why did Zhazha have to stab me in the back? That fucking Brutus. Everyone fucks you over eventually. Everyone. Don't believe me? Look around at your friends. Think of everything they've done that pissed you off. What kind of friends are they? Shitty ones.

Dr. M has tried to get me to deal with this. But even he will fail me eventually. That's what people do. They fuck you over and then blame you, lash out at you. It's exhausting. It makes me want to run off to some deserted island.

"You have to learn to trust someone sometime," he lectured.

"Why?"

"Because that's part of growing. And you need to grow."

Sometimes he asked too much of me. We both knew I couldn't. That I'd fall in love with someone and then it would end badly. It always did. Zhazha was dead. Meredith was dead. But I still had a chance with Sarah. She could be my person, my meaningful connection. I had to make the effort. If you tried hard enough, you got what you wanted, right?

* * *

Sarah decided a new corpse meant it was time to go shopping. She waited until after lunch to saunter in, whistling to herself, carrying a few shopping bags from Barneys and Bergdorf full of bright colors from ODLR, Gucci, and Valentino. Good-bye, goth Sarah. She glowed, her skin looking luminous.

"You have got to see what I bought!" She dropped her bags at Zhazha's desk.

"I think Celia is looking for you."

"Oh, okay, be right back then!" She trotted off to Celia's office, her hair bouncing like a horse's mane. In only few hours since the news broke about Zhazha, Sarah's hair was already blonder, shinier, and if it were possible, sparklier. It was as if with Zhazha's death, Sarah had somehow grown more powerful and gorgeous, righting the fashion power pyramid. Or she'd just booked a hair appointment. Whatever, she looked damn good.

"This is so unfair!" Sarah yelled, stomping back to my cubicle.

"Problem?"

"I can't move back here yet. Out of respect for Zhazha."

"Well, it's only temporary, right?"

"Who cares! She's dead! Fuck her, fuck this desk!" People in the cubicles near us started whispering. "It's not like she cares!" She moved to sit down, but I grabbed her arm.

"Don't sit, Sarah."

"Why not? She's dead, Anya."

"This is not your desk." It wasn't anyone's desk. But I had to give Zhazha one day of respect even if she was a shitty friend. Fine, *and* I wanted to remind Sarah that she wasn't the queen anymore. She belonged with the copy department.

"You know what? I'll burn this desk. How would you like that?" She grabbed her bags and continued her tirade down the hall.

"Are you all right, Anya?" Dalia peered around the cubicle wall. She tilted her head to the side, angled in the perfect your-loved-one-is-dead tilt.

"What do you want, Dalia?"

"I-I just wanted to see how you were, that's all. It was really awesome what you did."

"Fine. You can leave now. You really need to stop hovering like that. It's creepy." I hurt her feelings. But I didn't need her fake sympathy today.

That night I set the building on fire and killed everyone inside.

Just kidding. I watched three back-to-back episodes of *Law & Order*. A girl needed a release. It was all work and no play lately.

* * *

That evening, Dr. M watched me from my orange armchair. I hated that thing. I'd bought it on a whim. I was no good with colors. He took off his glasses and cleaned them on his shirt.

"I think you've been surrounded by death, and this latest one isn't helping. You need time to process."

I stared at my nails. What I needed was a manicure. Desperately.

"Anya? What are you thinking about?"

"Jack," I replied. "I'm trying to figure out where I stand with him. He acts like my friend, but then he texts about me. Not cool, right?"

"No, it's not cool. So you're going to ignore what I said?"

I shrugged. "I'll deal with emotions later." Emotions were so messy. "Do you think if I asked Jack point blank what his deal was, he'd tell me?" I tuned out Dr. M's response.

I knew what I was going to do. I was going to find out whether Jack was my friend. I was the queen now, not Sarah. Being the queen bee meant I needed a royal court. Jack had to be mine.

He and Sarah were out together this second. They'd posted on Insta. They were celebrating. How tacky, right? At least pretend to be sad about Zhazha. If I could do it, so could they. But there the two of them were: Jack in one of his capes and Sarah in Valentino. Holding cocktails. I was staring at the photos long after Dr. M left.

A well-placed subtweet can do wonders. It can tell someone you hate them without actually saying the words. Or, in my case, it alerted Jack to my sudden interest in his favorite outerwear: *Must go cape shopping soon. Anyone have suggestions?* There. That should get his attention. The only thing he loved more than attention was buying clothes that got him seen.

I updated my Sarah and Jack board. I had to focus my chi, get my energy aligned with my goals. I had to split them up for good. I tore up photos of the two of them. I printed out tweets. Every use of my glue stick was like a pin in a voodoo doll. They would break up forever.

* * *

"What about this one?" Jack held up a shapeless swath of fabric. I wrinkled my nose.

"I need something with a bit more detail to it."

We were at Barneys, my favorite store. Bergdorf was my number two. But Barneys got my color palette. Their fashion buyers were the best in the world. I was dying to hang out with them.

"So, like, how have you been?" Jack asked as we wandered around. "With Zhazha and all, I mean."

"Honestly? Freaked out. How many more of us are gonna drop dead?"

Jack nodded sympathetically.

"The police don't even seem to care," I added.

"It's so scary right now. I mean, when you think about it, that could have been me," he said. "I wanted to work with you guys. Ugh, so glad I didn't." I patted his shoulder to show that I understood. I *felt* for him.

"That is scary. Ooh, what about this one?" I held up a wool and leather cape.

"So chic. You need to get it." He glanced around before leaning in. "So, can I tell you something in private?" His voice was low. "This is going to sound so weird. But like, the killer—or killers—are kind of chic."

I stared open-mouthed. Jack Archer contained multitudes.

"I mean, like the murder scenes they set up are so very editorial. Better than what any mag is running, right?"

"Yeah, I see what you're saying." He liked my styling. He thought my art direction was good. And he thought my work was chic. This was everything. Why couldn't Sarah say these things to me?

"I'm just saying if you have to die, it's a very stylish way to go." He looked in my eyes as he said it. "If I'm next, I want something really extravagant. Like, Chanel couture show extravagant."

I bit back a smile. "Of course you do. But I wouldn't tell a lot of people that." *Keep it between us. Our secret.*

"Oh, God no!" He laughed. "Can you even imagine?"

"You know, that means that the murderer—or murderers—must have an eye . . . and a grudge against everyone."

"Yeah. And for a good reason. Like, maybe . . ."

We said it at the same time. "Sarah."

Jack covered his mouth, then moved his hand indecisively. "I don't know why I said that."

"Um, because it's true?" I wrinkled my nose to show I was serious. "The police have questioned her."

He shuddered, then glanced around to make sure no one was listening. "Let's def keep this between us. I won't lie, I'm scared to be alone with her."

Eureka.

I reached out and grabbed his hands. "Me, too! And I've never been able to tell if she likes me. What if I'm next?" I tried to sound as terrified as I could. I wanted to make this moment perfect.

"Girl, I so get you. She runs super hot and cold. Totes the same way with me."

"Why put up with it then? Like, Jack, I'd never treat you that way." *I'd never kill you. Not if you were really on #TeamAnya.*

"Babe! Samesies. I love you so much. Let's go get a drink after this! Just us."

"Amazing. Let me pay for my cape first. Oh, hey, did you tell Zhazha all that weird shit Lisa said about me?" I had to know. "She mentioned it a while back before . . ." I waved my hand to mean *before she was brutally killed.*

"Oh, God, you know, I think I did." He grimaced. "I was saying how obsessed Lisa was with you. It was all good stuff, don't worry. You can trust me."

I nodded. He was lying; he'd probably said worse. But I found myself numb to it all. Everyone talks shit; it was the fashion way. Jack was my friend now. I could either kill him or forgive him. I took a deep breath and smiled. I chose the latter. Dr. M was going to be thrilled.

"You're such a good friend, babe," I said. I meant it. He slung his arm around me. This was what friendship was: hugs, shopping, and some major lies.

Later that night, I posted selfies of us together. I called Jack my true bestie in the caption. He commented, *You know it.*

When Sarah texted Jack later complaining about me, he screengrabbed it and sent it to me. I was ecstatic. Jack loved me, not Sarah. He was going to be my friend only. He was scared of Sarah, which made it easy to convince him she wasn't a true friend. Not when she treated everyone like dirt and killed them. Dr. M wasn't pleased with my tactics but conceded I needed a new friend, one who actually liked me.

I made a mood board of me and Jack. Just the two of us. Looking so cute and happy. And *chic*. I trimmed Sarah out of some photos. And then I tore up her cutout heads and giggled.

17

eather leggings are very versatile. You can wear them with just about anything. That's why they were my unofficial uniform, worn with a black cashmere sweater, black platform boots, and some chunky jewelry. There's no such thing as too much black.

"Dressed for a funeral, I see." Sarah smirked. It was Monday morning and too early to deal with anyone.

"Very funny."

"When is what's-her-name's service, anyhow?"

"In a few days. Her family is flying over from Russia." Some of them, at least. The rest were in Brooklyn.

"So why are you dressed all somber and shit?"

"Because my friend died."

She shrugged. I wanted to remind her she went all noir for Lisa. But what was the point? Sarah would always be Sarah.

"Jeez, why so sensitive? I was just coming to say hi."

"Fine, hi." I was in no mood for her antics today. She eyed the desk and all the flowers that had arrived for Zhazha.

"Wow, why is everyone sending flowers here?"

"Out of respect. Something you know nothing about."

"But she's dead. Whatever, maybe I'll take some—"

"Put those down and leave. Now." They weren't for her. Sarah was a taker, just like Dr. M said. She'd take everything from me. She couldn't even let someone have their death flowers. I wanted to deny her everything.

"Um, you aren't my boss. I'm yours. And last I recalled, we used to be friends."

"Were we?"

"Whatever, Morticia."

Dr. M said my relationship with Sarah was a "sunk cost fallacy" and that I should move on. I had to Google it. But think of all that wasted effort! I couldn't just let her go.

"You need to decide if you're going to move on or if this is your life now. And you know what I'd suggest," he said in our last session. I nodded. Yes, I had to do something. Something that would make Sarah really see that if she continued to reject me or threaten me, there'd be a hefty price to pay.

So I was playing it cool. Sometimes, when you really want to tell someone how you feel, the best thing is to act the opposite. Clam up and shove your feelings and emotions so far down, it will take Dr. M a decade to get to them. Yes, that was living the right way.

I could feel eyes on me the whole day. The entire office knew about my spat with Sarah, and they were all on my side. It was awesome. *Be above it, Anya.* But they were all still doing that head-tilt thing. The death tilt. It was infuriating. The next person who did it was going to get a pen shoved in her eyes. Between that, all the "How are yous?" in lilting tones, and the white flowers delivered by the truck full, I was going out of my head. Death was so fucking annoying sometimes.

But my day got marginally better when Detective Hopper called. He needed to see me, asking if he could come up to the office. I wanted to be flattered, but we both knew this was about Zhazha. Even in death, that bitch was mucking up my life.

When he showed up wearing a killer gray wool coat and a black suit, I nearly swooned. Disarming your opponent with your amazing fashion sense was quite the skill. I ushered him into Celia's empty office.

"We won't be bothered in here," I said.

"Where's Celia?"

"Emergency Botox," I replied. If she had to do another funeral with the requisite press, her forehead muscles would need time to settle.

"No, seriously?" I stared at him until he got the point and cleared his throat. "This is such a bizarre world you work in. I don't know why you do it."

"Let me guess . . . I'm too smart to work in fashion?" I rolled my eyes.

"Try too sane."

I snorted at his response. "Right. So what's up?"

"Where were you December twenty-fourth at eight PM?" Right to the chase, no foreplay.

"Christmas Eve? I was home."

"Alone?"

I shrugged. "I don't have any family to spend the holidays with," I reminded him.

"Can anyone verify that you were there?"

"I'm sure my doorman can." I had doled out hefty tips for Christmas.

"Okay, good. Now tell me all you know about Zhazha."

"Everything?"

He nodded.

"Well, she definitely wasn't who she said she was."

"She was a fraud?"

"Her whole story of being Russian royalty was bullshit. She was just a pretty girl with an accent."

"Who brought her in to *La Vie*?"

"I did. But that was after she was making it big as a blogger."

"Can you explain that to me?" He was adorable.

"Of course. So there's street style, you know? Like photogs snap pics of girls with great style. And those girls with huge social followings cash in with campaign deals."

"They make money just from the photos?"

"Well, yeah. It's their brand. Anyway, Zhazha was getting pretty big. Here, look." I pulled up her Instagram. "See, she was fabulous. Look at how natural she was when she posed. The camera loved her. Such great angles. Anyway, we met during Fashion Week, and then I brought her on here."

He nodded. He was a logical, just-the-facts kind of guy. Logic was good. Emotions were too messy.

"So if she was outed as a fraud, you'd be held accountable? That's a lot of motive right there for you, Anya."

I shrugged. "No one cared if she wasn't really from Siberia. They cared how she looked wearing clothes. You know what they say . . ."

He raised his brow. Just one. God, it was hot.

"Fake it till you make it. She did."

"So who didn't get along with her?"

"Oh, that's easy. She and Sarah hated each other. Just because Sarah fell with Z nearby and swore that she'd been pushed. And then Zhazha kind of stole her boyfriend."

The look he gave me wasn't happy. I had been holding out on him. "You didn't tell me any of this."

"You didn't ask. You know how Sarah was sleeping with Greg and was superjealous? Well, then Zhazha came into the picture. Sarah was furious." Okay, look, I know we weren't BFFs anymore, but should I be doing this? Snitching on Sarah? *Be logical, Anya.* What would Sarah do in my place? She'd rat me out and then put on lip gloss.

"So she had issues with Mulberry, Cassie, and Zhazha . . . all of whom are dead."

"Oh, and Lisa. She and Lisa Blitz fought a lot." His jaw did a hot thing when he clenched it. I could see the muscles. "I don't want to say she killed them because I have zero proof. But if anyone had motive . . . She and Z even had a very loud fight in the office. It was a scene."

He kept writing in his notebook. What had he written about me? *Show me yours and I'll show you mine, Detective.*

"This is all very helpful. Oh, one more thing. You mentioned we could talk to your therapist."

Dammit. "Shrink. Yep."

"What was his name?"

"Dr. M! He's the best. Dr. Moritz."

He gave me a strange look before nodding. "Jacques Moritz?"

"Yes, why?"

"Nothing, just something I need to check on. Listen, you should probably keep your distance from Sarah Taft until we have everything sorted out. She could be a very dangerous person."

What did he need to "check on"? Dr. M and I had nothing to hide. Absolutely nothing. I was a model patient, he'd tell the police. He'd say he wished everyone was as compliant as me. That's what good shrinks do. They help you.

I nodded solemnly. "I'm trying. I asked Celia to not have her sit near me. But unless she's locked up or I quit, we will have to work together."

"Just be careful."

Was he worried about me? O-M-G, he was! It was a start, right?

* * *

Making amends is supposed to be vital to helping you move forward. You have to recognize the damage you've done in order to become a better person. That was what I had to do now. So here I was, laying my soul bare, telling all my sins to the world, waiting to be judged. Come on, throw your stones, people. I deserved it. I hit publish on my opus, my grand confession, letting everyone read it.

"Why I Cheat on My Diet: A Confession" told the horrible truths about eating bacon, bread, macaroni and cheese, and fried chicken. How I detoured home from events to stop at Popeye's because no one made biscuits quite like them. And that every time I was pushed to eat less and do more, I binged in the security of my apartment.

Dr. M and I had both agreed that this was a huge step forward for me, being so open and personal like this. He even made sure I had extra Klonopins around in case I got too stressed out over it all. And it *was* stressful. The comments were pouring in, mostly supportive, some asking how I wasn't five hundred pounds. (Metabolism? My insane workout routine? Lugging dead bodies around really did burn the calories right off.)

But it was Celia's response that I was most curious about. She read it and asked me to come in. I sat across from her in silence, waiting for her to speak.

"You know, Anya, we're a lot alike. When I get stressed, I eat. Just last week, I had some Pinkberry. So I understand you completely. What you did was so brave. So brave. Especially with everything going on here."

"Thanks, Celia—"

"And it was smart. We needed a distraction, to get everyone talking about something besides the bodies piling up." She grimaced. "Sorry, that sounded so crass. But you know what I meant. This is a new news cycle. Well done. Now have you spoken with your police friend?"

"Detective Hopper? Yes, he's looking into Zhazha's history and people who didn't like her."

"You mean Sarah."

"He heard about that big fight she had with Zhazha."

"Sarah is going to be the death of us all." She rubbed her temples.

"I hope you're joking, because honestly, she just may be."

"Ugh, I can't take this stress. I'm going for a massage. If anyone needs me, I'm unreachable. Oh, and Anya? Get back on your diet."

I wasn't sure who'd need her. No one knew where Sarah was, and Greg wasn't going to pop by. He had gone low profile since the cameras were discovered. Once the videos went online, he all but disappeared. He had said something about not trusting the office anymore. But so far, Sarah hadn't faced any repercussions. There was no proof she put the cameras up without permission. And her lawyers told our company's legal team that there was no expectation of privacy in the office. Sarah could get away with anything, it seemed.

Celia was right about one thing: distractions were needed. I was obsessing—what to wear to Zhazha's funeral, what to say next to Detective Hopper, how I was ever going to get Sarah to finally let me braid her hair. I needed to give my mind a rest. Which was why I decided that weekend was time to redecorate my apartment. Or decorate it at all. I'd kept the walls pristine white. Barren. Just furniture and clothes, nothing more.

Though I hummed at the thought of bloody red walls, I decided against painting—the smell would drive me crazy. Instead, I opted for hanging some framed magazine covers—vintage ones from *La Vie*'s past. Start small, and if I liked the way they looked, I could add more. I got out my hammer and nails (every girl needs to have her own toolbox) and attempted the job—but the nails sank right through the dry wall. New York apartments were total crap. Next I tried the whole stud-finder thing, but that didn't help much either. The prints would have to be in very odd locations if I used the beams.

Finally, I gave in and bought those anchor thingies, a nail gun, a new drill (mine was a bit worn down), and I tried again. It took three hours, but the prints were on the wall. I had to admit, they looked kind of cool—five separate ones in a gallery format. I was pleased, if a little tired. Determined to relax and enjoy the fruits of my labor, I posted photos of my work to my Twitter account.

Sarah immediately replied, *Sucking up even at home, Anya?*

That fucking cow. I typed my reply and then stopped. Celia would probably yell at me for fighting publicly. I had to take the high road. I ignored Sarah, and instead, I took the nail gun and used it over and over and over on another part of the wall, on pillows, on shoes I didn't like—until the *Pop! Pop! Pop!* noise soothed me. I imagined it was Sarah's head the nails were going into. *Pop!* Into her eyes. *Pop! Pop! Pop!* Nailing her mouth shut. *Pop! Pop! Pop!* Into her forehead like a metallic bindi. *Pop!* That's what you get for not liking me! *Pop! Pop!* BFFs support each other, you stupid bitch! *Pop!* The exercise almost calmed me down, but I needed more. I needed to know what it felt like going in to actual flesh.

I pulled my rib-eye steak out from the fridge. I was planning on cooking it later, but fuck it. This was better. I pumped it full of nails until the meat was officially tenderized. Oh, God, that felt heavenly. I shot more nails into it, spelling out, *FUCK YOU.* Childish, yes. But damn it felt good. Something was still missing though. I needed to see blood oozing out. Meat juice hardly counted. There was only one option.

I took the gun in my right hand and aimed it over the fleshy part of my left hand, where the thumb and palm meet. Taking a deep breath, I pulled the trigger, the nail shooting into my tissue.

"Motherfucker!" I screamed, blood pouring everywhere. But holy fuck, that felt good. The pain was almost blinding. The thing with intense pain is that it forces you to focus; it almost clears your mind. It's like the fast-track to meditation. You can either close your eyes and chant for ten years or just shoot yourself in the hand. Either way, you'll get clarity. I wondered how long I could leave the nail in my hand. I Googled heavy-metal nail poisoning, but the results were disappointing. I finally grabbed pliers and pulled the nail out, gritting my teeth. I yelled the entire time. So much for being strong. Thank God Frank couldn't hear me.

I ran the hand under water. It no longer seemed like *my* hand. It felt removed from me. After washing it, I mopped up the blood and wrapped it up, covering it with Band-Aids. Shit, I realized belatedly that I needed a Tetanus shot.

Four hours later, I was injected, stitched up (seven stitches!), and bandaged. Looking good, Anya. I tweeted a photo of my hand with the caption *I'm no Martha Stewart. Ow! #Notsohandy.*

My apartment was decorated *and* I had an alibi against power tools. Two birds, one nail gun.

* * *

The next day at the office, Sarah decided she was going to sit at Zhazha's desk no matter what. And she was wearing Z's heinous Georges Pike bracelet, from his new Zhazha line. It had been left in one of the desk drawers. Of course Sarah pounced on it. She was a taker.

"Wow, what happened to your hand?" She gestured to my overly bandaged wound. The doctors at Mt. Sinai had been a little overeager, but I was still proud of my little show-and-tell.

"Ugh, decorating accident. I was not put on this planet to wield power tools." I made a face.

"Ha, apparently not. You should just hire someone to decorate for you."

"You know, that's not a bad idea. Maybe I can do a story about it."

"Yeah, probs."

"Isn't that Zhazha's bracelet, Sarah?"

"This? Yeah. But she can't wear it, so I may as well keep it."

"But it was made for her, so people will know. That may come off as tacky. Maybe you should send it back to Georges?"

"Send it back?" She looked at me blankly.

"Maybe he'll send you one for yourself?"

"Ohhh! A Sarah bracelet! Great idea, Anya!" She picked up the phone and started dialing. It was strange that the girl couldn't remember what she had for lunch yet somehow knew every designer's phone number by heart.

"Georges? It's Sarah. Taft, from *La Vie*. Hi, darling. What? Oh, I know, what horrible news. Listen, I'm going through all the boxes on *my* desk, and I see a bracelet for Zhazha. Can I send it back? It's not in my taste. Perhaps you can send something that's more . . . me? . . . I see. It was a special gift . . . What do you mean you can't send me anything? Don't you know who I am? Well, see if you ever land in *La Vie* again!" She slammed the phone down.

I grinned. "Did it not go well?"

"How dare he! He said no! To me! Well, I'm keeping it. I'll show him." Before Zhazha came along, before me, no one said no to Sarah. I felt a moment of satisfaction. Sarah held her wrist up, admiring the tacky piece of shit. Why would anyone combine leather, chains, crystals, beads, studs, and charms on one piece of jewelry? Georges Pike had never heard of editing. No wonder Zhazha loved him so much.

"Maybe he's doing you a favor, Sarah. That thing is hideous."

"It is not! He's a genius."

"A genius who's not interested in you. Seriously, toss it."

"No." She pouted. "I am going to prove him wrong. By the time I'm done with him, he'll be begging for my forgiveness."

I rolled my eyes and went back to work, adding a jewelry story to our editorial calendar ("Ten Statement Jewelry Pieces to Die For"). Sarah sighed loudly. I ignored her. I was working on being more logical. And my brain was telling me to not give in to Sarah's needs. She sighed again, this time setting her head down on her desk dramatically.

"Jesus, what?"

"Jack's ignoring me."

"So sort it out. What the hell do you want me to do about it?" I was dancing with fucking joy on the inside. Jack and I were chatting and texting nonstop. I had to reinforce to him what a bad friend Sarah was so I'd been typing up my (real and fictitious) conversations with Sarah: *Jack, she said she hated your capes today. Ugh, what a see-you-next-Tuesday.*

That bitch, he wrote back.

"I thought you'd care." She looked wounded, as if I'd nail-gunned her hand instead of mine.

"We're not friends, remember? You said so yourself." *Be strong, Anya.*

"Ugh, I was just mad at you, hello?"

I didn't reply. My mind was ultraclear still after my nail-gun experiment. I could actually think. I could see outcomes in ways I hadn't before. This was what I needed to be doing. Clarity was such a precious gift. I was going to go see Dr. M today. He'd be so proud of me.

* * *

When I got back from my lunch, Sarah was gone, making the rounds at all the jewelry designers and pointedly skipping Georges Pike. She was determined to write the roundup to end all jewelry roundups and wanted everyone to know.

Greg finally showed up while Sarah was out. He was pacing up and down the hallway, walking in the shadows, jumping when anyone came near him.

"Greg?"

He jumped. "Oh, Anya. Hi." His skin was sallow, almost waxy looking. He'd been skipping his spray-tan sessions, and his hair looked like it hadn't been washed in weeks.

"Um, can I help you?"

"Y-you haven't seen Sarah around, have you?"

"No, I think she's at an appointment. Do you need something?"

"No, no, that's good. D-Don't tell her you saw me."

"Greg, is everything okay?" I asked. He motioned to me to follow him into Celia's office. She was at some spa.

"She's crazy!" he stage-whispered.

"Who is?"

"Sarah! When she found out about me and Zhazha, she went ballistic. She put cameras up! She spied on me." He lowered his voice to a whisper. "I-I think she killed her."

"Greg, did she threaten you?"

His eyes widened.

"Do you need help?"

He somehow grew paler.

"Listen, why don't you call the detective working the cases? He'll help you, okay? Here's his number." I wrote it down on a Post-It.

"Okay. Thank you, Anya." His eyes teared up.

I recoiled. Greg was a mess. He needed to be more logical, like me. He should fire her. But he wouldn't. He was so weak. Sarah could claim harassment, but she hadn't yet. I'd seen several suit-wearing people going in and out of Greg's office over the past few days. Legal was working on it, figuring out how to come out on top. Circling the wagons, assessing risk . . . insert jargon here.

I should give them something to really worry about. And I would.

18

Before Zhazha's memorial that Thursday, Celia took me, Dalia, Evie, Sarah, and a few others to Narcissa for dinner. She figured if we were going to drink vodka in honor of Z, we needed actual sustenance too. I couldn't fault her reasoning, except none of us were actually allowed to eat in front of her. She ordered tuna tartare, a pear salad, carrot fries, oysters, and a few entrées. We had four bottles of wine and nibbled on the salad. When Celia got up to say hi to someone at the bar, Dalia leaned over and whispered, "We are getting pizza later, right?"

"Oh, obvi," Sarah answered.

"We're going to have to," Evie added.

"Just don't tell Celia," I chimed in.

"Meanwhile, Anya, that's a rather colorful dress for such a solemn occasion," Sarah noted. Everyone's eyes swiveled over. I was wearing a Mary Katrantzou dress. It was black with an explosion of color. I wore a black bandage on my hand.

"Well, I decided to wear something that would honor Zhazha. She'd hate all black. She'd think it was boring."

"Oh, God, you are so right!" Dalia exclaimed, downing her third glass of wine.

"Still, don't you think it will look bad?" Sarah was trying to bait me. But my outfit was fucking perfect. I had tried on four different looks before deciding on it. I steeled myself. Sarah's taunts would not faze me.

"Well, if anyone is offended, they can come talk to me." I shoved a forkful of lettuce into my mouth.

"Offended by what?" Celia asked, rejoining our table.

"By Anya's obviously inappropriate dress." Sarah rolled her eyes.

Celia took in my outfit thoughtfully. "I think Mary Katrantzou is an inspired choice. Exactly what Zhazha would have wanted. And just enough black to make it occasion appropriate. Really, Sarah, when did you stop taking fashion risks?"

I bit my lip to keep from laughing. *Always win* sounded off in my head.

"Hey, Sarah, what did you do to Greg?" I asked, silencing the table.

"What? I didn't do anything to Greg." Her voice rose in pitch.

"Oh, weird, that's not what he said. He said you were crazy and, like, watching him? And then he asked for help and then called the police." I calmly took a sip of wine. Evie was grinning like a cat, enjoying the drama. Dalia's face went ashen; she was too nice for the fashion world.

"Whatever. He's so dramatic. We just had a fight."

"So he won't be telling the police anything? I don't know how much more you can afford to have leaked."

Her eyes went wide. She looked around at the table in disbelief. Sarah's mouth opened and closed like a fish.

"Are you threatening me, Anya?" she growled. "Because I know plenty about you . . ."

I grinned. "Why would you think that's a threat? Isn't that interesting . . ." I stared at her until she looked away. I wanted to hug her. To gossip with her. But all of that was shoved so far down that I could only be cold. I turned to Celia. "Shall we go soon?"

* * *

The Russian Vodka Bar was dark. So dark, you felt like you couldn't breathe. It was not a fashion destination.

Celia wrinkled her nose at the loud electronic music playing over a speaker. "Well, it's a look" was all she said.

"Hello! You must be . . . Anya?" A man with dark, thinning hair and one gold necklace came up to me. "I am Dimitri, Zhanna's cousin. Thank you for coming."

"Dimitri, so good to finally meet you," I said, trying unsuccessfully to dodge his hug. His cologne—Thierry Mugler's Amen—enveloped me. I started coughing.

"Ah, you must be so upset still. Here, drink." He handed me a shot and watched me expectantly.

"To Zhazha," I choked down my shot. He nodded approvingly before pounding his own.

"And you must be Celia, yes?" The ritual was repeated until all of us had taken shots. Finally, Dimitri led us to a table and sat us down, joining us briefly. I hoped it would be brief, at least.

"So, Dimitri, are the shots traditional in Russian memorial services?" Celia asked.

"We leave vodka and black bread for the body in Russia. Tonight, we do it up Brighton Beach style." He gestured to the waitress to bring more shots.

"Brighton Beach style?" Sarah asked, shooting me a look.

"Yes, it's where we live for last eight years."

"I thought Zhazha was from Siberia?"

"Zhanna? No, no, she worked as waitress in my uncle's bar. But then she became a model—Zhazha." I felt Sarah's accusatory eyes on me. "I should go say hello to more people." He hopped across the room, greeting other guests, drinking more vodka.

"Did you know she was a fake when you brought her to us?" Sarah glared at me.

"She was a huge blogger. We needed her. What does it matter?"

"But she was a nobody!" We were all nobodies. Except for Sarah.

"Sarah, is this really the time or place? Zhazha's dead."

"Yes, yes it is!" Her voice bordered on hysterical. Then again, she had been beaten by a dead Brooklyn waitress. "You would like her. Both of you, fucking phonies. You're both frauds!"

I kept my face still. I'd come too far to be taken down by her now. No one reacted to her accusation. I let out a breath. I was relieved no one cared.

"Girls, let's not," Celia said at last. "How long do we really have to stay here?"

"Twenty minutes; otherwise, it looks bad," I noted.

"Then let's get more vodka." Celia gestured for another round while I scanned the room. It was mostly fashion people (including Jack, who sat down at our table, perched next to me), some bloggers, some of Zhazha's weird fans (Flower Power and Simon were there but too scared to approach us). My Lauren-bot was in the corner, her shard glistening in the dim light. I thought I spied Zhazha herself, carrying her head around, but she ducked down a hall before I could catch her. She wouldn't be tacky enough to show up to her own funeral, would she? Even Mulberry hadn't done that. Well, this was Zhazha we were talking about. I kept staring, looking for her, and instead caught the eye of Detective Hopper. He walked over. Strutted. The man could do a mean catwalk. Jack let out a low whistle.

"Hello, Detective. You know everyone here."

"Evening, everyone." He nodded.

"Detective!" Sarah said. "Did you know that Zhazha was a fraud and Anya knew? Wouldn't that give her, like, grounds for murder?"

He glanced at me before answering. Those eyes. "Yes, I did, actually. We've looked into Zhazha's background. Anya told me, as a matter of fact." I smiled to myself. He *did* like me. "But . . . say someone has had a lot of public fights with

Zhazha and threatened her with witnesses around. And filmed her ex sleeping with Zhazha. *That* person would be a prime suspect."

The color in Sarah's face drained. "You don't mean . . . me, do you?"

I fake coughed to cover up my snort.

"We'd like to speak to you tomorrow, Ms. Taft," Detective Hopper continued, ignoring me. "Anya, may I have a word?" He grabbed my elbow and escorted me ten feet away. This was the most we'd touched in a while. My mind was doing cartwheels.

"You need to be careful with Sarah. Don't hang out with her, cut down how much you're alone with her."

"So you definitely suspect her?" I wanted to hug him. If Sarah wouldn't be my bestie, she'd have to pay for it. Her entire life was going to be an ode to me. I could kill her. It's not like I hadn't thought about it. Debated it. Made pro and con lists. But what I learned with Meredith is that it was over too quickly. Sarah wouldn't suffer if I killed her. I wanted her whole life ruined. Love me or else.

"I can't comment, you know that. All I can say is that I'd sleep better knowing you weren't around her. We don't know what she's capable of."

"Wait, you think about me before you sleep?" I grinned.

"That—that's not the point. Anya, are you going to listen to me or not?"

"I am, but I had to come tonight. I promise, I'll stay away from her."

"Good. Also, we spoke with Greg Davies. Did he tell you anything?"

I nodded. "Just that she had filmed him. He was pretty hysterical."

Detective Hopper looked grim as he shook his head. "We saw the footage."

"We all saw the footage. She posted it online."

"Listen, just stay away from her," he repeated. He squeezed my arm and glanced at my bandage. "What happened to your hand?"

"Oh, home decor accident. I tweeted all about it." Apparently he didn't follow me on Twitter.

"Looks painful. Be safe." He pointed at me. His finger was so close, I could lick it. (I refrained.) He left me standing there.

Back at the table, Sarah sat glaring, no doubt hoping she could kill me with just her eyes.

"What's the matter, Sarah? Not in the mood to toast to Zhazha?" I asked.

"Fuck you, Anya."

"What did the detective want?" Evie asked, aiming for innocent but failing.

"Oh, Greg went to see him. Something about you threatening him?" I stared at Sarah as I said it.

Jack gasped. "Oh, shit. Sarah, you need to get your ass a lawyer."

"Shut up, Jack. You're so not helping!" she wailed. He looked hurt for a second and then rolled his eyes. He held my hand.

"God, Sarah, you are such a psycho!" Evie grabbed a drink and threw it back.

"Sarah, I think you should leave," Celia said while motioning the waiter for yet more drinks. Sarah dropped her head and then got up. No argument. She grabbed her coat and ran out of the bar.

"Wow, she's going to take us all out," Dalia said.

"Probably." I shrugged. Jack hugged me. He was my friend now.

* * *

The next day, I wore a new Rick Owens dress (black with a sheer skirt attached) along with motorcycle boots by Givenchy. Was it a bit much? Yes, but after Sarah's freak-out in front of everyone, I needed a solid look. Wearing four thousand dollars' worth of clothing just for a Thursday may have seemed excessive, but welcome to fashion.

I was going to ascend today. Become a true *La Vie* woman. I wasn't running around, making a scene at memorials. I wasn't accused of killing Zhazha or Cassie or Mulberry or Lisa. I was keeping calm, dressing well, and doing everything Celia wanted. I hadn't bled at work in days! I was her ideal *La Vie* girl. I had done it.

Sarah's voice wafted over to me. "And this is my desk. Say hi, Anya!" she said, waving at me. With her was a teenage girl holding an iPhone, filming her.

"What's this?" I tried to duck out of the video.

"My vlog, duh! The police want to account for my whereabouts, so I thought why not just put it on YouTube, right? Brillz, huh?" She grinned. It *was* brilliant. Why didn't I think of that?

"Who's she?" I asked.

The girl behind the phone smiled at me.

"My intern, obvi. This is Amanda. Say hi, Mandy!"

"Hi!"

"So this is Anya. She works for me." Sarah moved to stand next to me.

"I don't want to be on your stupid vlog, Sarah." I covered my face.

"Anya, chill. No one cares about you. I mean, what is this outfit? Wait, you have like a tag or something. Hold on." She yanked on my collar. Nothing happened. I was too aware of how close her hands were to my neck. She yanked harder.

"Just cut it, Jesus."

"I got it!"

A horrible ripping sound filled my ears.

"Did you just tear my Rick Owens dress?" Deep, cleansing breaths. Inhale and exhale. Everything was going to be fine.

"O-M-G, I did. Ha ha, oopsies!" She giggled.

"You'll have to pay for it to be fixed." I was furious. My dress was ruined.

"Ugh, whatever. Don't wear designer if you can't handle wear and tear. A real fashion girl would know that."

Right there, in front of little Mandy, I smashed Sarah's head into my knee. And then on my desk. Over and over and over, blood splashing—

"Okay, we're off! Toodles!" Sarah grinned. Then to the camera, "Anya is very tightly wound. I think because she's totes in love with the detective we work with."

This was not how I expected my day to go. I didn't think Sarah would go full Kardashian with a camera. Or that she'd ruin my new dress. Or announce to the fucking world I liked Detective Hottie—Hopper. It was too much. It was as if the world had collectively decided to throw me in the trash. How could you fight that?

Sarah skipped happily down the hall, colliding into Celia and Bronwen. (The assistant wore a literal crown of thorns today.)

"What are you doing, Sarah?" Celia asked.

"Sorry, boss! Wow, Bronwen, doesn't that hurt?"

"Have you gone down to the police station yet?"

"Not yet. But I'm recording my vlog for them."

"Get down there, now. Straighten all this out. If I find out you didn't talk to them today, so help me God, I'll put Anya in charge of *you*."

Sarah actually screamed then. I didn't take offense. I'd make her grovel if I were in charge. Every menial task, every mean thing she said, I'd take out on her several times over.

"That's what happens when you kill people," I called out.

"I didn't kill anyone!" she yelled back. Something flew my way.

"Sarah! If you throw one more thing, I will call security," Celia scolded. She looked tired. I wondered if there was trouble at home, though I didn't really care.

Sarah sobbed as she ran out. God, she was so emotional. She really needed to learn how to keep cool. I picked up the phone from where she had thrown it. It was still recording.

"We need to do something about her," Celia muttered.

"The police will probably take care of it."

"Will they?"

I shrugged.

"Bronwen, go get me a half-soy, half-almond milk latte," Celia said.

And then I was alone.

I could erase the whole video. But I didn't. A Sarah tantrum was pure gold. I could blur my face. Or the part about being a real fashion girl. But I left it. They were the ravings of a lunatic. I went to Sarah's desk, giving her future audience a tour of her belongings. Her desk, not Zhazha's.

I narrated as I opened each drawer to show what she had inside. Her collection of lipsticks and glosses, hair brushes, a box of tampons—and voodoo dolls.

"What's this?" I held up six dolls. Each were named. Each had pins in them. Mulberry, Cassie, Lisa, Zhazha, Jack. And me. "Oh, shit." I panned over each one before hitting stop. I couldn't wait to send it to Detective Hopper. Should I cut that part about him out? No. The less edited, the better. I emailed myself the file and forwarded it to him along with a note, *This happened today.* No love notes. No emotion.

"Anya! What the fuck is this?" Celia bellowed twenty minutes later. The video was live and spreading on Twitter. Uploading took a bit, but the world had to see it. I was merely doing everyone a favor.

"Um, Sarah's vlog. Did you see the voodoo dolls? There's one for me. I can't work here if she's going to be allowed unfettered access. She's a murderer, Celia!" I wiped my eyes with shaking fingers. A good touch, I thought. One of us had to go. And it would be Sarah. It had to be. A *La Vie* woman didn't draw the wrong kind of attention.

"You're right, you shouldn't have to. But I'll be real with you—if we don't up our numbers, there'll be layoffs. And right now, Sarah is the only reason people are coming to us. Her infamy is great for our traffic."

"So you're keeping a murderer over me?"

"No, no, of course not. We want both of you to stay."

Commit, Anya. Commit to this moment. I stood up.

"No. I will not work with her. I quit. Effective immediately." The words came out before I could stop them. Dr. M would say my ego was taking over.

Dread, that's what I felt. Dread and panic and total and complete fear. My heart drummed in my ears. Have you ever lost a job? You know that moment when shit hits the fan and you have no choice but to accept what's happening? I wasn't fired. But how could I stay there? How could I go to work every day knowing Celia would always pick Sarah over me? That no matter what I did or who I did it to, Sarah Taft would win. She was born lucky and would always be lucky. The rest of us would have to claw our way up, make luck happen.

Okay, maybe emotion and ego won out this time. But how much is a girl supposed to take? I did all the hard work. All of it! And Sarah was reaping the benefits. I was supposed to get the promotion. I should have been in charge. It was *me, my work*. I packed up my desk shoes in various tote bags and walked out.

Celia Avery would pay for this. She'd regret not choosing me, not making me her star editor. I giggled as I left the building. I felt better just thinking about what I was going to do to her.

19

ersonnel changes at magazines are like celeb breakups. Every other fashion site and blog has to run who left, why, and who the winner was. Usually, that's the magazine. But I'd be damned if I'd let *La Vie* win anything. They picked Sarah over me again. The insult. So I made sure to talk to a website or two, mentioning all the videos (Greg's romps included). I dropped hints about the fingernails found in Sarah's desk too. I'd been wronged, and Sarah was a murderer. Dr. M thought I was desperate for attention. But what did he know? He didn't even read magazines.

Zhazha would have been by my side, laughing the whole way. I really did miss that stupid bitch. Why'd she have to go behind my back? If only she could have been a normal friend instead of such a needy soul sucker. But at least I wasn't dealing with her whining right now. I was also kind of over Detective Hopper, especially since he insisted on calling me not to chat but to yell at me. I hated when people yelled at me.

"Did you have to drop the information about the case?"

"I said they should contact you. I didn't give out any new info." I didn't, not really.

"Yes, you did." His voice was stern. And sexy.

"Like what? And did you tell me it was confidential or off limits? Did you ask me to sign anything? No. And was any of what I implied wrong?"

I could hear him sigh. "First off, we haven't connected Lisa's case to Zhazha, or any of the others."

"Oh, come on—"

"Second, no one needed to know about the fingernails. And now because of you, we have to do a press conference."

"Well, it's about time. People are getting antsy."

"Hey, don't tell me how to do my job!" he snapped.

"I'm not! But people want to know what's going on. They're scared."

"Fine. The press conferences aren't up to me. I don't decide when those happen. Anyways . . ." He paused, calming himself down. "I can't reach your doctor. Have him call me. We can't clear you without talking to him."

"He's so forgetful. Just email him. It's probably easier." I gave him Dr. M's email address. He checked it often, but I had to remind him. I even had to check his email for him some days. We were close enough that he didn't mind.

"Thanks." He hung up.

Our relationship was clearly in a rough patch. That was to be expected. Seventy percent of office romances don't work out. Proven fact. Some things were beyond even my control. (Maybe I could pitch a story to someone about not dating coworkers. "Workplace Romance: Road to Disaster or Honeymoon in the Conference Room?")

* * *

I needed to focus on plan C (for Celia). I had to bide my time, because it would be really suspicious if anyone dropped dead right now. Sure, I'd just thrown Sarah's pretty little head under the bus, but I'd also walked out in a huff. Too risky. So I waited a week, pacing around my apartment, drawing up contingency plans, and coming up with my final exit strategy. Then I wardrobe-planned because outfit changes were key. Okay, fine, I also binge-watched *Law & Order*.

* * *

233

It was finally C-Day. I had a meeting at two PM at the *La Vie* offices with Celia, Greg, and possibly human resources. Celia had been really vague on the phone about the whole thing.

"We just need to clear the air. How's two? I have Botox in the morning, so you know." (I did. I had copies of everyone's calendars.)

Celia and Greg were either hoping to lure me back or trying to see if I was going to sue them. (Emotional distress? They pushed me to murder?) Companies didn't care about retaining talent anymore; they only cared about covering their asses. That was the real problem with the editorial world these days. The grand old days of developing real genius on your staff had died out. Now it was all about marketing dollars and social engagement.

At one PM, I put on a Stella McCartney metallic sweat shirt with matching sweat pants—thank god for athleisure. I added gold Jimmy Choo pumps. No black; I had to shine. The rain outside wouldn't ruin my power-bitch dressing.

Twenty-five minutes later, I was sitting in Greg's office waiting for Celia. The forced small talk was making me suicidal. Every time there was any noise—someone's phone pinging; a computer ding; his own squeaky, farting shoes—Greg would jump out of his skin. Poor guy. He was such a nervous nelly. I wish I'd been there for his conversation with Detective Hopper. But even some things I wasn't privy to.

Greg paced the room, looking at his watch like a nervous tic. Pace, pace, pace, stare. Pace, pace, pace, stare. "I don't know where Celia is. She's never this late."

"She did say to come at two, right?"

"Yeah. Let me call her assistant."

By 2:30, we both knew Celia wasn't coming.

"Okay, well, I'm leaving. This was a waste of my time, Greg."

"Anya, no, wait! Look, I know the situation with Sarah is tenuous, but we need you to stay. You're a key member of the team." The team. There was no team. He just wanted someone to do the work. "I don't know where Celia is, but I'm asking you to reconsider." He leaned in and quietly added, "Please don't leave me alone with Sarah."

"What you and Sarah do is none of my business. I can't stay at a publication that doesn't want to protect its employees." I had practiced my speech, trying to balance the perfect amount of outrage and boredom.

"Excuse me, Mr. Davies?" Bronwen stood at the door, her crown of gardenias slightly askew on her head.

"Is she here?"

"No, she hasn't returned and isn't answering her phone. Um, should we call someone?"

"Call who?"

"I don't know. With everything that's happened here . . ."

"Has Sarah been here all day, Bronwen?" I asked. She shook her head. The gardenias bounced around.

"No, she's out today. I don't know where."

"Try Celia's husband first, and then if you get nowhere, we can call the detective I know." She smiled, looking relieved.

"See, Anya—" Greg started.

"Don't. This is your mess."

I wrinkled my brow in worry and checked my phone. I opened the Kardashian app and watched a makeup tutorial. I knew exactly where Celia was: where I had left her. Barely alive, unable to see or speak, but probably able to breathe. Maybe able to breathe? I was, like, 99 percent sure she could still inhale oxygen.

When no one had heard from Celia by 3:30, I suggested going through her calendar to see where she'd been earlier.

"She had a ten AM, but that's it," Bronwen said.

"But where, Bronwen?" I asked.

"Oh, at her Botox doc." She smiled, crinkling her nose.

"And have you called them?"

"Should I?"

Greg and I stared at her until she picked up the phone. I tapped my foot impatiently, pointedly checking my watch. Greg's eyebrow twitched. Was that a new tic?

"I see, okay, which hospital? Thank you." Bronwen hung up. "She had an accident and was sent to Beth Israel."

"What happened?" I asked, frowning.

"They said she had a reaction to her Botox and is in the ICU."

"That doesn't make sense. She's not allergic to Botox. She practically gets weekly injections."

"Anya's right, something is off. I think we should call the police." Greg's whole head was twitching.

I was already dialing Detective Hopper. "Hi, it's Anya. Listen, I'm at *La Vie*. I was supposed to have a meeting with Celia, but she didn't show up. She supposedly had some accident with her Botox doc, and we're worried something happened. Can you meet us at Beth Israel? Great, thanks." I turned to Greg. "I'm going to the hospital. If you want, you can join me."

When we got to the emergency room, Celia's husband, David Avery, was already there, pacing. He filled us in, though he hadn't heard much. I wanted to ask him, Did she plank through dinner? Make him eat kale every day? Poke his stomach to see if he had gained weight? Did she intone that an Avery didn't leave dirty dishes in sinks? Or was she actually nice to him?

We waited for Detective Hopper to come, hoping he'd be able to find out more. He walked in the doors looking grim but hot. His suit looked a bit disheveled. I tried my best to not lick my lips.

"Walk me through what happened."

No hello, no kiss on the cheek. Two steps forward, five steps back.

David told him what he knew, and we jumped in with what Bronwen had told us. Hopper went to speak with the nurse.

"Okay, I'm going to go to this Glowing Skin place," he said when he came back. "If there's any change in her condition, please call me." With a nod of his head, Detective Hopper left. Just like that. No *Be careful, Anya*, no *See you later, Anya*, nothing. No mention of thinking about me or anything. Rude.

* * *

I'd like to say that I was at Celia's side when I heard the news, that I was holding her hand, feeding her ice chips or some shit when the phone rang. But I was getting a much-needed manicure. Good beauty maintenance cannot be avoided. And all my extracurricular work was hell on my hands. I glanced at the caller ID while the woman filed my nails. Hopper.

"Hi. Any news?"

"We arrested Sarah Taft today."

"You what?" I said a little too loudly. The nail tech glared at me, and I smiled apologetically.

"She was identified as the person who attacked Celia."

"So it wasn't an accident?"

"No, the amount of Botox in Celia's bloodstream was enough for a toxic overdose. A woman fitting Sarah's description checked in for an appointment and was seen fleeing Celia's room. A nurse at the doctor's office said Celia identified Sarah in a brief moment of consciousness."

That blonde wig was worth its weight in gold.

"Wow. Just . . . wow. I didn't know you could overdose on Botox."

"The amount in Celia's system was the highest ever recorded. It's a miracle it wasn't lethal. There's more. When we arrested Sarah, we found needles and Botox vials in her apartment. It's pretty open and shut."

"She really did it. Oh my God."

"We're waiting on her lawyer, and we're going to arraign her soon."

"For just Celia or for the other cases too?"

"Right now, just this. We don't have any proof she committed the murders, though she's our number-one suspect right now. But we're questioning her and hoping to get more evidence." He hesitated. "Anya, if and when she gets out on bail, I want you to be very careful. She's very dangerous."

I tried not to smile. "Yeah, okay, I will. This is a lot to mull over. I just can't believe it. I mean, I know we all suspected it, but it's still so shocking."

"Take care, Anya."

"Thanks, Detective." I hung up, nodding to my nail tech. "You know what? Maybe we should do bright red. I think it's a far more festive color, don't you?"

I smiled while she buffed my nails, picturing Celia passed out from the Haldol injection I gave her, unable to move or do anything while I topped off her Botox. Seriously, the security at those boutique medispa joints was ridiculously lax. Any lunatic could walk in, claim she has an appointment, and do whatever she wanted. Injecting a full syringe worth of Botox into each eye had seriously been *so* much fun. *Squish squish!* I had no idea what it all would do to her, but I was pretty positive she was going to be blind, at least. If she lived.

As a bonus, I was fairly certain she'd wet herself in the end.

"Oh, Celia, a *La Vie* woman never makes a spectacle of herself," I said, mimicking her voice. I giggled again, the nail tech watching me. "Sorry, that tickled," I said, making a face.

* * *

Sarah was charged with one count of attempted murder in the first degree, one count of assault, and one count of impersonating a doctor. The DA was still mulling over revenge porn charges, but that was a separate case. Her bail was $500,000, which was paid by her parents—though they didn't want her home with them. Sarah was released with an ankle bracelet to monitor her comings and goings. If she was found guilty, she'd get life in prison.

Can you imagine, poor Sarah Taft in jail? I tried to keep a serious look on my face as I imagined her in an orange jumpsuit for the rest of her life. No highlights. No facials. Would she go to the same prison as Martha Stewart?

The papers went wild the second they found out. *"Killer Fashion Editor Sarah Taft Gets Caught! Botox Butcher Heads to Big House!"* And then of course came the think pieces, the long essays about what could possibly drive someone like Sarah to maim and kill, about the pressures of the fashion industry. One of them quoted Dalia. (Finally, her day in the sun.)

The evidence against Sarah was pretty bad. She just hadn't been that careful. Apparently, she'd rented a mailbox nearby where the Botox had been delivered. The employee there identified her as the blonde who'd rented it—under the name Cassie Sachs but paid for with Sarah's credit card. The Glowing Skin Institute identified her as the person who came in (under the name Frou-Frou Taft) that morning and then disappeared. And Sarah herself couldn't offer up an alibi, mainly because she had been passed out in her apartment with no one to verify her location. She didn't remember me dropping by with Celia's supplies. Why would she? I snuck in while she was asleep and gave her a Haldol injection in her thigh. Intramuscular injections were the best. The tiny needle hole would never be found. So Sarah snoozed her way through Celia's attack. No alibi, no way out.

With Celia incapacitated and Sarah essentially on house arrest and not allowed within twenty feet of any *La Vie* employee, the only person overseeing the magazine was Greg. Which was how I found myself on the phone with him, agreeing to come back to work.

"Anya, come back now. It's safe!"

"Why should I? You guys screwed me."

"I know and I'm sorry. We'll fix it. Promotion and raise."

"Fine." I hung up.

I had conceded, but I had nothing else cooking at the moment. Sarah was ruined. Celia was pretty much dead. Greg jumped if you so much as said his name. I had won. I had everything I wanted. So why was I feeling so meh? I was missing something. I needed to get back to work, and that meant going back to *La Vie*.

I wore a black lace Moschino pencil skirt, black studded Valentino ankle boots, a tuxedo blazer (also black, obviously), and bright-red lipstick. I was the HBIC now. We were in the smaller conference room for our editorial meeting. There was a pall over the entire office. As if everyone was in mourning. Or realized they could have died too.

"Like, everyone only wants to talk about Sarah and the murders!" Evie was also wearing black. I glanced around. In fact, everyone was in dark colors. Was this what it meant to belong?

"I know, it's really annoying." Dalia nodded.

"So let's give everyone what they want." Too many uncomprehending eyes swiveled my way. I sighed. "Let's write about life with Sarah, working here, first person and all that. People will go bananas."

"Can we do that?" Evie asked.

"Why not?" I shrugged.

"Okay, so who writes it?"

"Well, I can write what it was like to be her work BFF and sit next to her every day. And maybe one of you can pull together a slideshow of Sarah's best photos?"

"O-M-G, that's so good," Dalia said.

"What can I write?" Evie asked.

"What was your relationship like? Maybe something about going out with Sarah?"

"I can do that. We did do a beauty trip to St. Bart's together."

"There you go. Let's get to work."

* * *

It may have been crass to turn Sarah and her legal woes into a story package for our readers, but it really helped with traffic. Celia was right about that. We could never say she was a killer, only an alleged one, but we could write what it was like to work with, travel with, and hang out with an alleged murderer; how it made us feel; and how we barely escaped with our own lives. "A *La Vie* Special Report: Our Lives with Sarah Taft" did exceptionally well, breaking our records and, at one point, breaking the site. The jail-themed fashion spread may have been a bit much, but if we didn't have a sense of humor now, when would we?

"This is awesome!" Greg raved. He had gotten some of his color back. How disappointing.

"Thanks, Greg. You know, I think just adding that personal touch really helps."

I sat at my desk at lunch eating sushi with white rice (suck it, Celia). Taking Celia's office would have been inappropriate. People would have talked, and appearances were everything. After all, her body was still warm. Until she died, I had to toil away back where I had started. And from what I could glean, David Avery had no interest in pulling the plug as long as *La Vie* was paying the bills. Some bitches got killer condos. Celia got to be a vegetable for the rest of her life. Them's the fashion perks.

I dipped my spicy tuna roll in some high-sodium, gluten-full soy sauce while reading the latest news about the case. Sarah's lawyers and PR team were working overtime to sow seeds of doubt in the populous: "There are other editors at that magazine who had more reason to kill. Why aren't we looking at them?" Sarah's legal team was smart. The DA had a strong circumstantial case against Sarah, and any jury would probably convict her. The best thing her lawyer could do was introduce an alternate theory.

Like, say, that I did it.

I wish I'd had a lawyer like this when I was a kid being questioned about Meredith. But whatever, the past is the past. No do-overs, no backsies. I wasn't going to let lawyers or Sarah Taft or anyone else pin this shit on me. I wouldn't rest until Sarah was locked up, until little Miss

20

Planning your own death takes a lot of effort. It's not just the way you're going to die; what you wear also matters. When the EMS guys came, I wanted to look fabulous. I think I'd gone through my entire closet twice before I gave up and went shopping.

I combed through the racks on Barneys' eighth and ninth floors before taking a break in the fifth-floor shoe mecca. This was home. I decided I needed to buy a new pair of Manolos. After all that hard work, it was the least I could do, and some metallic d'Orsay pumps were screaming my name. After all, I did get that promotion—in the end. And Greg gave me a $20K raise. Imagine that! If only Celia could see what I was doing to the site—she'd have a fit. But she was still in the hospital, sucking on that tube with no visitors. Her husband and Bronwen had abandoned her for some peace and quiet in Tulum.

My phone rang in the middle of shopping. To my surprise, it was Detective Hopper. He'd gone a little radio silent on me after Sarah's arrest. Some people just don't handle breakups well.

"I hope you're not calling with bad news . . ."

I heard him cough. "Sort of. I hate to tell you this, but Sarah Taft made bail."

"I know. I saw it online."

"Yeah. Right. Look, just steer clear of her and you'll be fine. And if anything happens with her, anything at all, call me. Okay?"

"Um, sure."

"Anya, be safe."

"I will, Detective. Thank you for everything." I hung up. That was all the good-bye he was going to get from me. We had a good run, but nothing lasted forever. I needed to find someone new to obsess over. Someone who didn't need to talk to my shrink.

* * *

It was strange, but I was actually looking forward to dying. It was going to be painful, sure. I imagine a lot of deaths are. But think of what it would accomplish. The end goal was what mattered. I would win. Not just this battle, but the war. And don't kid yourselves: this was a war. Against Sarah, against Celia, against all of *La Vie*. They were all against me. Even when things went my way, even when they let me do what I wanted, they were against me. They'd never let me be one of them. They were just biding their time, waiting. Lulling me into a false sense of security. But eventually, they'd attack. I couldn't let that happen. Just imagine the public outcry over my death. It was going to be glorious! It's kind of like when you want to stage your own funeral just to see who goes and what they say about you.

Frankly, all my work still didn't feel like enough. Sure, there had been Cassie. And Zhazha. And poor, dumb little Mulberry. Lisa. Sad Diana, who nobody knew but who had impacted *La Vie* so much. And, okay, Celia, but she was kind of alive still. My death would hit them hard, but I was sure some people (cough, cough, Evie) were expecting it. I was, after all, Sarah's main rival. So I needed one big coup de grace before I died. *La Vie*'s deathblow. A final mood board.

I wanted to reach each and every employee at *La Vie*, from the interns to the sales team, from the credits assistants to the stylists. Publishing has always been about the numbers.

244

Metrics! We need metrics! A splash. Numbers were what mattered the most. If you don't reach the largest audience, you're a failure. And sometimes the answer was right in front of you. I wanted to slap myself, it was so obvious:

I was going to kill everyone.

* * *

I went about assembling the parts for this penultimate act, something for *La Vie* to remember me by. To curse my name. Or Sarah's, actually. All this work only to have the credit go elsewhere. It kind of sucked, but it was either this or be a credit hog locked away. Still, I'd know who did it all. That's what mattered.

My tools: a couple boxes of plastic tampons, a dropper, glue, an X-Acto knife, tweezers, and fentanyl. I had other poisons I liked better, but fentanyl was just so easy to get. (Dr. M wrote prescriptions like they were candy. He was the best.) Besides, I had a surplus in my apartment that needed to be used.

Someone was always on her period at work. The staff was 95 percent women. And for whatever reason, *La Vie* didn't offer free tampons (though everyone knew that tampons should be free to the world; it was a basic human right). Every week another editor or assistant went wandering the halls asking if someone had one to spare. Keeping boxes in your desk was the norm. We'd pilfer from a drawer whether the owner was around or not. Bloody vaginal emergencies were important.

And that's how I thought of it; the idea was just staring up at me when I went to the bathroom one day. Poisoned tampons.

So there I was, spending an evening carefully slicing open tampon wrappers, sliding the cotton plug out of the applicator without damaging the plastic, adding a tiny amount of fentanyl to the cotton—enough to do damage but not warp the material—sliding the tampon back into its applicator, and then gluing the packaging back together. It took me thirty minutes to do my first one, but by the end, I was averaging eight minutes per tampon. The mistake pile had to be redone, and I went through two boxes to get thirty-six wrappers to look just right. But my masterpiece was ready.

The next day, I left the box of perfectly gorgeous tampons in Sarah's abandoned desk. Most of her belongings were still there, though people had already stolen a few things. Slowly, her pens, notepads, and other supplies had disappeared. It was only a matter of time before the rest of her desk was reabsorbed into the office ecosystem, feeding the rest of the fauna and flora that made up our sad drone lives. If anyone "borrowed" Sarah's tampons, they'd learn to keep their hands, and vaginas, to themselves. They'd die in waves, over weeks. Then again, staff turnover at fashion magazines was notoriously high.

"Hey, Anya. What are you doing?" Dalia asked as I sized up Sarah's desk.

"Oh, just wondering if we should return some of the personal items to Sarah."

"Why? She can't use her lip gloss collection in prison." She laughed at her own joke.

"Because it's her stuff."

At my various schools, whenever someone would leave—whether because they were lucky enough to reintegrate or they'd given up, gone crazier, or landed in jail—their leftover belongings were never returned to them. Most of the family members didn't want the sad mementos we kept. Other girls would descend upon the dog-eared books and magazines like assistants at a sample sale. It was soul crushing.

Sarah deserved to have her things returned. It was only right. And going to her apartment gave me the perfect opportunity to stash my mood boards, right where the police would find them. Just the key ones: Mulberry, Cassie, Lisa, Zhazha, Celia, the entire staff, and now, one for me. (Mine included photos of me with cutouts of knives.)

I found an almost empty box in the supply closet, dumped it out, and brought it over. It would suffice for most of Sarah's things. Three pairs of shoes (minus the boxes), two bags, six lip glosses, two bronzers, Band-Aids, tweezers, a small mirror, and a framed photo of Frou-Frou. Lisa's long-dead phone and the mood boards. I picked everything up with a plastic bag.

"Bad vibes," I muttered.

Dalia watched me for a moment and then shuffled off. She had given her two weeks' notice, and would soon be free of *La Vie*. Of Sarah. Of me. I envied her. She was moving on to the retail world: Barneys. To oversee accessories buying. Her boss was Aiko, the head buyer. One name only. She was the source for everything I bought. I wanted to take Dalia's place. Maybe later.

"I loved my time at *La Vie*," she said when she told me, "but my future is elsewhere." We both knew she'd put up with too much shit here. "Besides, with all the murders . . ."

I'd actually hugged her. It felt weird.

When I was done with her desk, I emailed Sarah and asked her if she'd like us to send a box of her items. She called me right away.

"O-M-G, Anya, I didn't kill anyone. You have to believe me," she said instead of a greeting.

"Sarah, um, that's great. Listen, I really shouldn't be talking to you."

"You have to. This is really scary. Jail is bad. I don't want to go back!" She sounded terrified. Joy radiated through me.

"So what do you want me to do with your things?"

"Who cares about them! I just want to see my friends. Can I come over maybe? Wait, I can't. Can you bring my things to me tomorrow and we can watch TV?"

"I don't think that's a good idea—"

"Please? I'll order food!"

I sighed. "What time?"

"How's eight?"

"Fine, but I'm still not sure this is smart."

"Oh, it'll be great, you'll see! We can do manicures!" She giggled for a few seconds too long. She was cracking.

I knew Detective Hopper would be pissed at me if I went over, but I felt sorry for Sarah. Besides, she was an integral part in my plan to die. I had to see her. I could show her my new toy: a selfie stick. She'd be totally into it. A way to take more photos of yourself? How could she not love it? Besides, she had technically bought it. Well, her credit card had. I wondered when she'd realize that she had lost it and that I was running up charges. Oh, well, I would leave it at her apartment tomorrow.

* * *

My new Cornejo dress did look pretty fucking spectacular. Such a shame I wouldn't be able to wear it again. You can't wear something after you died in it. That was so gauche. Besides, blood was a bitch to get out.

Black and white with gold d'Orsay pumps. It was kind of perfect. My hair was in loose waves, and I kept my makeup natural looking, with hints of pink. I wanted to look innocent and sweet.

I picked up Sarah's box, the selfie stick, and the folded-up mood boards. My Uber was waiting, I had to go. It was now or never.

Sarah was overly excited when I arrived. It was as if two dogs were jumping on me, not just her and her tiny, over-stimulated pom.

"Anya!"

"Jeez, Sarah, calm down."

"Sorry, I'm just excited to see you." Her eyes were wide, and she was grinning. Jesus, she meant it.

"Look, I really shouldn't be here . . . *La Vie* will get pissed, and the NYPD—" She dug her nails into my skin. That was going to leave marks. Good. For once, I wasn't worried about evidence. "Do you mind?"

"Anya, please. I haven't seen anyone. And they're going to send me back there. Please don't leave me alone tonight!" Were those . . . tears?

Had I finally broken Sarah Elizabeth Taft?

"Okay, I'll stay. Let's just get inside before anyone sees."

She smiled, relieved. I should have felt sorry for her. But pity was a useless emotion. Pity and guilt, ugly sisters who should never exist. Sarah had taken my promotion. She'd betrayed me and everyone else. She'd threatened me, her friend. Blackmail is never a good relationship foundation. Sarah had wanted to be the star of *La Vie*. Well, I was going to make sure everyone knew her name forever.

"Where can I put this?" I nodded to the heavyish box I was carrying.

"Oh, wherever. You didn't even need to bring it, but I'm glad you did. Seriously, Anya, thank you."

Sarah could change moods and personalities faster than anyone I'd ever known. Dr. M would have had a field day with her. Imagine all the sessions, the dream journals, the medications. The bills. The man could have retired on Sarah alone.

I walked beyond the foyer and glanced hesitantly around. It was a mess—and that was being kind. Clothes were piled up everywhere, dog toys strewn about. The pungent smell of stale dog pee hung in the air. Frou-Frou wagged his tail, waiting for a treat. I should have brought him a tampon to gnaw on.

"So what have you been doing with yourself, Sarah?" I asked, setting the box down on the kitchen counter. The smell was worse the deeper you went into the apartment. It was like something died in here. Fitting. I was pretty sure food was rotting away. I handed her the mood boards, and she absent-mindedly took them, not even looking at them. She put them on the counter next to the box.

"Oh, nothing really. It's hard to go out—the paparazzi are everywhere. Did you see them outside?"

"Uh, no, no one was out there." Was she delusional now? Hallucinating? Maybe I had pushed her too far.

"Oh, well, they usually are."

"Can we open a window? It's a little ripe in here."

"Is it? Sorry, the cleaning lady quit."

"Do you have any perfume you can spray? I think the dog peed or something."

She sprayed some Le Labo Jasmin perfume, which sat on the room funk, adding a spicy level to the ammonia-scented air. I tried not to gag. The buzzing noise started up.

"There!" She smiled, satisfied. She breathed deeply.

"Maybe we should go out?"

"No. I can't." She pointed to her leg. I looked down at her ankle bracelet and nodded. Old Sarah, *my* Sarah, would have bedazzled it. "And anyways, I look awful. My highlights aren't done, and I don't want any more photos in the paper. Daddy said he was going to cut me off if there was one more—and then I'll have to use a public defender!" She started sobbing.

"It's fine, really. I just need to get used to the smell. Don't worry."

"Are you sure?" She wiped her nose. A *La Vie* woman would never use her hand to wipe. Gross, Sarah.

We moved to the living room to watch TV while Sarah babbled almost incoherently about what she was going to do once she was found not guilty. Her lawyer planned a not guilty defense by reason of insanity.

"You do understand what that means, right?" I said.

"That I'm not guilty."

"No, Sarah, it means you're incapable of being found guilty because you're insane. They'll send you to an asylum."

"Oh, I know. Isn't it great?" She beamed. "Mommy said I could go to one of those places and rest, like Passages Malibu. I mean, I am, like, totally exhausted." Her fake cheery voice almost drowned out the buzzing noise. I wondered if it was coming from her voice box. What if she was a bot? That would explain so much. "And then you and Jack can come visit me!"

"I don't think it's like that—"

"Anya! Stop being so damn negative!"

"You're right. What do I know? Your lawyer obviously wouldn't steer you wrong. Um, I'm going to get some water." I debated leaving. Maybe I could just make a run for it. She was already being tried for Celia. That could be enough. Surely I could come up with a new plan. Nothing was worth this.

No, I had to do this. I'd come too far. Sarah had to fall, especially if she wanted real fame. She had to become a *Dateline* special with Lester Holt, not just a Wikipedia entry. *Keep going, Anya. Don't turn back.* I had to finish her. I had to end this. I closed my eyes. I could picture her locked up, her hair matted and her highlights grown out. She'd get puffy from all the carbs she'd have to eat. The vision motivated me. Pushed me on. I remained calm. Everything was going to work out just fine. I would have done my breathing exercises, but I didn't want to choke on the stench.

"You know, you keep saying you're going to be found not guilty. But what if they find you guilty of the other murders?"

"The other murders? I'm not being tried for those."

"Not yet. But what if they find evidence linking you to those?" I had taken my hunting knife out of my a plastic bag in my purse. The same knife I used on Cassie. Bought with Sarah's card. I carried that and the selfie stick, which I dropped on the floor.

"How could they when I didn't do them?" She smiled, showing all her teeth. It was her beauty pageant smile. All rich, pretty girls have one.

"I don't know. So many bodies have piled up. Celia. Cassie. Mulberry. Zhazha, Lisa. And, well, me."

"You? I never tried to kill you."

"Yes, you did. Tonight. You stabbed me. I nearly died. And you had something against all of us."

She laughed nervously. I laughed with her, then louder, throwing my head back and cackling.

"Anya, you're so funny."

"I know. I have a *wicked* sense of humor."

Have you ever stabbed yourself? Not just cut yourself—anyone can cut themselves—but really, honest-to-God stabbed yourself? Plunging a knife into your body isn't as easy as the movies make it look. But I had to do it. I had to die, and I had to die in Sarah Taft's apartment.

I took a deep breath, holding the knife in my left hand. No hesitation. They can tell when you do that, you know. One deep, purposeful plunge. Shove it like you mean it. *One, two . . .*

"Holy motherfucker!" I yelled. Sarah screamed.

Don't ever let someone tell you being stabbed doesn't hurt. It's painful as all hell.

"What are you doing? O-M-G, O-M-G!" She kept repeating that idiotic acronym.

I hated her more than life right now, which was okay since I was pretty sure I was going to bleed out. I pulled the knife out of my flesh, groaning the entire time. Yeah, I was definitely going to die. I looked at Sarah. "I did it all for you. You could have loved me. But no. You had to be a fucking bitch about everything. You took and you took and not once did you think about me. Did you?" I spat the words out. "You did this. You made this all happen. It's your fault!"

"But . . ." She didn't finish her thought. Sarah still didn't realize what was happening. She didn't get it. Not because she was dumb, but things like this didn't happen to people like her.

I knew this part would suck, but I had to do it. I lunged, landing on top of her. My abdomen seared with pain. I held the bloody knife in my right hand and stabbed her before she could move away. And then I felt wetness as the knife slid into Sarah. Shit, did I go too deep? I wasn't supposed to kill her. If only she were more cooperative. I should have drugged her the second I walked in, but I wanted to watch her realize she was going to die. Or almost die. See it in her eyes. All of this could have been avoided if she'd only loved me back. We were officially broken up.

"You're the killer," she whispered. "It was you!"

"Duh," I replied. "I wouldn't pull the knife out if I were you. You'll bleed out before anyone can get here." I grinned before pulling my head back and smashing it into her nose. Cartilage crunched. She'd need to get that fixed.

Sometimes, when you hurt the ones you love most, you're really hurting yourself.

I smoothed her hair a bit. "I deserve to be at *La Vie*. I deserved to be your friend. To be you." She didn't stir. She probably had a concussion.

I didn't have long before I passed out. I had to keep going. I had to finish this. I felt blood in my hair—was it hers or mine? It didn't matter. Sarah's eyes were closed but she was still breathing. Good. I got up and grabbed the selfie stick and Sarah's phone, took a photo of myself looking dead, making sure to get some of my blood on the stick.

The photo was the best one yet. Eyes nearly closed, blood seeping—I looked like someone had just stabbed me to death and was taking a kill shot for a trophy. I looked like Bloody Sarah had struck again. I uploaded the photo to her Instagram account leaving it logged in. Each tap was slow and excruciating. Time stood still. This was the end.

I picked up Sarah's hands and wiped my blood onto her. It was a holy communion. With my blood, she would be reborn as Bloody Sarah. She didn't move, except for shallow breaths. I set the selfie stick in her right hand, curling her fingers around it.

Finally, I lay back down, gasping as I positioned myself, and called 9-1-1 from Sarah's phone, being sure my bloody fingerprints were all over the screen.

"Sarah Taft. Stabbed me. Help," I panted. For real. This wasn't an act.

I closed my eyes, 70 percent sure I was going to die. I was okay with that. Sarah was still passed out, I'd be fine. Even if she did manage to get up, what was she going to do? Kill me? I started laughing, holding my side in pain. "Jesus fucking Christ."

* * *

My aim was better than I realized. While I needed thirty stitches in my side, I hadn't nicked any organs. All my prep work with Cassie had made me a stabbing pro. I did need some blood though; I bet Sarah's apartment looked like the set of a horror movie. The doctors said it was lucky I was such a fighter. Sarah could have taken out my liver or intestines. It was the fat on my stomach that saved me. See, Celia? Not being skin and bones was good for you. #Neverplankingagain.

But Detective Hopper wanted to talk.

"Walk me through everything that happened."

"I went over to bring Sarah her things. We were talking about her case, her lawyer, the murders . . ."

"Did she say anything about them?"

"Just that she wouldn't be found guilty. That she was going to an institution." He nodded, prodding me to continue. "Then she mentioned *my* death. And I froze. She pulled out a knife. We fought, I hit her in the face with my head, and she just stabbed me." I paused to show how overcome I was. "It was awful," I sobbed.

He nodded. "When did you stab Sarah?"

"After she stabbed me. I pulled the knife out and . . . I had nothing else, no way to defend myself." Tears streamed down my face. "It was all I could think of doing. I didn't mean to hurt her."

He looked grim. "The blood spatter will tell us who stabbed first." He sighed. "You should never have gone over there."

"I was so stupid going there. I don't know what I was thinking." I looked down, tears rolling down my nose and onto my chest.

"Yeah, what were you thinking?" he asked, staring at me.

"Honestly? I know you said it was Sarah. That she attacked Celia. But I couldn't reconcile that with the person I know. Knew. Was it all a lie? I mean, I sat next to her for two years. How is that possible? Ugh, you wouldn't understand." He wouldn't. He didn't know Sarah, not like I did.

"That was pretty damn stupid. You could be dead now."

"I didn't think she'd come after me. I was helping her with her things. So . . . why?"

"Well, you got her job, right?"

I nodded.

"So maybe it was payback."

I shuddered, tears forming in my eyes. "This is all just too much. I need to rest, I feel so tired." He nodded and left the room. I gave myself extra points for the emotions. The tears were worth two cookies.

* * *

I spent a couple days in the hospital. I kept waiting for the detective to come in and arrest me. Each time the door opened, my heart beat faster. And the monitor showed it.

Sarah had lived. I was pleased with that. She was in the same hospital as me, in surgery, since her wound was deeper. I even showed relief when an officer told me the news. I didn't want her dead. Honest to God.

Finally, they let me leave. Jack came to get me and take me home.

"They've been grilling me," he said. "Like, did I know that Sarah was homicidal and all that. I mean, we did know, but we didn't?"

"I'm so happy you're here." I hugged him. And I was happy. Nothing sadder than having no one to pick you up from the hospital. "How's Sarah?"

"Um, so busted. She doesn't remember anything, she claims. Like, I guess she lost a lot of blood or something?" He shrugged and grimaced. Like it was all so ghastly.

I hid in my apartment after that. Reporters camped out-side the building, trying to get a story with the victim of the *La Vie* Slasher. I had no interest in speaking with them. A little press was good. A shitstorm paparazzi fest was bad. It made me anxious.

Greg called repeatedly to find out if I was alive, okay, happy, going to sue. Let him sweat. I paced around wearing black Gap yoga pants and a tank top. This was my veg-out, no-one-can-see-me outfit. I wore it for days.

Don't get me wrong, I was happy. I got what I wanted. I was free. I could walk away from everything right now. I was the queen. Sarah would take the fall for most, if not all, the murders. All the supplies—the Botox, the handsaws, even the mood boards and glue—were bought with her credit card. (Sarah had five different cards, all paid by her parents. She never checked the bills. She never noticed when one went missing.)

Both our prints would be on the mood boards from when I handed them to her. But I'd worn gloves when I made them, each and every time. The selfie stick had her prints and my blood. Her phone had both of our prints, but that was easy to explain.

I had done a good job. I felt happy deep down for helping all those people achieve their big goals in life. Mulberry was more famous than her mother. Cassie learned to be an origi-nal. Lisa learned to never, ever threaten me. Zhazha became the biggest fashion blogger in the world. Celia would never have to worry about wrinkles again. But right now, I felt depressed. This must be what that postpartum shit was all about. I'd given birth to a masterpiece, and now I was bored. I had nothing. I had . . . just Stabler.

I think I was on hour seven of an *SVU* marathon—thank God for small favors—when there was a knock at my door. Dammit, someone let a reporter in.

"Anya? It's Detective Hopper." My heart jumped to my throat. I glanced down at my outfit and shrugged. He probably liked girls who looked homely. I did an armpit smell test, smoothed my hair, and went to answer the door.

"Um, hi."

"Hey there. Can I come in?"

I nodded.

"I'd ask what you've been up to, but . . ."

"The reporters won't let me go anywhere. I don't like the attention. And I'm not ready to go outside." I sat down.

"Are you doing okay? Do you need me to call someone?" he asked, concern dripping from his voice. This wasn't a date. It was pure charity.

"No." I glared. "I'm fine. I just need time to process everything and figure out what I'm doing next."

"Just making sure. You don't seem like your usual self, is all."

"Even fashion girls need downtime, Detective. It's how we stay sane." I felt a bubble of laughter rise up on that line. I fought the hysteria. Now was not the time to laugh in his face. "What can I do for you?"

"Well, I've come to talk to you about Sarah."

I flinched when he said her name. I'd practiced this. I'd watched hours of SVU and forced myself to pay attention to the victims, their movements, their simpering faces. It was a subtle flinch, not a don't-hit-me flinch. Just enough for him to notice.

"She doesn't remember the attack on you. But the evidence backs up your story. She stabbed first, you defended yourself. She even had planning boards in her kitchen. Her lawyer has agreed to a deal, so there won't be a trial. However, part of the deal is that she is going to be sent to an institution."

"Like a mental one?"

"Yes. The DA had her examined and found her incompetent to stand trial. She's not right in the head. They said she has," he pulled out his small notebook and read, "'disassociated personality, paranoid delusions, and psychotic episodes brought on by her depersonalization disorder.'" He stumbled over the last part. "She basically had no recollection of the murders but fantasized about them. It was an out-of-body experience for her."

"So what, she gets sent away for ten or eleven years and starts a new life?"

"No, she never gets to come out. And she won't be in such a nice facility. She has to go to a state hospital."

I grimaced. "That's . . . dark. Wow."

"I wanted you to know before you read about it anywhere. Also, Sarah wants to see you. She's asked to meet with you to apologize. The judge and the doctors think it might help."

"But she doesn't remember."

"It may still help her to make amends."

I sighed. "Do I have to?"

"Only if you want to. She's being held at Bellevue right now."

I nodded.

"There's just one other thing. Your shrink. Are you sure his name is Jacques Moritz?"

"Of course I'm sure," I snapped. Why wouldn't he drop this?

"Anya, Dr. Jacques Moritz hasn't practiced in years."

I blinked at him.

"What? That's not right. You must have the wrong info. Let me call him." I dialed. Straight to voice mail. "He's not answering."

Detective Hopper gently put a hand on my arm. "Anya, Dr. Moritz has been dead for five years."

I sat down, wincing from my stitches. "This has to be a mistake. Look, he gave me prescriptions." I tossed a pill bottle his way. Right on the label was the name *Dr. Jacques Moritz*. Detective Hopper stared at it.

"It's possible his prescription pad was stolen."

"By who? Some freak who wants to hear my problems? That's not right. Did you email him?"

"Yeah, he never replied. Who have you been seeing?"

There it was. Pity. It filled his eyes as he gazed at me. Like I was the victim of some weird con. He felt sorry for me.

"I think I need some rest. Thank you for coming to see me."

He had to leave. Now. He was bringing my world crashing down. That's not how things were supposed to be. He needed to leave me and Dr. M alone.

"Of course. We need to get to the bottom of this. When you're rested."

I nodded as he opened the door and left. Was he lying to me? All of this some clever ruse to get me to confess? They do that, you know. Lie. All the time.

"Anya, you always pick people who betray you," Dr. M said. He was sitting on the sofa, holding a bowl of popcorn. He had watched everything. He was my best TV buddy. "You need to break things off with the detective. For good."

He was right. He was always right.

* * *

Every time I heard mention of Bellevue on TV, I assumed it was a nuthouse, but it's not. It's a regular hospital. They just happen to have an inpatient psychiatric ward. The area for the criminally insane was separate from the rest of the psych ward, and that's where Sarah was being kept. Where she was going next wouldn't be as nice. Overcrowded, dirty, and no amenities. I didn't know why she didn't fight for a private institution. Even I wouldn't wish this on her.

I stood across the street on First Avenue in a black Saint Laurent leather jacket, a Helmut Lang black jersey pencil skirt, Valentino boots, and a ripped white tee from Alex Wang. I wore a McQueen skull necklace. It seemed fitting.

I met Hopper outside the hospital, and if my nerves gave me away, I played them off like I was scared to see Sarah. He smiled and rubbed my arm. I pulled away from him.

"It'll be fine. There will be guards there too."

"Will she be medicated?"

"Probably. The doctors said she's had a psychotic break."

I let him check us in and take us to the nineteenth floor. We had several more check-ins before being buzzed through even more doors and then into a visitor's area. This was where these wards became more like prisons. Doors onto doors onto doors. *Buzz, buzz, buzz.* The patients here were criminals, and no one let them forget it. I shuddered. Bile rose up in my throat as I smelled that distinct disinfectant odor all state facilities have.

"You'll be fine. We'll leave here soon."

I nodded, trying to not panic. *I'm not checking in. I'm not checking in. I'm not checking in.* This wasn't a trap; I'd get to go home after this. Fuck, what if this was a trap? *Deep breaths.* My Xanax wasn't working.

I sat down and waited for Sarah. I was in a medium-sized room, no windows, no air, nothing to stab anyone with. There were a few comfortable armchairs, nothing that anyone could easily pick up. A stained sofa was against one wall. Everything was in those horrible coral-pink and sea-green colors that only existed in hospitals. I imagined this was the room the nurses and orderlies slipped into for late night fun. Except there was a camera in the corner. Nothing was private. They would record everything. This was a trap. They wanted to catch me slipping up. I knew it! Detective Hopper was not on #TeamAnya. He was a faker. The worst kind—he made you think he liked you. The buzzing noise started up again. I ground my teeth.

"Are you okay?" Detective Hopper asked.

I didn't reply. I sat looking at my nails. I'd gotten them painted black and gold because I was a rock star.

"Okay, she's coming. I'll be right in the hall."

The guards showed her in.

I was ready for goth Sarah or tough and dramatic Sarah. But this was not who I thought would shuffle in. Her hair was stringy and oily, her skin waxy and pale. She was wearing an overwashed, threadbare pajama set with a mismatched robe. Her nose was bandaged, and the bruises under her eyes were a deep purple. This was intake Sarah. And she was a hot mess. My heart fluttered. My Sarah Taft had been replaced by this version. And the pain, the neediness that wafted off her (along with some pretty bad BO) was almost overwhelming.

Then it hit me: I was her only friend now. I was all she had. I had taken everything from her. I had won.

"Hey, Sarah . . ." I started tentatively, testing the waters.

She raised her head, squinting. "Anya?"

"Yes, it's me." The guards sat Sarah down on one of the armchairs and then moved to stand in the doorway. I sat in the chair across from her—not so close that she could claw my eyes out, but close enough that we could speak.

"How are you?"

"Are you dead?"

"No. I'm not dead. Don't you remember?"

"There was blood."

"Yes, there was blood."

"What happened? Why am I here?"

I sat back, watching her. Was this an act? Sarah was craftier than I'd given her credit for, but this acting job was too much for even her. Unless Detective Hopper put her up to it?

"You tried to kill me, Sarah. Don't you remember?"

She shook her head, holding her hair in her hands. "No. No, I didn't."

"You stabbed me with a knife. And you tried to kill Celia. And Cassie and Zhazha—"

"But . . . I don't remember . . ." she whispered.

I sighed. This was getting me nowhere. "You wanted to talk to me. Why?"

"I . . . I didn't do it. Help me . . . ?"

"You did do it—I was there. You tried to kill me. If that's all, then I'm leaving." I stood up to leave, and she grabbed my arm. Alarmed, the guards moved in, but I shook my head, motioning for them to stay where they were. "What is it?"

"I know who killed them."

"Who killed them?"

"You did." She grinned. "Mariana."

It was like the air had been sucked out of the room. She knew me, the real me. This was it. She was going to signal the officers and arrest me at any moment. I braced myself. "You did! You killed them! You did!" She grinned wildly.

A bubble of hysteria started sliding up my throat. I was going to laugh. I knew it.

"You killed them, Anya! I know what you did! Admit it! You were always a liar. Mariana! Your name is Mariana!" She threw her head back and laughed. "Your boyfriend told me who you really are." She cackled. "You killed everyone. I saw you do it." She practically sang the last part.

I had pictured how I'd tell her about myself. One day, after we'd had decades of friendship between us, after I knew all her secrets, I'd tell her mine. But this wasn't my fantasy. She knew. And Detective Hopper was the one who told her. He'd betrayed me just like Dr. M said he would. My heart was racing so fast I couldn't distinguish between each beat. Sarah knew everything. My mouth was dry. I swallowed. Panic engulfed me.

Stop, Anya. You can do this. The evidence all points to Sarah. Dr. M's voice was loud in my ear. He was right. Still, I glanced at the guards. They hadn't moved; they weren't even paying attention.

Deep breaths, Anya. Don't smile, don't show anything, Anya.

"Are you serious?" I asked loud enough for everyone to hear. "You are nuts!"

Her eyes widened. She was the crazy one. She was the one locked up. She'd taken the deal. This was Sarah's fate, not mine. She could have been by my side instead of sitting here, making fish faces.

"I mean, that's just crazy, Sarah. Totally. Fucking. Crazy."

You've got this, Anya. You can walk out of here, Dr. M whispered. *No one will stop you.*

I smoothed my skirt. It was just like Sarah to try to bring me down, even when she was at her lowest. We could have been the closest of friends. BFFs. Forever and ever.

Before I walked out, I leaned in and whispered in her ear, "You're nobody now. A nothing. How's it feel, Sarah? All you had to do was love me. You did this to yourself." I wanted to grin. To taunt and leer. But Dr. M was shouting at me about restraint.

Detective Hopper was waiting for me outside the room. "How'd it go?" I nearly ran from him. Was he going to charge me? Was this it? I couldn't end it here, with the ugly walls.

"She didn't want to apologize at all. That was . . . wow."

"Yeah, she's accused several people of being the killer. She has good moments when she's lucid. Sorry this wasn't one. What did you whisper to her?"

"Just wished her well. I hope she gets better."

"She may never recover."

"Is there anything else you need from me?" I asked stiffly. I needed to get out of there. I needed to be free.

"No, that's it. You know, even if she hadn't taken the deal, we had enough to convict her. You didn't see her plan boards . . ." He smiled encouragingly. "It doesn't matter. It's over for you.

"You should know, however, we're looking into the death of Dr. Moritz. It looks like there may have been foul play involved. We're thinking it was a former patient of his. Can you work with a sketch artist so we can get a better idea of what this impostor looks like?"

"Of course, anything I can do to help," I heard myself say.

And I would help them with Dr. M. Why wouldn't I? Dr. M was always there when I needed him. He was the most attentive shrink I'd ever had. We almost broke up once though. Almost. He said I wasn't making progress, that I was too obsessive with people. He was just mad because I made mood boards of him. After that, our little fight, he became *so* helpful. And he really took a personal interest in my life. He even gave me his prescription pads for when I needed them. He was the best. Really.

Epilogue

It was that time of year again, and though I'd sworn it off, I found myself in the crush of stilettos and sequins, moving through the crowds at Spring Street Studios. It was Fashion Week again. It was always Fashion Week somewhere. But this time it was *my* Fashion Week.

I was attending a presentation for Georges Pike's latest jewelry show. Everyone and their mother wanted to show this season, and when jewelry designers got in on it, your calendar just exploded. Having gone through everything I had last year, I was the most in-demand person at every show and dinner—even without a magazine tied to my name. It was a coup to get me to actually come. Gimmick seating will always get you a few flashbulbs, and what could be cooler than the girl who survived Bloody Sarah's reign of terror? Fashion loves a tale of survival and redemption.

Of course, I wasn't covering the collections for anyone. I was now a consultant, whatever that meant. *La Vie* was in limbo, restaffing and relaunching, and I didn't want to lead the new team. Greg had been fired; legal decided his sexual misconduct in the office was too big an issue for them. They had enough on their plates with all the dead bodies.

265

Dalia had dodged the great tampon massacre and was thriving at Barneys. I was 100 percent jealous of her. Imagine, working with those shoes all day? Heaven. We'd had lunch a few times but only because I wanted to see her boss in person. Aiko always said hello, and she seemed genuinely happy to see me each time we ran into each other. She wore red lipstick. (I bought five different shades of red from the beauty department downstairs.) And she had an *A* name, like me. I'd already started my Aiko mood board.

Jack met me outside in front of the show, photogs snapping away. The streets were clogged with black cars. He gave me a once-over before grinning. "Chic."

I was wearing a black crepe jumpsuit with Balenciaga's dad sneakers. Aiko had helped me pick it out. Or rather, the Barneys sales email did. Whatever. I know it came from her.

"Thanks, boo," I replied to Jack. He was wearing a mustard-yellow suit. It was a look, but he made it work. We needed each other today. This week, especially. Ever since Sarah, I had avoided going to fashion events, avoided the cameras. But Jack had embraced the attention. There had been profile after profile on him. He always made sure to mention me. He was such a good friend.

We exchanged glances and then struck poses for the photographers out front. We were to stay together, that was our pact. Jack was my first male friend. A proper gay bestie. He told me when I had lipstick on my teeth and everything. We moved from pose to pose before heading inside.

A new PR bot was overseeing the entry list. She was a Brittany. Perky and peppy, Brittanys were never not smiling. She waved us in without checking our names. Clearly an updated model from the Laurens.

Once we got inside, we paused for more photos. The flashbulbs were giving me a headache.

"Ugh, we need to wear sunglasses," Jack muttered. I put my arm through his.

There were police officers watching over things now. That was a change from last year. I didn't know what they thought would happen, but the city wanted to be proactive. Detective Hopper wasn't there. After his betrayal, after he told Sarah all about me, I cut him out of my life. Just like I did with Sarah. Except he was dead.

He'd insisted on digging up what happened to Dr. M. I tried everything to make him realize it wasn't important, that Dr. M was happy with me. But he wouldn't listen. Hopper's death was a tragedy. A decorated detective turning to drugs, overdosing on a Xanax, Vicodin, and alcohol cocktail. There were now task forces set up to help the NYPD combat prescription drug use within the ranks.

I still saw him from time to time. Hopper would pop up somewhere and stare.

Sarah was still locked up. She had been moved to a facility in White Plains. How unchic is that?

"Anya! Jack! Over here! Pose for a photo!"

I smiled, throwing my hand on my hip and did my best Sarah imitation while Jack sucked his cheeks in. She would be so proud of all that I'd learned from her. I was wearing five coats of lip gloss for that perfect shine. I was momentarily blinded by the flashbulbs, but my smile didn't waver. After all, a bad photo can ruin months of hard work. A true fashion girl kept her photo game on point at all times.

I spotted Georges surrounded by well-wishers. We went over to say hello.

"Anya! Jack! My loves, you made it!"

"Georges, *mon cher*! The collection is so chic." One of us said it. It didn't matter who. Fashion lies just fall from the tongue during shows.

"Did you see the Anya necklace? It's made just for you!"

"Oh, you shouldn't have!" He really shouldn't have. Jack stifled a laugh. I hated Georges's work, but he'd become extrafamous as the unofficial reason that Sarah had killed Zhazha. (Technically, that case was still unsolved. As were

267

Mulberry's, Cassie's, and Lisa's. But everyone knew it was Sarah.) As the designer chattered on and on, I saw Aiko swan in, and I waved to her. She was with Dalia.

"She's so *maje*," Jack said when he saw her. He got me. He got my style. But still, we needed a third. We needed Aiko.

Two guys were whispering behind us. I stiffened.

"Who are they?" one said.

"That's Anya and Jack. You know, they survived Bloody Sarah at *La Vie* last year."

"Ohhh, wow. You know what I heard? I heard Anya's the one who killed everyone, not crazy Sarah."

"*No*! Seriously? I heard it was Jack."

"Wow. That's so edgy."

"Totally. Way chic."

"Let's get selfies with them!"

"O-M-G, totes!"

Acknowledgments

I want to thank my family for not only encouraging me but also putting up with me for so long. A huge thank-you to my incredible agents Deborah Schneider and Josie Freedman at ICM for never giving up on me or Anya. Giant bolt of gratitude to my patient and thorough editor, Chelsey Emmelhainz, and everyone at Crooked Lane Books. Daniel Ross Noble: you know I adore you. And a big merci to Daniel and Mark Waters and Jessica Tuchinsky for being #TeamAnya and Katrina Escudero for first introducing me to everyone. Karen Robinovitz, for starting this whole thing off, and Dara and Gwen, thank you.

A huge shout-out to Jessica Morgan and Heather Cocks for encouraging me to write this book. Miranda Burgess and Alex Hestoft, thanks for the drinks and constant support. Toni Hacker and Ben Harnett, thank you for reading the earliest of drafts. Thank you Tali and Ophi Edut for always being there and Catherine Townsend for keeping me inspired. To all the fantastic writers and editors I've been lucky to work with, I'm forever thankful and grateful. To all the ridiculously talented people in fashion I've met over the years, you're amazing.

And last but not least, I couldn't have written this without Beanie, my very patient dog and writing partner. You get all the belly rubs in the world.

About the Author

Amina Akhtar is a former fashion writer and editor. She's worked at *Vogue, Elle, Style,* NYTimes.com, and NYMag.com, where she was the founding editor of *The Cut* blog. She's written for numerous publications, including *Yahoo Style, Fashionista, xoJane, Refinery29,* and *Billboard,* and for brands like Bergdorf Goodman and H&M's *10 Years of Style* tome. After toiling in the fashion ranks for more than fifteen years, she now writes full time in the desert mountains, where she's detoxing from her once glam life. *#FashionVictim* is Amina's first novel.